Lulu Goes

to College

Barbara McGillicuddy Bolton

ISBN 1508907668   ISBN 978-1508907664

Photos and design by Francis X. Bolton

© 2015 Barbara C. Bolton
All rights reserved

To the Class of 1965

This is a work of fiction.

Chapter One

Lulu Delaney arrived to begin her first year at Lovejoy College, Lovejoy, Maine, the day after Labor Day, 1961, carrying the two baby-blue plastic suitcases her uncles and aunts had given her for high school graduation. Had she made a fuss, her parents would have driven her the two hundred miles down from Meduxnekeag in Aroostook County, but because she knew the trip would have been a hardship for Old Nelly, as her father called their Ford — whose underbody, transmission, and tires weren't what they might have been — she had been just confident enough to say her goodbyes at the Paradise Diner, where the bus stopped once in the morning going south and once in the afternoon going north. She was wearing a white wash-and-wear Ship 'n Shore blouse with a Peter Pan collar and a plaid wraparound cotton skirt made by her mother. Her brown pumps were from Dux Shoes, the best shoe store in town. Her scarab bracelet was a graduation gift from her aunt and uncle in Bangor. The gold circle pin on her collar was a going away present from her friend Alice, who the summer before senior year had "had" to get married and drop out of school and who had sat in the audience at graduation with a baby on her lap.

The bus deposited Lulu at the door of Chubbuck, her dormitory. She walked between white pillars through the open doors into a lobby as cool and dim as deep woods.

"Lulu? Lulu Delaney?"

Lulu turned in the direction of the melodious voice that sounded thrilled to have located her. She wondered what it was about her that identified her as Lulu Delaney from Meduxnekeag. "I'm Lulu."

"I'm Deb, your Junior Advisor." As Lulu's eyes adjusted, she beheld a straight, slim, smiling coed. "Welcome to Lovejoy. And to

Chubbuck." Lulu had learned in Home Economics class that faces had four basic shapes. Deb's face was heart-shaped. Lulu had also learned that by maximizing her assets and minimizing her liabilities every girl had it in her power to make a striking impression. Lulu's slender build and clear complexion were assets, her freckles and glasses minor liabilities, her height surpassing the ideal but not impossibly tall, her limp brown hair something that could be worked with. Not everyone was blessed with the feminine ideal, which was blonde, blue-eyed and petite.

Deb fit the feminine ideal. No wonder she was chosen to be a Junior Advisor, Lulu thought. "Gordon Linen?" Deb asked, her perfectly arched eyebrows lifting slightly.

"Oh, yes!" At home, Lulu had helped with hanging laundry on the line and taking it down again. It was her mother, however, who pulled the wringer washer into the middle of the kitchen every Monday morning, attached a hose to the faucet of the sink, filled the tub with dirty laundry sorted by color, and fed each steaming wet article through the wringer. Lulu and her mother had debated the merits of Lulu washing and drying her own sheets in the coin-operated automatic machines in the basement of Chubbuck versus paying for linen service. In the end, it was her mother who decided on the service to assure Lulu's getting a clean start once each week. Lulu set down her suitcases and tucked under her arm one of the sets of sheets and towels lined up on a parson's bench. A warmth spread through her as though the linens were fresh from the clothesline at home.

With a wave of her hand, Deb indicated the door propped open at the far end of the lobby. "Room 104 is second on the left. Your roommate Jill arrived an hour ago. There's a meeting next door in my room right after supper." She smiled as if to make light of her list of information. "See you then."

Lulu was just able to pick up her two suitcases and walk to the doorway of Room 104.

"Roomie!" Arms held wide, the coed who must be Jill crossed the room to greet Lulu. Lulu was not accustomed to hugging someone she was meeting for the first time. Blushing to the roots of her hair, she bent briefly to meet her petite roommate's embrace and breathed in her aroma of cinnamon and soap. Jill had on a red wraparound dungaree skirt and a white blouse with a gold circle pin on the Peter Pan collar. She had said in an introductory letter in the summer that she routinely ironed her hair. Either she had been too hurried that morning or the humidity had had its way because soft curls framed her round face like a dark halo. "These are my parents," she said with a sweep of her hand and a sweet smile, "Mommy and Daddy."

Jill had mentioned her parents in such cavalier fashion in her letters that Lulu was surprised by the warmth of her introduction, and "Mommy" and "Daddy" sounded positively babyish. "Hello." She nodded to short, smiling, ovoid Mr. and Mrs. Stassio, sitting side by side on an unmade bed like painted eggs in a cardboard carton. She was unsure whether to cross the room and offer to shake hands.

Jill's parents stood up and Mrs. Stassio walked to Lulu with her arms out, and so Lulu stooped to hug her roommate's even shorter mother. When she straightened, she found herself face-to-face with Mr. Stassio, who held out his right hand. When Lulu took it, he put his free hand around her shoulders, pulled her close and kissed her cheek. In Meduxnekeag, her father greeted men with a handshake and women by touching his forefinger to the brim of his hat — or to his forehead if he was inside. Her mother greeted both men and women with a smile and a nod. No telling whether they would have risen to the occasion of all this hugging and kissing.

"I've taken the free-standing bed and the wardrobe," Jill said. "I hope you don't mind." The three Stassios stood in a huddle, their expressions polite.

"No, no, you were here first."

The three Stassios beamed at Lulu.

Jill's bed was in the corner furthest from the door. A wardrobe and a bureau stood next to it, and a scatter rug, no doubt brought from home, lay alongside. Bunk beds stood against the wall on one side of the threshold. On the other side, a door stood open to a closet. All the rooms had originally been designed as doubles, but, as the Dean of Women had explained in the welcoming letter she sent during the summer, more students than anticipated had accepted Lovejoy for the class of 1965.

"Take the lower bunk, okay?" Jill said. "We can use the top one for storage."

A separate enclosure in the Dean's letter had listed Lulu's roommates as Jill Stassio from Fall River, Massachusetts, and Elise Robinson from Greenwich, Connecticut. A few days later a letter arrived from Jill, and she and Lulu had corresponded for the rest of the summer. Jill wrote that she had written the third roommate as well. Eventually, as time went on and Elise Robinson did not respond, Lulu and Jill concluded that Elise, unlike the horde that had accepted Lovejoy above all others, must have made a different choice.

Lulu placed both her suitcases on the lower bunk and opened the larger one. The desk between her bed and the door would be more convenient than either of the two by the windows, she told herself; so maybe she was just as well off getting second pick. By the look of things, Jill had already unpacked. She and her mother began making up her bed with Gordon Linens. Lulu loved her three younger brothers dearly, but she'd always felt she'd missed out by not having a sister. Living in a dormitory of women with the warm and lively Jill as her roommate would supply the experience she'd lacked.

"Oh, Angela!" Jill's mother sounded so dismayed Lulu looked up from laying her clothes out on the lower bunk. "There's only one pillowcase! Should Daddy and I drive downtown and get you another one?"

"That's okay, Mommy." Jill sounded brave. "Next week, when we change linen, I'll get a second pillowcase."

"It wouldn't take Daddy and me long. I'd send him by himself except…"

"Ha-looh!" There was a tap on the door and a young woman strode into the middle of the room, stopped and pivoted slowly like a Miss America contestant. Her face was a perfect oval. Her pixie haircut fit her head like a sleek cap, accentuating her delicate cheekbones. Her eyelashes were dark with mascara, the high color in her cheeks had been effected by a subtle application of make-up, no doubt, and — strangely — her lipstick, unlike Lulu's pastel pink or Jill's fire engine red, was an inhuman silvery color. A multi-colored silk scarf wound around her neck and draped almost to her fanny. She wore a white, tailored shirt — no Peter Pan collar — a madras skirt, and highly polished cordovan loafers.

"Elise Robinson," she said, pronouncing her name with a slight lisp. She extended her hand first to Jill's parents, then to Jill, then to Lulu. There was something so formal in her manner that none of the Stassios, and certainly not Lulu, offered to hug her.

"You have the top bunk," Jill said very smoothly and sweetly to Elise. "You have the left side of the closet. Lulu has the right." Since Lulu hadn't yet hung up a stitch of clothing, she couldn't see how she had claim to either side. Now that she looked through the open closet door, she could see that, although the built-in bureaus looked identical, the floor on the left side had a hump having to do with electrical equipment or the like. Lulu felt a sisterly pride in Jill for having asserted herself with this classy new roommate — and gratitude that the action had been taken in her behalf.

"*Que sera, sera.*" When Elise tossed her head, only the feathery ends of her hair moved. "A room is a room. A bed is a bed. A rose by any other name....I'll just go get my *pater* and get myself moved in." She swept out of the room and returned with her *pater*, a set of Gordon Linen under his arm. Like his daughter, Elise's father was of only medium height, but he carried himself tall. He was tanned and his black wavy hair was slightly longer than Lulu was used to seeing on a man. He dropped the linens on Lulu's bunk and shook hands all around with a warmer, less formal manner than his daughter's. He and Elise made several more trips to the lobby to bring into 104 what appeared to be an entire station wagon full of belongings.

All at once, as though a whistle had blown, the three parents began to say their good-byes. Elise presented her cheek to her father to kiss. Short of a shopping expedition to purchase a second pillowcase, the Stassios had done everything there was to do to set Jill up in the room. As the family hugged goodbye, tears rolled down the cheeks of all three.

"Goodbye, Mommy." Jill said in a broken voice. "Goodbye, Daddy."

"Goodbye, Angela dear," Mrs. Stassio said.

"Goodbye, darling," Mr. Stassio said. Lulu, who wasn't used

to seeing a grown man cry, gave her full attention to straightening the blotter on her desk.

Once the parents were gone, Elise slung two of her suitcases to the top bunk and, leaving her other luggage strewn across the floor, stretched out on the scatter rug next to Jill's bed. "I'm so tired, I may just sleep on this rug tonight. I'll make up my bed tomorrow."

Jill threw Lulu a worried glance. "You wouldn't be very comfortable there."

Elise laughed and sat up. She put both hands behind her head and stretched her back. "Don't worry. I'll make everything decent before supper." She got to her feet and heaved a box of books from the floor to one of the desks under the windows — the desk with the most room around it and on which Jill's handbag lay. "I'll need this desk, okay?" She picked up Jill's handbag and tossed it lightly to the desk under the other window.

Jill opened and closed her mouth without saying anything.

"I think that's only fair, considering." Elise pulled bookends out of the box and placed them at either end of the desktop. Without turning to look at Lulu, she said, "And I'll take the right side of the closet, if you don't mind. I don't want my Bass Weejuns getting all squeezed and scuffed."

Lulu looked down at her own brown pumps. The motto of Dux Shoes was "Boston Bred," and until that moment, she had been pleased with her purchase.

Elise walked to the closet, looked into the full-length mirror on the inside of the door, put a hand to her hair and smiled at herself. Still smiling and humming, she set about unpacking her books while Lulu hung clothes and filled bureau drawers. When Lulu unfolded one of her sheets, Jill sprang from where she was seated on her own bed and took hold of one corner.

Her books arranged, Elise stepped out of her Bass Weejuns and climbed part way up the ladder to her bunk. "Maybe I'll leave this for later," she said half aloud.

Jill and Lulu exchanged glances. At home, Lulu was used to heading off quarrels among her little brothers. Besides, she had spent the summer making up beds and performing even more menial duties as an aide at Our Lady of Sorrows Hospital in Meduxnekeag. She wouldn't object to executing one more set of hospital corners in order to keep the peace. She took a deep breath. "I'll make up your bunk while you finish unpacking." Jill widened her eyes in disapproval. Elise gave Lulu a look that was either a simper or an affront and moved off the ladder.

By the time the bell rang for supper, all three roommates were completely settled into Room 104 Chubbuck and had lugged their empty suitcases to the basement trunk room. The dining hall was a two-story-high wing on the downhill side of Chubbuck. After they had descended the stairs and gone through the cafeteria line, Elise waved to someone already seated and, without explanation, left Lulu and Jill holding their trays and looking around. They found two seats together. As Jill chatted up their tablemates, Lulu looked around the room noting the abundance of gold circle pins and Peter Pan collars. Tall windows on three sides filled the hall with a late-afternoon amber glow. The wood-paneled walls, the golden brown of maple syrup, were hung with American primitive paintings, flat, stark portraits of homely men and women and of children who resembled miniature adults. Lulu recognized the type from illustrations in her American history book. She felt honored to be eating in the presence of genuine art.

Back in Room 104, Elise said she had a friend over at one of the men's dorms who had been at her "brother" school. She and "Muffy" would be going over to call on him.

"But we have a meeting in Deb's room," Jill said.

"Tender my apologies." Elise stood smiling at the closet mirror and freshening her makeup until a coed she'd eaten supper with appeared at the door dressed like her twin in a tailored white shirt, madras skirt, long silk scarf and cordovan loafers. Without introducing Muffy, Elise tucked a pack of cigarettes into her purse and started out the door. She turned back briefly, her eyes on a spot over Lulu's head. "Kindly tell Deb I'll do my best to make the next meeting."

After the door shut behind Elise and Muffy, Lulu turned to Jill. "What is a brother school anyway?"

"That's when a boys' private school is within shouting distance of a girls' private school, and every month or so the inmates have a dance together before their keepers lock them up again." Jill kicked off her shoes and unbottoned her blouse.

Lulu had been raised with the principle that if one had nothing nice to say one should say nothing at all. She changed the topic. "Your mother calls you Angela?"

"That's my full name. I shortened it in high school."

"Shortened?"

"Yeah. An-JILL-ah, get it? Shortening names is a family tradition. My grandfather shortened Anastassio to Stassio. So I could have been Angela Anastassio. Sounds more Catholic, doesn't it?"

Prettier, too, Lulu thought, but she had been raised not to make personal remarks. "Nice that we're both Catholic. We can attend Mass together Sundays."

"Actually, my family is Christmas-and-Easter Catholic, not Every-Sunday-Go-to-Church Catholic." Jill spoke as matter-of-factly as though Not-Every-Sunday-Go-to-Church-Catholic were as legitimate an alternative as the Eastern Rite or Greek Orthodoxy.

Lulu squelched an impulse to argue over name shortenings or religious practices. "Almost time for Deb's meeting. I'm going to get ready." She turned her back to Jill to remove her clothes and slip on a brightly colored cotton print muumuu that was elasticized around the neck and hung loose to her ankles.

"Oooh, yours is so pretty." Jill had also put on a muumuu. "Where did you get it?"

"My mother made it."

"Your mother made it!" Jill put her hands to her cheeks and widened her eyes. "Wow!"

Next door in 102, Deb, in a muumuu that brought out the blue in her eyes, sat in her turned-around desk chair, her legs crossed at the ankles, her hands folded over a sheet of paper on her lap. The blue gingham curtains at her windows framed tropical plants, their scions cascading halfway to the floor and dancing in the breeze. Blue gingham spreads covered the beds, posters decorated the walls and on one of the windowsills goldfish drifted around in a glass bowl.

The freshmen, each in a brightly colored muumuu, arranged themselves cross-legged on the floor, roommate by roommate, like books by the same author on a library shelf. Deb pointed to one after another and said each one's name. When she had named eight, she looked down at the sheet of paper, looked up again, and said, "Where's Elise?"

"Over at the men's dorms," Jill said.

Deb lifted an eyebrow and pursed her Cupie-doll lips.

"Visiting a friend from her brother school," Lulu said. "She said she'd make it to the next meeting." Lulu didn't know why she felt she had to defend Elise. Jill certainly didn't feel the need to. Lulu looked around at the other freshmen. Most likely, it was among these women, not with Elise, that she would find, in the words of Anne of *Anne of Green Gables,* kindred spirits.

Roommates Mimi, in a mostly red muumuu, April, in a mostly yellow, and Janet, in a mostly green, were of medium height and weight with medium length hair of a medium shade of brown. If they continued to wear the same muumuus day and night for the next few days, Lulu hoped she might be able to keep straight who was who.

Roommates Bridey, Kateri, and Dottie were more distinctive. Bridey and Kateri each had wavy hair that fell almost to their shoulders. Bridey had the coloring of Snow White — hair as black as ebony, skin white as snow, lips red as blood. Her features were skewed in a way, however, that made her look comical rather than beautiful.

Kateri was beautiful. She also had hair black as ebony and lips red as blood. Her skin, though, was as coppery as a new penny. In her orange and red muumuu, she looked like the one authentic Hawaiian at an imitation luau.

Sitting between them, Dottie looked oversized and underwrought, like a *Snuffy Smith* character in a *Mary Worth* comic strip. She had frizzy blonde hair and round, tortoise-shell glasses. Her shoulders were rounded, her body much too square for the feminine ideal. She smiled and nodded in appreciation as Deb recited what she called the cardinal rules of Chubbuck Dormitory.

"Heeding curfew is the first cardinal rule." For the first nine weeks of the semester, freshmen women had a nine pm curfew six days a week, 10:30 on Saturdays. The second cardinal rule was that men were not allowed on the floor. The milling about of fathers and brothers earlier in the day was an exception. In future, if a custodian, for instance, or a plumber needed to put in an appearance, the cry *Man on floor!* would precede him and be taken up by anyone and everyone until he finished his business and was safely off the floor. If a date came to pick someone up, the scholarship student stationed at the lobby desk would buzz the coed's room and inform her she had a *caller*. If a man deemed not to be a date inquired at the lobby desk for a coed, she would be buzzed and informed that a *visitor* awaited her. Either caller or visitor must wait in the lobby. Of the several common rooms off the lobby, there was only one that a woman and her caller or visitor were permitted to sit in. Under no circumstances was a caller or visitor to ascend above the first floor or descend to the basement. A woman could invite a man to join her for the formal Sunday dinner. Men were not allowed in the dining hall at any other time.

As Deb talked on, Lulu's mind began to fill with images of the exciting social life that lay ahead. She pictured the fuzzy form of a guy entering through the white pillars of Chubbuck and stopping at the desk to ask for her. When he raised his head to watch her emerge, she recognized him as Keith Sinclair, the summer orderly at Our Lady of Sorrows Hospital. After graduating from Lovejoy, Keith had joined the army and served as a medic in Southeast Asia. He was at this moment in medical school in Boston and would never come back to Lovejoy. Lulu gave her head a little shake and tried to concentrate on what Deb was saying.

"About the phones…" Incoming calls came to the front desk, which was covered from seven in the morning until ten at night. Late night phone calls went unanswered. In the hallway between the lobby and the stairs descending to the dining room, there were three phone booths. Since they served the entire dorm, it was important to keep all calls short and to the point.

Lulu didn't expect to make any phone calls. Long distance calls home would be prohibitively expensive, and, besides, she could express herself more easily in letters.

"I want to say something about neatness." The maids, Deb explained, would come in every weekday to sweep, mop, and dust. It was up to the students to make up their beds each morning, stow books and clothes neatly away and pick up any clutter. The maids also cleaned the bathroom, and it was imperative that the women keep the bathroom free of their personal belongings.

Deb shifted in her seat and put her hand over her heart to indicate that what she was about to say next was of a personal nature. "When I was a freshman, I had a terrific Junior Advisor. I thought maybe she'd become my best friend, but what I learned is that she already had her friends and that I needed to make my own friends among the women in my own class." Deb lowered her hand to her lap and spoke more briskly. "So, I am here to help you get started in Chubbuck and at Lovejoy. You may knock on my door at any time from eight in the morning until nine at night, and if I'm in I'll be glad to talk with you either right then or whenever we can set up an appointment." She stood up and walked to the door and held it open. Lulu, who had warmed to Deb like a little sister, felt stung by her concluding remarks and brusque dismissal.

On the other hand, she thought, maybe Deb's manner was exactly that of a big sister with little sisters.

"Welcome, everyone." Jill threw open the door of Room 104 and gestured for the others to enter. Compared to Deb's cozy nest, 104 looked rather Spartan.

"Wow! Look at all those books." Bridey walked across the room to Elise's desk. "Someone's already read everything in *Great Thinkers of the Western World*, by the looks of it."

The only book Lulu had brought with her was a *Webster's Collegiate Dictionary*, given to her by her parents as a graduation gift. "You know what books are in *Great Thinkers of the Western World*?"

"You might as well know — I've already told my roomies...." Bridey laid one hand over her heart. "...I was here last year but I got kicked out for plagiarism." She made a fist and struck her breast three times. "*Mea culpa, mea culpa, mea maxima culpa.*"

"It was only a suspension," Dottie said. Through her thick round glasses she bestowed on Bridey the sympathetic and encouraging look of a teacher soothing an over-excited kindergartener.

"Yeah, the college said I could come back this year. I lived at home and took a couple of classes at the community college and worked part time and — ta da! — I'm back!" Bridey flung both arms into the air. "So if there's anything you need to know about the first seven weeks and four days at Lovejoy, just ask me. My main advice is don't copy stuff out of a library book without giving attribution. You never know what the professors have read."

Everyone decided to look at the two other freshman triples. Because of the space taken up by the lobby, First Floor Chubbuck had fewer rooms than the two upper floors. Bridey, Dottie and Kateri lived down the first short hall and around the corner. "What a pretty bedspread! Is it Indian?" Jill ran her hand over the red and black blanket on the free-standing bed.

"Yes," Kateri said quietly. "Indian like me."

"American Indian?"

"American Indian."

Jill placed her hands on either side of her face, opened her eyes wide and breathed out. "Wow!"

Lulu, too, was surprised. In Meduxnekeag, the Indians lived in shacks on the road to the dump. A couple of Indian kids had been in her classes in elementary school, but none that Lulu knew of ever graduated from high school. When she worked in the children's ward at the hospital, she had seen plenty of Indian mothers no older than she was. "What do your parents do, Kateri?" As soon as she blurted out the question, she wished she could take it back. The adult Indians she knew of in Meduxnekeag picked potatoes alongside the school children in the fall and scrounged in the dump year round.

"They're both high school teachers." If Kateri had taken offense, it didn't show in her tone of voice. "What do your parents do?"

"My father's a clerk in the Five and Dime. My mother's a housewife." Lulu wished for a moment she had Kateri's complexion so that the blush sweeping up her neck and onto her face wouldn't show. She didn't know whether she was more embarrassed by her lack of tact or by what suddenly struck her as her parents' low stations in life. She might have added that her father was an inventor and her mother a poet, but she knew that those were mere avocations.

The little crowd of new floor mates crossed the hall to the third triple. Although Janet, April and Mimi looked similar, Lulu found she could distinguish them by their accents. Janet's New Hampshire accent was most like Lulu's own, while April sounded like a female version of President Kennedy. Mimi had a harsh — to Lulu, almost comical — New York City accent so that even when she was perfectly serious — especially when she was perfectly serious — she sounded like Groucho Marx. The three roommates sat side by side on the freestanding bed, in front of what appeared to be an entire girlhood's worth of stuffed animals, and smoked Kents, tapping ash into the little lady-like metal ashtrays they held in their hands.

From their summer correspondence, Lulu knew that Jill, like her, had gone to a public high school where nice girls didn't smoke. Lulu fully intended to take up smoking sometime in the future, sometime when she had extra money to throw around, but that wouldn't be during her stay at Lovejoy. It occurred to her that maybe the reason Dottie didn't smoke was that she, too, was a scholarship student, but Lulu didn't feel like asking. She'd already embarrassed herself enough with her question to Kateri.

As curfew approached, all eight freshmen got ready to retire. The bathroom on First Floor Chubbuck contained a tub and three shower stalls. Standing in front of one, Bridey grinned at Lulu and said, "New showers always give me that 'Psycho' moment. You know, when you think maybe a hand will reach in and grab you. Oh, well, here goes." Bridey pulled off her muumuu and, stark naked, hung it on a hook. Then she blessed herself, opened the frosted glass door and stepped in.

Lulu stepped into a second shower and shut the door. She pulled her muumuu over her head, opened the door slightly and hung the garment on the hook outside. She studied the faucets, hoping not to scald herself. The bathroom in Lulu's home had just a tub, no shower. She had taken a bath once a week and used the bathroom sink for twice-weekly sponge baths and shampoos. Her friend Lenore's house had two bathrooms, one with a tub, the other with a shower stall, where Lenore had showered every single morning of high school. Lulu moved to one side and turned both faucets at once, twisting her hands one way and another until the temperature looked okay. She stuck one hand under the flow — just right. As the water pounded her scalp and ran down her body, she doubted she'd ever bother with a tub the whole time she was at Lovejoy.

She turned off the water and reached out for her towel and then for her muumuu, which she slipped on before stepping out. Deb, Janet and April were standing at the sinks. Although Lulu hadn't seen any other coed with glasses that day, she realized she wasn't the only one who was nearsighted as, one after another, Deb, Janet and April popped out contact lenses and placed them in little containers. Lulu was nearly finished rolling pink sponge curlers into her hair when Bridey returned with Kateri, both wearing curlers identical to Lulu's. "Triplets!" Bridey squealed.

Triplets! Sisters! Living in Chubbuck was going to be like inhabiting the world of *Little Women*. When she was in grade school, Lulu had seen herself as Jo, the tomboy sister who, in the sequel, grew up to have a houseful of boys.

Back in 104, Jill stood in front of her wardrobe mirror in baby doll pajamas vigorously brushing her curls and singing. She smiled at Lulu when she came in and then at her reflection. *"I'm a beauty, oh, what a beauty, I'm a beauty and clever and kind."*

Lulu laughed at the "I Feel Pretty" parody that so suited her self-confident little roommate. "Bravo!" Jill was *Little Women's* Amy, the youngest sister, fun loving and slightly spoiled but generous, too, as long as she got her own way.

Jill set down her brush and pinched her cheeks. Then she picked a paper up off her desk and waved it at Lulu. "The Freshman Week Schedule," she said, her mood switching from silly to sober. "I'm going to read this over again in bed."

The evening before and for as far back as she could remember, Lulu had knelt by her bed, blessed herself, made a short examination of conscience and recited silently an "Our Father," a "Hail Mary" and a "Glory Be." At the end of summer, she'd decided that kneeling in a dorm room would call too much attention to herself and that she would say her morning and evening prayers in bed.

The bell in the lobby rang, signaling ten minutes before lights out. "I'm not covering up for her, and I'm not letting her in through the window," Jill said. "If she misses curfew, she can sleep on the lawn."

"Oh, she'll be along. She wouldn't miss curfew." Missing curfew the first night at Lovejoy, considering how Deb had stressed it as a cardinal rule, seemed inconceivable, even for someone as sophisticated in her manner and her reading tastes as Elise.

The door flew open and Elise strode in. "I'm in love!" She put one hand on top of her head and twirled around and around until she collapsed at the foot of Jill's bed. "I'm in love," she repeated. "And just a wee bit tipsy."

"You're drunk!" Jill sat up and pulled her knees up away from Elise. "And it isn't even the weekend."

"It's so much more civilized on the men's side of campus." Elise twisted herself to a sitting position and looked from Jill to Lulu. "Didn't you hear me?" she crowed. "I'm in love."

"So soon?" Lulu had also sat up.

"Not soon, you goofball. Sammy and I have known each other for ages. Tonight he said he wants to marry me."

"See how you feel about that in the morning," Jill said. Her expression added, *and get off my bed*. When Elise stood up and took off her jacket, she looked disheveled. "Your shirt's not buttoned up right!" Jill said. Lulu was pretty sure Elise had been buttoned up right when she left the room earlier.

"*Que sera, sera.*" Elise threw her jacket and the rest of her clothes onto the floor of her side of the closet and slipped over her head a men's tee shirt that fell to her knees. She climbed the ladder to her bunk, stopping midway to hang off with one arm and proclaim, "I'm in love, I'm in love." At the top, she fell onto her bunk, and it sounded to Lulu that, although the night had turned cool and there was no heat in the dorm, she had not bothered to get under the covers. "Did I ever thank you two dears properly for making up my bed? Well, I'm thanking you now."

"You're welcome," Lulu said. Jill said nothing.

Lulu turned out her light and blessed herself. As she began her examination of conscience, the thought intruded that Elise wasn't like any of the sisters in *Little Women*.

Chapter Two

Elise was asleep when Lulu and Jill left for breakfast. When they returned, she was applying her makeup at the closet mirror, dressed in a fresh white shirt and the previous day's madras skirt, crumpled from its night on the closet floor. "Where're my Bass Weejuns?" she asked her reflection. She reached into the closet, pulled out her shoes and slid them on while holding onto the closet door and smiling at the mirror. Without closing the closet, she crossed to her desk, picked up her purse, and walked to the door of the room. She took one step out, turned halfway back, raised one hand, said, "Ta ta," and closed the door behind her.

Lulu smiled at Jill and pushed the closet door shut. "Good grief."

Jill stuck her tongue out at the door of 104. "And good riddance."

The two roommates walked across the road from Chubbuck to the auditorium/gymnasium in Hesseltine, the Women's Union, where the freshmen men and women were seating themselves on folding chairs. As they glanced around, Jill nudged Lulu and whispered, "Our future husbands could be in this very room." Lulu wasn't exactly looking for a husband, but she did hope that at Lovejoy she would find her first real boyfriend. Although she'd had a crush on her hospital co-worker Keith Sinclair and had shared a memorable embrace with Wesley Carmichael the night his younger brother arrived at the hospital in an ambulance, she'd never had a real boyfriend. She'd never been the one to ride in the front passenger seat of a boy's car as though she owned it, or to wear his class ring around her neck, or to know she had a date for every single Saturday night and every single special event. She certainly didn't want to get married anytime soon like her high school friend Lenore, who had eloped the day of her eighteenth birthday. Or like her friend Alice, who spent her days in a remote farmhouse in the sole company of a baby. But, after so much vicarious yearning, Lulu did want to experience romance first hand.

Dr. J. Prescott Livingstone, President of the college, stood on the stage at the podium and beamed at the students while they settled themselves and finally, mesmerized by his frozen smile, fell silent. "Welcome!" Dr. Livingstone's smile thawed and he came to life. "Welcome to Lovejoy, Lovejoy where you will receive a strong liberal arts education. To paraphrase St. Paul, when you were children, you talked like children, thought like children, reasoned like children. Now, you are children no longer, but men and women, men and women in this community of scholars known as Lovejoy. It is time to put away childish things — and childish thinking." With much gesticulation and head wagging, he informed his audience that their average SAT scores were Lovejoy's best yet and that much was expected of them. He turned and pointed to a sign behind him that read: *In Loco Parentis*. Lulu had seen the motto on posters in the lobby and dining hall of Chubbuck — it meant parents were crazy, Bridey had said. "It means the college stands in the place of your parents," Dr. Livingstone said.

"Permit me to address the topic of student life, if I may," Dr. Livingstone went on. A strong liberal arts education, he said, did not consist merely of going to classes, reading the assignments, writing papers and taking tests, although those things were important. No, a strong liberal arts education meant taking part in all of campus life. Each student should familiarize himself with the college's nature preserve, with its rare book collection, especially the prized manuscripts of Maine's own Sarah Orne Jewett, and with its art collection, especially the prized works of Maine's own Winslow Homer. Each student should support the athletic teams, the student newspaper and the guest lecture series.

Especially the guest lecture series. Dr. Livingston said that, as he was the one to do the inviting, he knew how difficult it was to attract first-rate speakers. "I made tentative plans with one eminent scholar on several occasions only to have him cancel at the last minute. Finally, the man wrote me that we had better give up trying to fix a date. 'You see,' he wrote, 'I try to schedule my speaking engagements on my way to somewhere else.'" Dr. Livingstone paused before delivering the clincher. "And Lovejoy, Maine, isn't on the way to anywhere.'"

Lulu was surprised by how heartily her classmates laughed. She knew Meduxnekeag was an out-of-the-way sort of place, but Lovejoy was in central Maine and central Maine seemed not so very far from Portland and Portland not so very far from Boston. She found Dr. Livingstone's speech exhilarating, nevertheless. She loved his stately phrases and what she imagined would be called "rhetorical flourishes." And she loved his message. She'd already decided she'd settle for B's rather than A's if it meant taking full advantage of what the college had to offer.

Looking pleased with himself, Dr. Livingston tucked his notes into the inside breast pocket of his tweed jacket and turned halfway around to introduce the others on the stage: the stoic-looking Dean of Men, the giddy-looking Dean of Women, the head nurse of the infirmary and the President and Vice President of Student Government.

After the nurse and student officers had spoken, the Dean of Men instructed the freshmen men to stand and follow him across campus to Conwell, the Men's Union, where their orientation would continue. Lulu scanned the crowd that filed out behind their Pied Piper. A college romance wouldn't be like a high school one. Instead of jalopies and class rings and silly talk, there would be serious discussions over coffee about the Impressionists, the Existentialists and the Expatriates. There would be fraternity parties with alcohol — Lulu had made up her mind to be a sophisticated, if cautious, drinker — and long walks hand in hand and warm embraces and sweet murmurings of love. Suddenly, she was once again in the night time hallway of Our Lady of Sorrows Hospital wrapped in Wesley's arms, his shirt damp with sweat and tears, his chest shuddering with the relief of knowing that his brother would be okay. Shaking her head to put the picture out of her mind, Lulu reminded herself that she had very little in common with Wesley Carmichael.

At the podium, Dean Diller was all smiles, the spiky ends of her black hair shooting off like sticks in a twig wreath. She composed her expression so as to convey one basic principle: all restrictions had been instituted by the college *in loco parentis* with the women's best interests in mind. She herself, she was at pains to explain, had very little leeway when it came to adjusting the rules or making exceptions. Sometimes a student approached her about changing rooms or roommates or classes, but, sadly, none of these matters were within her power. "If I had a magic wand" — her smile returned at the thought of this fancy — "I'd make all your wishes come true." The smile vanished. "Alas, I have no magic wand."

Bridey turned in her seat, looked Lulu straight in the face and briefly crossed her eyes. Lulu put her hand over her mouth to keep from laughing out loud. To distract herself, she studied the room, which with its dark wood and white plaster resembled a courtroom. She imagined a trial taking place with herself as judge, then prosecutor, defense lawyer and, finally, defendant, not guilty as charged. She awoke from her reverie when everyone clapped and stood up.

Outside, on the top step of the Union, Lulu stood with Jill and surveyed the campus. Lovejoy had been founded as a Baptist college in the aftermath of the Civil War. After World War II, with the arrival of the GIs and their government-paid tuitions, the college sketched an ambitious plan to move out of the moldering former mansions and squat utilitarian buildings in town to higher ground on the outskirts. By 1961, the trees planted in bare fields had matured enough to shade the buildings, all Federal style in a uniform red brick with white wood trim. From the steps of Hesselton, Lulu could see the four women's dorms in front of her and, to her right, the president's house. On a rise to the left, the plain white conical steeple of the chapel poked above the trees. From seven in the morning until nine at night, its carillon chimed the quarter and half hours and, on the hour, "The Old One Hundred."

Halfway down the hill from the chapel, at a ninety degree angle to the four classroom buildings, stood the library, Lovejoy's most imposing building, the tip of its elaborately tiered steeple the highest point on campus. Beyond the library lay the quadrangle of the men's dorms, fraternity houses and Conwell Union. Beyond that was a pond, a field house and playing fields — and, so Lulu had been told, a little theater.

Lulu counted a total of seven tiers on the library tower. The bottom tier was a square with clock faces, the top a tall skinny cone from which protruded a wrought iron bird that turned in the wind.

"It looks like a wedding cake," Jill said.

"What?"

"The library steeple. It reminds me of a wedding cake."

It occurred to Lulu that Jill had marriage on the brain.

The two spent much of the rest of the day together, reconnecting after splitting up to take separate language exams. Summer heat clung to the campus as though reluctant to depart from such a uniformly beautiful and well-kept place. The flowerbeds surrounding the red brick buildings looked artless, but there was nothing wild or weedy about them. The maples lining the pathways were well spaced, each given room to spread and grow symmetrically, to fulfill its potential like an indulged only child.

Here and there, Lulu and Jill would spot Elise, but they didn't acknowledge each other. Lulu felt as though she'd be intruding. Jill said she wouldn't stoop so low. Elise was never alone. Once, Lulu saw her walking arm in arm with a blond athletic-looking fellow, Sammy presumably. He was wearing loafers without socks, a madras shirt and Bermuda shorts, his wire-rimmed eyeglasses pushed to the top of his head. Another time, Elise, Muffy, the presumed Sammy and several others also in madras and loafers were sitting together under a spruce on the grassy rise leading to the chapel laughing and carrying on as though they had known each other for years. Perhaps, Lulu thought — wistfully — they all belonged to the same set of sister and brother schools. Perhaps they were like an enormous family of siblings — oddly all the same age. Yet, the way Elise clung to Sammy's arm and looked up into his face did not make the two of them seem like brother and sister.

Late in the afternoon, Lulu walked up the wide steps in the middle of the terraced lawn between the classroom buildings and through the library's main entrance to attend a meeting for students on scholarship. She would have to work ten hours a week at a campus job. Considering the price of room, board and tuition compared to the minimum wage she had been paid at Our Lady of Sorrows, the deal was overwhelmingly in her favor. At the threshold of the meeting room, she looked around half expecting to see Dottie. The only other woman from First Floor Chubbuck, however, was Janet, who waved and pointed to an empty seat next to hers. Lulu sat and looked around. It looked as though all the freshmen with amateur haircuts and plastic-framed glasses had been skimmed off for this meeting. The exception was a boy — man, Lulu reminded herself — on the far side of the room. His curly blond hair fell past his earlobes, and he lay back in his seat with an insouciance no one else matched. Perhaps every student in the room except him and Janet was from Maine and wouldn't otherwise be able to afford any college, including the University of Maine.

Janet wasn't exotic looking like the guy with the golden curls, but with her contact lenses and her smooth brown pageboy, she looked as polished as her roommates Mimi and April. Lulu guessed that if Janet hadn't gotten a scholarship to Lovejoy, her parents could have afforded to send her to the University of New Hampshire.

Lulu's parents had been in favor of her going to college somewhere or other but had had no idea how they could afford the board and tuition anywhere. Her father, who was on an even keel after a history of unhealthy high and low spirits, avoided thorny problems of a personal nature. It was her mother who one weekday morning put on the hat she wore to church and went up to the high school to get Lulu out of class to consult with the guidance counselor. The University of Maine was too expensive, she told Mr. Cyr, but she wondered if Lulu could work out a way to attend one of the teacher training schools.

"She should apply to Lovejoy," Mr. Cyr said.

Her mother sat back and blinked and Lulu knew what she was thinking: *If we can't afford the U of M, we certainly can't afford the likes of Colby, Bates or Lovejoy.*

"You see, Mrs. Delaney, starting this coming year, Lovejoy is offering full scholarships to Maine students, especially ones who wouldn't be able to go to college otherwise."

"But could Lulu keep up at Lovejoy?"

Lulu was shocked. Her mother had always encouraged her and told her she was smart.

"She's in the National Honor Society and her test scores are excellent — excellent for Meduxnekeag High but at the same time decent enough for Lovejoy."

Decent enough for Lovejoy? Lulu spoke up. "Couldn't I go pretty much wherever I could afford the tuition?"

"Lulu," Mr. Cyr turned to her. "Lovejoy, Colby, Bates and Bowdoin are in Maine, but they aren't really Maine schools the way the U of M is, not any more. Those colleges draw students from prep schools and top-notch suburban schools all over New England and beyond. We've had only a trickle of graduates go there in recent years. Sad to say, most of them drop out."

"I got six hundreds in my SAT's!" Lulu felt her face reddening. She couldn't believe she had to plead her case with Mr. Cyr.

"Yes, and we at Dux High are proud of you. But, as you know, Lulu, those tests range even higher. Some of the students at Lovejoy score in the high seven hundreds. I'm not saying they're smarter than you are. What I am saying is that they've been pushed and, truth to be told, force-fed to perform at the top of their potential."

Mr. Cyr turned his attention to Lulu's mother as though Lulu herself were a small child who couldn't be expected to have a say in her own future. "She'll have to work hard and sharpen her study skills, but by junior year I predict she'll have caught up with the best of them. That's what happened with the Sinclair twins, who graduated a few years ago, and that's what's happening with Jimmy Taylor, who's there now."

"None of those boys behaved all that well in high school," Lulu's mother said.

Lulu thought her mother's comment must have popped out unbidden — it wasn't like her to make personal remarks. As for Mr. Cyr's cautious appraisal of Lulu's prospects, she felt insulted but not dismayed. Except for a TV course on New Math junior year, she'd never worried about her grades or had to kill herself trying. How much harder could college be? She loved to read and that's what college work would consist of, more and more reading.

Lulu emerged from her reverie to find assignments being given out. Hers was in the library. The library! More and more reading!

She was glad she didn't get Janet's detail in the dining hall. Lulu feared she herself would be too clumsy for waitressing.

Supper, like all the meals so far, was cafeteria style. As Lulu stood with her tray in the elegant wood-paneled dining hall, she was glad she had Jill beside her. Otherwise, she would have had to sit with strangers. But, of course, she realized, everyone there was among strangers — or almost everyone. Elise and Muffy and two other coeds Lulu had seen them with earlier were laughing and talking at one of the tables. There was room for two more, but Lulu wouldn't think of joining them, and she was sure Jill wouldn't want to either.

"I see First Floor Chubbuck!" Jill set off and Lulu followed.

Mimi looked up as they took the last two seats at a table for eight. "Welcome to our table, folks, and to our humble repast, such as it is."

Because of her Groucho Marx accent, everything Mimi said sounded to Lulu like a joke. Lulu put on a goofy-looking smile and fluffed up her hair. "I'd change this potpie into filet mignon…if only I had a magic wand."

Everyone laughed and Lulu, who was used to amusing her family and friends with her imitations, felt almost at home.

"When do you think Ricky Nelson will get here?" Bridey looked around at the others.

"Ricky Nelson?" Lulu spread her napkin over her lap.

"Yeah, Ricky Nelson. They say he's in our class."

"But Bridey…" Dottie spoke in a gentle, reproving tone. "…just who is *they*?"

"People are talking about it all over. He's skipping Freshman Orientation because he doesn't want to draw attention to himself. He wants to blend in and have an ordinary college experience after spending his whole life in a fishbowl. He'll arrive in time to start classes." Bridey took a mouthful of food and chewed slowly, savoring her bombshell.

After supper, the eight First Floor Chubbuck freshmen walked out onto the lawn that lay between the two sets of women's dorms. Men and women sprawled on the grass listening to the golden-haired man from the scholarship meeting, who sat cross-legged strumming a guitar and singing. Some in the crowd were singing along. When her new friends plopped down, Lulu did too, although it crossed her mind she was risking grass stains. After the verses of "Michael, Row the Boat Ashore" were repeated over and over and as the crowd sang more and more zestfully, she joined in, softly at first and then with abandon, her voice drowning in the chorus of Lovejoy Class of 1965 lustily urging Michael to shore through rough seas.

A girl — woman — with curly blond hair that matched the guitarist's rose from the grass and danced free-form among the others. The long silk scarf around her neck, like the ones Elise and Muffy wore, danced in the air behind her. She whipped it off and, laughing, let it float onto the bent curly head of the guitarist.

When the warning bell rang, the women rose almost in a body and walked the short distance to their dorms. The men seemed in no hurry to leave. Apparently, Lulu realized, they had a later curfew — or perhaps no curfew at all. She didn't mind. She was going to have a wonderful four years at Lovejoy, she just knew it.

She hadn't been asleep long when she woke up to a roaring sound. She and Jill ran to the windows. After a minute, Elise joined them. A mob of freshmen men was outside chanting something at the tops of their lungs. Dottie, Katerie and Bridey and then Mimi and Janet came running into Room 104. "Can you believe it?" Mimi said. "April is sleeping right through this."

Out in the hall, Deb yelled, "Panty raid!"

Dottie, Katerie and Bridey and Mimi and Janet rushed from Room 104 back to their own rooms. "Panties! Panties! Panties!" The guys roared. Already panties were flying through the air from the upper floors. Jill, Lulu and Elise ran to their bureaus and pulled open drawers. Each grabbed a pair of panties and ran to the window Jill had flung open. Jill and Lulu threw theirs willy-nilly; Elise hung back, searching the moonlit faces outside.

"Throw, Elise, throw!" Jill was jumping up and down like a child.

"I'm looking for Sammy!" Elise's lisp was gone and she, too, sounded as excited as a child. Lulu felt as though maybe Elise was a regular person, after all. Elsie threw her panties in a wide arc, and all three roommates put their hands to their faces and shrieked.

The underwear had been flung out into the dark, but when Lulu got back into bed and shut her eyes, she saw a blue sky raining panties. They were almost all sheer and lacy and high cut. One pair was all cotton with thick cuffs and a wide waistband. Lulu opened her eyes and sat up in bed. She had gone with her mother to Penney's to buy new underwear. "You've bought the last pair in your size," the saleslady said. "Myrtle Marshall was in here last week and bought your size to take with her into the Army." Lulu and her mother had sewn tiny personalized labels into every article of her clothing.

Lulu pictured the men's dorms festooned with panties, the one pair perfect for a WAC bearing her name.

Chapter Three

The next day everything changed, and it was obvious to Lulu things would never be the same again. The upperclassmen returned. They descended in waves, taking over the dorms and dining halls and walkways as the formerly bold freshman class fragmented into meek little huddles, scuttling about campus as directed and tending to such matters as filling out index cards with temporary faculty advisors.

After breakfast on Friday, Lulu walked with Jill to Hesseltine where the folding chairs had been packed away and the auditorium/gym converted into a sort of bazaar. Each department had a table surmounted by a large hand-written sign and manned by a professor. This was the class fair. The system was handicapped, Deb had explained, in favor of the seniors and juniors, leaving the sophomores in the least desirable position. The freshmen were slated mostly for 101's, which, Deb assured her advisees, were plentiful.

The auditorium was already full, and many students, no doubt the sophomores, were moving from booth to booth at a trot. Clutching the index card she'd filled out the day before, Lulu hurried first to French 201, then to Latin 101, Math 101 and English 101. At each booth, she filled out the class times on her card. She saved *Great Thinkers of the Western World* for last, where there were four lines and four professors instead of the usual one.

A blush rose up Lulu's neck and face as though she were standing in line on the sidewalk outside Dux Theater to see an x-rated movie, an occasion of sin or near-occasion of sin, she had never courted. In the diocesan paper that summer, the Bishop of Portland had warned students attending non-Catholic colleges against taking courses that could undermine their faith. By the time Lulu read the bishop's words, she'd already set her heart on *Great Thinkers*. For one thing, it was a prerequisite for a major in any of the social sciences, and practically every freshman took it. Besides, Keith Sinclair, her charming co-worker at Our Lady of Sorrows, had recommended it. Lulu didn't intend to give up belief in a personal God the way — she discovered chatting with him during slack periods on the night shift — Keith had, but she did want to expand her thinking. She wanted to understand the sorts of things he understood.

After supper, eight of the First Floor Chubbuck freshmen congregated in Room 104. "The Thunder Thinkers," Bridey said. She was speaking of the heads of the various humanities departments, the professors who gave the *Great Thinkers* lectures. "They're showing off to get people to major in their field." She tapped her cigarette against the ashtray she held in one hand. "That's how college works. The professors compete for the best students."

"What about the rest of us?" April looked worried. She brought a tissue to the pink tip of her nose.

Lulu wasn't worried. She figured some department would spot potential in her. If several departments wanted her, she'd have to make a choice — even though she always hated to disappoint anyone.

Bridey brought the cigarette level to her mouth. "If you're not a junior thunder thinker, you can always major in psychology or sociology." She took a puff.

"They're not too hard?" April scrunched the tissue in her hand.

"At Lovejoy everything's hard," Bridey said. "Psych's got probability and Sosh has statistics…." She frowned. "Or maybe it's the other way around. Anyway, probability and statistics are really hard, but otherwise most of the tests are true or false. Also, there's not much writing and a lot of people major in them. So you can sort of get lost in the crowd."

"I'm interested in Psych but I wouldn't major in it," Mimi said. She lay across the bottom of Jill's bed, her head leaning on her hand. "Biology's the best preparation for med school."

Lulu felt a sudden admiration for Mimi. She herself planned to take only the minimum requirements in math and science. She'd avoid music as well as she had a tin ear. Art, too, as she wasn't good at drawing and she figured to appreciate art properly she'd have to have some talent in executing it.

"By the way, did anyone notice an odor in the trunk room when you put your suitcases away?" Bridey looked around at her audience.

"EEEyoo!" A collective expression of disgust went through the group. Also a wave of interest as all leaned towards Bridey.

"They say that one year a woman in this dorm, on this floor, had a baby and put it into her suitcase in the trunk room and left it there."

"And what happened?" Jill opened her eyes wide.

"Well, it died, of course. And the first person who went to get her suitcase at the end of the year opened the door and this awful smell came rolling out. The poor thing nearly fainted. Well, she told the housemother and the housemother told the Dean and the Dean came right over and the police got involved..."

"Did they find the mother?" Jill was pitched so far forward on her desk chair she looked about to fall off.

"Yes, it hadn't been that long since the birth and when she was examined internally, gynecologically, it was easy to see she was the mother and then she confessed."

"And then what happened?"

"I think she went to prison. I'm not sure about that. It just about ruined Lovejoy's reputation. People were afraid to let their daughters come here."

"Bridey," Dottie tilted her head and gave her roommate a gently skeptical look. "When did all this take place?"

"Well, I don't know exactly. In the fifties, I think."

Dottie slowly shook her head. "Sounds like one of those things that didn't really happen."

"No, no! It really happened. It was in all the papers."

Saturday morning, Lulu and Jill bought their books at Hades, the combination snack bar and bookstore located in the bowels of the library. As they walked back to Chubbuck, their arms loaded, Jill said, "Let's go downtown after lunch and buy stuff for the room."

"What kind of stuff?"

"You know, matching bedspreads and spider plants like the

ones in Deb's room and maybe some goldfish in a bowl, stuff like that."

Lulu had just written a check and carefully tallied the stub. Except for a few days' work during Christmas and Easter vacations, the money she'd earned in the summer would have to last the whole year. If she joined a sorority, there would be an initiation fee. Most students belonged to sororities or fraternities, and, as Dr. Livingstone had advised, Lulu wanted to be part of all aspects of the college. Maybe if she said nothing, Jill would drop the idea of more spending.

In the lobby, Jill went immediately to the pigeonholes along the wall next to the sign-in desk where she had been checking every day for a letter from Ronnie, her boyfriend back in Fall River, Massachusetts. She let out a squeal, set her books on the desk, plucked out an envelope, studied the front, kissed it and pressed it to her heart.

Lulu set down her own books, pulled out a letter from her own pigeonhole and was surprised the handwriting was not her mother's. There was something familiar, however, about the geometric shape of the writing. In the upper right hand corner, she read "Wesley Carmichael" and a Boston address. She had a visceral feeling of herself and Wesley holding each other, his chest moist through his cotton shirt and surprisingly solid.

Jill stuck her letter between her teeth and picked up her stack of books in both hands. Lulu did likewise. In 104, each dropped her books and sank onto her bed to read her mail.

Dear Lulu,

I am still in Meduxnekeag, but I put my college address on the envelope because I expect to be there by the time you get this letter. I'll be glad to get back to Boston because not much is happening here at home. I keep thinking about you and what a good friend you were to me the night it was touch and go with Wade.

He's coming along pretty well, by the way. He'll be home in a few weeks and maybe even back to school before Thanksgiving. He's sorry to be missing out on the beginning of senior year. If you ask me, it's just as well that he's missing out on certain things, if you get what I mean. He keeps saying he's sorry and that he's not going to hang around with a drinking crowd any more. Let's hope he can continue to stay right with Jesus.

I hope you are off to a good start at Lovejoy. What I found out freshman year was that Dux High did not prepare me as well as I thought it had. Some of the other students here were much better prepared. Also, there are so many distractions. I really like Boston, however, and everything there is to do in a big city (not much like Meduxnekeag, ha!) Maybe in Lovejoy there aren't so many distractions.

Lulu, I'm remembering you in my prayers. Don't let college get you down — or turn your head. Keep in mind Elijah's still, small voice. I look forward to hearing from you and all about how you are getting along at Lovejoy.

Your friend,
Wesley Carmichael

Beneath his signature, Wesley had sketched a city skyline and in the foreground a potato barrel standing in a field. A human figure stood between background and foreground facing the city. Neither Wesley nor Lulu lived on a farm, but compared to their new classmates they were both country people.

Lulu folded the letter back into the envelope. She didn't get the allusion to Elijah and it gave her a funny feeling to think of staying right with Jesus. That was Pentecostal talk. No doubt it was common parlance at Nott Bible College. Every year one or two graduates of Dux High went on to Nott, which, behind their backs, classmates who thought of themselves as more worldly, Lulu included, referred to as "Not College," "All for Naught" and "Not for Real."

Lulu pictured Wesley sitting down to write this long letter to her. His square face and even features, which were as geometrically precise as his handwriting, were assets. His inflamed complexion and reserved manner were liabilities. The total might have shaken out to allow for a measure of popularity beyond the couple of boys who were his friends except that, in the eyes of his schoolmates, he possessed a fatal flaw: he had no personality.

When he was a senior and Lulu a junior, they had been in an experimental TV math class that met mid morning in the cafeteria. As a result of sitting across a table from him five mornings a week watching him take carefully diagrammed notes, which he would swivel for her to look at, she had developed a crush on him, a secret crush she'd scarcely admitted to herself. Now, she wasn't sure she would have much to say to him in an answering letter. Aside from taking a class together, all they had in common was having been thrown together in a crisis, a once-in-a- lifetime, unrepeatable kind of event. It was by chance that she'd been working at Sorrows the night screaming ambulances delivered Wade and five other teenage boys, by chance that Wesley showed up *in loco parentis*, that she stood with him outside the open emergency room door and that, at the moment they knew Wade would be okay, he enfolded her in a shuddering embrace. There was almost no chance they'd ever be thrown together again.

Elise strode in leaving the door ajar. "Three little maids from school were here looking for you."

"Who?" Lulu and Jill both looked up.

"April, May and June from down the hall."

Lulu smiled. The variation on the names April, Mimi and Janet was pretty funny in spite of Elise's dismissive tone of voice.

Jill folded her letter and put it back into its envelope. She looked over at Elise, who dropped a few books onto her desk and began humming to herself. "Lulu and I are going downtown this afternoon to buy matching bedspeads and stuff," Jill said.

"Matchy-matchy, too bourgeois for me." Elise took a drag on her cigarette. "But you two go ahead." She tilted her head and blew a column of smoke into the air.

"Knock, knock." Mimi lifted her fist and let it fall against an imaginary door. In her other hand, she waved a brochure. "Look at this, mail order bedspreads. We can order them through Veronica." She read from the brochure: "*Top quality and prices you can't beat.*" Mimi had a more decisive manner than her roommates, Lulu decided, like the lead puppy in a litter of look-alikes. She had pulled her hair up into a messy chignon.

"We're trying to decide between the blues and the pinks," The whine in April's voice suggested an underlying resentfulness, as though she were the pup the mother dog couldn't spare a teat for and got bottle-fed by its human family, setting up a tug-of-war between feelings of abandonment and privilege. She had pulled her pageboy back into two short ponytails that waggled as she spoke.

"I like them both," Janet said, like the perfect mid-pack animal. A plaid plastic band running from ear to ear kept her hair off her face.

Jill took the brochure from Mimi and paged through it. "I like this pink one."

Elise glanced over Jill's shoulder. "So ess, ess and gee." She took a drag on her cigarette.

"Ess, ess and gee?" Jill looked up from the brochure.

Elise smirked. "Sweet, simple and girlish."

Jill frowned and Lulu felt sorry for her. Maybe Jill's being an only child accounted for her not knowing when she was being set up. Lulu pointed to the brochure. "How about that green one with the pink stripe in it?" If Janet, who was also on scholarship, could spring for a bedspread, then so could Lulu. It was a practical purchase, too, because without spreads the beds looked a little unkempt. The fact that Elise wasn't buying one wouldn't matter because her bed was above the sight line.

"Perfect!" Jill smiled at Lulu, a smile that said the two of them were a team even if Elise was a spoiler.

After lunch when Lulu and Jill were in 104 alone, Jill said, "Ready to go downtown? Bridey's going with us."

Lulu stiffened and blushed. She'd hoped the bedspread purchase had satisfied Jill's desire to buy stuff. "We can enjoy Deb's plants. We don't have to have our own."

"I can buy one for one window, and you can buy one for the other."

"Actually, my desk isn't by either window. So maybe you should ask Elise about buying the other plant." Lulu knew what she was saying verged on meanness in every definition of the word, but she was determined not to open her checkbook again in a hurry.

"I wouldn't stoop that low." Jill stuck out her lower lip, which made her look about as old as Lulu's four-year-old brother Neil.

Jill returned later in the afternoon, all smiles and carrying a shopping bag and two spider plants in hanging baskets. "Happy un-birthday!" She swung one basket in Lulu's direction. If she'd been upset with Lulu earlier, she'd gotten over it. She placed the baskets on her desk, dug into the shopping bag and pulled out a small brown paper bag. "I went to a hardware store and got hooks."

"You know how to screw them in?"

"Of course, my daddy taught me." Jill borrowed an electric drill from the custodian, stood on a chair and drilled a hole in the lintel above each window. She screwed the hooks in and hung the baskets. Lulu wouldn't have felt competent with an electric drill. Jill jumped down from the chair and gestured with the drill to the window over Elise's desk. "That plant is yours, Lulu. All you have to do is water it regularly."

Lulu realized a thank you was in order, but the words stuck in her throat.

Saturday evening the fraternities held parties — parties from which freshmen were banned for the initial weeks of the semester. To fill the social gap for freshmen and non-Greeks, Student Government had arranged for movies to be shown in Hessleton auditorium. The president of Stu Gov, Bridey informed the others, was headed by a non-Greek, the first non-Greek in its history. "He thinks the freshmen will think Saturday night movies are so neat, they don't need to join fraternities or sororities." She briefly crossed her eyes. "Ha!" The First Floor Chubbuck freshmen, minus Elise, walked across to Hessletine together to see *Death of a Salesman*. "Low-man, get it?" Bridey whispered early in the movie. When Willy Loman's wife said to his sons, "Attention must be paid to such a man, attention must be paid," Lulu put her face in her hands and wept. She felt Jill's hand on her arm and a tissue pressed into her hand, which made it even harder for her to stop crying. She took off her glasses and dug her hands into her eyes and tried not to cry out loud and embarrass herself and ruin the movie for everyone else. She stayed in her seat wiping her glasses for several minutes after the lights came up.

When she stepped out into the lobby, Jill disengaged herself from a little knot of men and women and once again put her hand on Lulu's arm. "You okay, Roomie?"

"Oh, sure, I'm fine." Lulu's laugh turned to a snuffle. She wiped her eyes and nose again with the tissue.

"Seth offered to walk me to the dorm, but if you need me…"

"No, no," This time Lulu was able to speak calmly. " I'm fine."

Quite a few men took it upon themselves to escort a new acquaintance across the road to the women's dorms. Lulu walked back with a remnant of the First Floor Chubbuck she'd come with. Dottie fixed on her the maternal look Lulu had previously seen her give Bridey and invited her into their room, but Lulu was sure Dottie's natural solicitude would cause her to burst into tears all over again.

Alone in 104, Lulu lay on her bunk with all her clothes on. All the people she'd met at Lovejoy knew only her, not her family, not her history. Each freshman was a cut flower in an assortment, no two from the same garden. No one at Lovejoy knew what in Meduxnekeag was common knowledge. That her father, for instance, when he got out of the Army had suffered a nervous breakdown and had had to leave farming and move into town where he took the job he'd held almost every year since, clerking at the Five and Dime. A stranger shopping there might assume that her friendly, well-spoken, handsome father in his dress shirt and tie was the manager or possibly a higher-up from away come to check up on the Meduxnekeag branch. Once upon a time, Lulu had thought his job wonderful, selling spools of thread, measuring out penny candy in small white paper bags, ringing up the purchases and handing back change all the while calling each customer by name and commenting on the weather and the prospects for a good harvest. For some time now, she'd realized that nothing he did in a day's work was more complicated than what her eleven-year-old brother Johnny could do. Johnny, in fact, with his paper route and lawn mowing and odd jobs already showed more ambition and business sense than their father.

The other fathers of Chubbuck freshmen were obviously successful enough to send their daughters to Lovejoy. If she tried to explain her father to any of her floor mates, it might end up looking as though she had no respect for him or, worse, that she was out and out ashamed of him.

She sat up and swung her feet to the floor. She picked up Wesley's letter from her desk and reread it. Then she sat at her desk chair, took a page from her box of stationery and wrote.

Dear Wesley,

Thank you for your nice letter.

I'm glad to hear that Wade is doing well. I'm sure he's learned his lesson.

I am getting along fine so far at Lovejoy. This evening a bunch of us went to see the movie Death of a Salesman. *It made me cry. I hope my brothers never lose respect for my father the way Biff and his brother did for their father. It was the saddest movie I've ever seen. I don't know much about Arthur Miller, but his story really hit home. The funny thing is no one else was crying — that I could see. Maybe coming from the same town as me, you would see the movie the way I did. Or maybe not. Your father owns his own business, after all. I don't know how easy it would be to see that movie in Boston, but I'd recommend it even though it's sad.*

Have fun in Boston and study hard!

Your friend,

Lulu

P.S. I know Elijah was an Old Testament prophet, but I'm afraid I don't know what you mean by the still, small voice. L.

Lulu addressed and sealed the envelope. She thought once more of the embrace she and Wesley had shared outside the emergency room. This time she didn't feel warmed by his radiant heat.

Jill came into the room. She closed the door and gave Lulu a searching look. "Have you been away from home before, Lulu?"

"I've been to Bangor overnight. I've been to pajama parties. But away like this? No, not really."

"I thought so!" Jill sat on the edge of Lulu's bunk and leaned forward to look at Lulu practically eye to eye. "Lulu, the first year I went away to camp, I was so homesick!"

"Homesick? I don't think I'm homesick, Jill."

"Maybe you don't think you are, Lulu, but that's the way you're acting — crying over little things."

Lulu wanted to tell Jill that what she had been crying over wasn't a small matter, but the explanation seemed altogether too arduous. "Maybe you're right."

Her diagnosis apparently confirmed, Jill gave a big smile and jumped to her feet. "Seth? The guy who walked me home? He's a junior. He doesn't believe in the fraternity system. That's why he was at the movies tonight. He's more mature than the fraternity guys."

Lulu and Jill were in bed with their reading lamps on ten minutes before curfew. Instead of looking at the book in her lap, Lulu was thinking how odd it was that she had felt comfortable confiding in Wesley about matters she'd never told anyone else. By now, her family would have received the long letter she'd sent them telling all about the exciting events of the past few days. Perhaps that very evening her mother had read it aloud at the supper table the way she always did with letters from relatives who'd moved away. Lulu pictured her parents and brothers seated at the kitchen table, and a sick wave surged through her. Was she now a relative who'd moved away? Was this what homesickness felt like?

The door flew open and Elise strode in and lay across the foot of Jill's bed. Jill prodded her with her toes. "Go lie down in your own bed!" Elise's mouth opened and she snored softly. "Good grief, get out of here." Jill prodded her again, this time harder. Elise sat up and leaned on her elbow. Then she bent her head and retched, filling the room with the stink of alcohol and stomach acid.

Chapter Four

Sunday morning Lulu put on one of the two cotton shifts her mother had made for dress up and sat at her desk writing her name and "104 Chubbuck" in the inside cover of each of her new books. Because she was fasting for Mass, she hadn't accompanied Jill to breakfast. Elise descended from her bunk and, without responding to Lulu's greeting, yanked her towels off the rack and left the room.

When Jill returned, she said, "I'm going to the Dean about Elise. This is impossible. Are you coming with me?"

"Well, maybe we should speak to Deb first."

"I talked to Deb at breakfast, and she isn't prepared to do one thing. Besides, it's not something she can do anything about. We have to go right to the top, to Dean Diller. She is the Dean, after all."

"But where would she put Elise? The dorms are crowded. That's why we're three to a room."

"She could room with Muffy. Maybe there aren't three in that room. Or she could room with one of the other boarding school snobs. They all love each other, and they all hate us."

"They don't hate us, Jill. They just can't be bothered with us."

"That's worse than being hated. I'm not speaking to Elise ever again."

"Good day, ladies." Elise walked in, one towel around her body, the other around her head. She gave Lulu an appraising glance. "All dressed up for Sunday-go-to- meetin' I see." She put on Bermuda shorts and another of her white shirts and began her make-up routine at the mirror. "If I didn't have plans with Sammy, I'd join you for Mass, Lulu."

"You're Catholic, Elise?"

"Episcopalian. But I'm interested in all religions. I actually have a big interest in ecumenism."

Lulu didn't feel like asking what "ecumenism" meant. If she could figure out how to spell it, she'd look it up later in her *Webster's*.

"Besides, Episcopalians believe in just about everything Catholics do except transubstantiation."

While she was at it, she'd look up "transubstantiation."

She dropped her missal into her purse and stepped out into the hallway where Bridey and Kateri were coming around the corner from their room. "Going our way, Catholic Miss?" Bridey asked, her lopsided smile an invitation for Lulu to join them.

Outside, the air was rinsed in evaporating dew and replete with birdsong and a green, green smell. A gang of crows feasting on spilled popcorn on the steps of Hessletine boldly held their ground as the three coeds walked by. Lulu wore a straw hat because her mother had counseled that an exception could be made after Labor Day if the weather was unseasonably warm. Kateri had on a black mantilla. Bridey was bare-headed. The sun brought out the red highlights in Bridey's hair and the intense, unrelieved blackness in Kateri's. Bridey's shift, like Lulu's, was pastel, while the yellow and orange in Kateri's was as bright and bold as a muumuu. Kateri tilted her head skyward, spread her arms and called out, "Good morning, Brother Sun!"

Bridey laughed. "You don't expect the sun to answer, do you?"

"Don't you hear him?" Kateri held the ends of her mantilla while she leaped and twirled as gracefully as a trained dancer.

"And what's he saying?" Lulu was curious.

"He says, 'Good morning, Catholic misses. God is simply wild about you.'"

Lulu was delighted with the idea of the sun lumping her in with these two new Catholic friends. It stood to reason Bridey was Catholic because her name was a nickname for Bridget, and Bridget was right up there next to Patrick in the Communion of Saints. And it made sense Kateri was Catholic because all the Indians in Meduxnekeag were Catholic — although Kateri seemed quite different from the Indians in Meduxnekeag. *Kateri!* Lulu stood still for a moment. "Kateri, like Venerable Kateri Tekawitha, Lily of the Mohawks."

"My parents named me for the Indian saint."

"Actually, she's not a saint yet." Lulu resumed walking.

"She is to me." Kateri twirled around and around spreading the ends of her mantilla like wings.

Lulu stopped herself from arguing further. People could be sensitive about names, she knew. Her mother had told her she wanted to avoid Mary, Margaret and Ann — and Mary Margaret, Margaret Ann, Anne Marie and all the other names and combinations so often given to Catholic girl babies. Once she was school age, Lulu wished her mother had thought fit to give her a saint's name at least. Her middle name was Mary, and for Confirmation she had taken Louise, but Lulu would always be the real, honest-to-God name her poetic mother had bestowed upon her.

At the door of Judson, the largest lecture hall on campus — big enough to fit all the freshmen who had signed up for *Great Thinkers* — Bridey fished a tissue out of her pocketbook. She smoothed it and placed it on top of her head. "They say Fr. Flannery had a nervous breakdown and that's why he got assigned to Lovejoy instead of being made a bishop or a monsignor or something." She spoke in hushed, churchy tones. "They say he's actually quite brilliant."

Judson was nearly full. Lulu wondered whether the chapel was too small — or too Protestant — for Mass to be celebrated there. She figured the women wearing hats instead of tissues were other freshmen. She followed Bridey and Kateri halfway up the raked seats, genuflected and bowed her head. *My Jesus, I adore thee.* There was no way they could kneel. Lulu closed her eyes, folded her hands and bent her head. "Pray to God…" Bridey whispered, "…we don't forget and genuflect tomorrow at *Great Thinkers*."

Lulu lifted her head and surreptitiously studied her surroundings. Judson Lecture Hall occupied the ground floor of the science building, which was built into a hillside. Coming from the women's side of campus, Lulu and her friends had entered from the lower end. The entrance from the top of the hall was closer to the men's side of campus. The lower half of the hall was predominantly women, the upper predominantly men, the middle mixed like a bungled layer cake.

Judson was wood paneled and handsome, but it lacked the mystique of Our Lady of Perpetual Help in Meduxnekeag. Only the Blessed Sacrament on a makeshift altar on the stage marked the place as sacred. No stained glass angels stood in the windows streaming color over the congregation. No Stations of the Cross progressed down one wall and up the other. There were no statues of the Holy Family — or of anyone else, for that matter. There were no bunches of flowers in season — chrysanthemums this time of year — no odor of incense or wax, no choir tuning up. Instead of a row of altar boys in white surplices over black cassocks — Lulu's brother Johnny often among them — a guy in khakis and a button-down shirt open at the collar stood at the edge of the stage, his hands folded. From where Lulu sat, he seemed at least two inches taller than she. Without those thick glasses, he would not have been bad looking. Possibly he would be Lulu's first real boyfriend. He was, after all, Catholic.

The priest, a big, shambling middle-aged blond with a florid complexion, stood fumbling with the cinctures beneath his chasuble as though encountering them for the first time. He raised his head, cleared his throat and stared. Lulu wondered if, in the effort to dress himself, he'd forgotten he was in front of a congregation. He walked to the makeshift altar, stood tall, lifted his right hand and in as amazing a transformation as Clark Kent to Superman, his awkward demeanor gave way to an authoritative one. "*In nomine Patris et Filii et Spiritus Sancti. Amen.*" The congregation stood and blessed themselves. "*Introibo ad altare Dei.*" The I-Will-Go-to-the-Altar-of-God pulled Lulu out of Judson Hall into the timeless world of the Mass.

"*Ad Deum, qui laetificat juventutem meam,*" the altar boy responded. The same seasick wave Lulu had felt the night before passed over her. She had helped Johnny learn the Latin responses and hearing this one, "To God, who gives joy to my youth," made her feel oceans away from her little brothers.

Before starting the sermon, Fr. Flannery stood at the lectern/pulpit in his shimmery vestment beholding his congregation with calm authority. His topic, the well-formed conscience, was the same as the curate's at Our Lady of Perpetual Help in his last Confraternity of Christian Doctrine meeting with the seniors. Like the curate, Fr. Flannery cited St. Thomas Aquinas's injunction that if one finds a discrepancy between a teaching of the Church and one's conscience, one is obliged to follow one's conscience. Like the curate, he added that a well-formed conscience would naturally align with the teachings of the Church. Fr. Flannery paused to gaze at his listeners. "My argument has become tautological." He smiled. "An empty exercise in logic." Next he talked about "invincible ignorance," which sounded to Lulu as though even a conscience as badly formed as an evergreen in deep woods must be heeded.

After the sermon, Fr. Flannery announced a forthcoming meeting of the Newman Club. Lulu made a notation in her mental calendar to attend. When the collection basket was passed, she was relieved that no one dropped in folding money. She put in a quarter like everyone else.

At Communion, she joined Bridey and Kateri in the line to the altar. Lulu had gone to Confession the week before and would receive Communion for another couple of weeks. After that, she'd refrain until she got around to going to Confession again. As a child, like the other Catholic children among her friends, she'd gone to Confession every couple of weeks and received Communion weekly. Adults tended to receive both sacraments less frequently, sometimes only in the first few weeks after they'd made their yearly Easter duty. In high school, Lulu and her friends had slackened their rate of Confessions to every month or so and stopped receiving Communion every single Sunday.

Most of the congregation received Communion. No doubt the others, like her, had recently gone to Confession so as to get the school year off to a good start. Back at her seat, Christ renewed in her and in everyone else who'd received, Lulu was careful to let the host melt on her tongue and not get stuck to the roof of her mouth, which was tacky from the morning fast.

"*Dominus vobiscum*," the priest intoned.

"*Et cum spiritu tuo*," the altar boy responded.

Glancing down at her missal, Lulu recited. "*In the beginning was the Word, and the Word was with God, and the Word was God…. And the Word became flesh and lived among us; and we saw his glory...*"

After the *Deo gratias*, Kateri's eyes were glowing the way they had when she danced under the sun. "I want to meet Fr. Flannery."

"Believe me," Bridey said. "You'll be disappointed."

Lulu got in a long line with Kateri to shake Fr. Flannery's hand. For a moment, she feared he would give such heartfelt and intelligent attention to each student that it would take forever like waiting for Confession behind a penitent with years' worth of mortal sins, but the line moved quickly. The persona of absent-minded professor had replaced Superman. Fr. Flannery's handshake was as lifeless as that of a stroke patient at Our Lady of Sorrows. When she said, "Father, I enjoyed your sermon," he nodded, cleared his throat and reached to shake the hand of the student behind her, who was Kateri and then the student behind Kateri.

Bridey was waiting outside in the sunshine. "So?"

"I'm disappointed." Kateri turned down the corners of her mouth and wiped an imaginary tear from beneath her eye, and for the moment she looked all the world like Charlie Chaplin. "Are either of you going to the Newman Club meeting?" Even when merely walking, Kateri moved like a dancer.

"Are you kidding?" Bridey briefly crossed her eyes at Lulu.

"I'm going," Lulu said.

"And what draws you two there, may I ask?" Bridey said.

"Music," Kateri said.

"Do you sing?" Lulu asked.

"When I dance." Kateri lifted her arms and executed a few dance steps. "*'Tis a gift to be simple, 'tis a gift to be free/ 'tis a gift to come down where we ought to be.*" Her smile was like that of the stained glass angels at Our Lady of Perpetual Help. "After dinner I'm going to the pond and sit on a blanket and read Plato." She began to dance again. "*And when we find ourselves in the place just right,/'Twill be in the valley of love and delight.*" She stopped dancing, wrapped her arms around herself and tilted her head to the sky. "Or maybe I'll just hug Plato and contemplate the heavens."

"You wouldn't get much out of the book that way." Bridey gave Kateri a sideways glance.

"Oh, I don't know. After all, Plato was a man first, not a book."

"Well, I'd rather hug a real man — wouldn't you, Lulu?"

Lulu pictured the pond's verge with its dark seed heads floating above tan stalks and herself on a blanket with a real man, the two of them reading aloud to each other from one of the classics of Western Civilization. She laughed and hugged herself in the bright sunshine. "I want it all."

"*Praise God from whom all blessings flow. Praise Him all creatures here below. Praise Him above, ye heavenly host. Praise Father, Son and Holy Ghost...Amen.*" Bridey's happy soprano rang out above the other voices at Sunday dinner, the first formal sit-down meal of the semester. Holding trays aloft, a row of coeds in white aprons burst from the cafeteria under the stairs and fanned out like cheerleaders at halftime. Janet lowered her tray to a stand and placed steaming bowls and platters on the table occupied by the First Floor Chubbuck freshmen — minus Elise. The look on her face reminded Lulu of how she felt the day she took the test for her driver's license. "Save room for dessert." Janet flashed an anxious smile. "It looks good."

After everyone had eaten, the servers made a second grand entrance, this time bearing crystal goblets of ice cream parfaits layered in red, white and blue bands. As Janet approached the table, her heel caught on a leg of the tray stand and she pitched forward. She righted herself but not before the parfaits slid off the tray like airplanes flying in formation and crash-landed on the table. The First Floor Chubbuck freshmen arched back and threw their hands over their faces as strawberries, blueberries, dollops of vanilla ice cream and shards of glass shot into the air.

After a stunned silence, Mimi and April leapt to their feet and put their arms around Janet, who put her face into her hands. Deb's roommate Veronica, who was dining room captain, made her way swiftly across the room. Dottie and Kateri picked up pieces of glass from the table and floor. Jill cast hopeful glances in the direction of the cafeteria. As two cafeteria workers appeared with a mop and a sponge, normal mealtime clinking and chatter resumed at the other tables. Thank God, I wasn't assigned waitressing, Lulu thought. Then she felt pity for Janet — and a little guilty for thinking of herself first — and then she was swept with giddiness. Funny as it was in an old-lady-slips-on-a-banana-peel sort of way, it would be awful to laugh out loud at her floor mate's misfortune. Lulu lowered her eyes to her lap, and was sobered to think that Janet might have to pay for the ruined parfaits and shattered goblets.

When Lulu lifted her head, Bridey caught her gaze and crossed her eyes. Lulu looked down and fought laughter all over again. It had been quite a pratfall and some day it would make a funny story, but not today.

After dinner, Lulu hurried to her first assignment at the library. Oak catalogs filled the left half of the sunny, high-ceilinged lobby; to the right was the long counter where Lulu was to report. The golden-haired boy — man — who'd played guitar on the lawn sat on a stool behind the counter. He had on the blue button-down shirt with rolled up sleeves of a boarding school boy, but if that was indeed what he was Lulu didn't think he'd be working at a scholarship job. Up close, his hair looked bleached — and not by the sun. Lulu had known a few girls in high school who'd peroxided their hair, and she herself had had a spell of using a product called "Light and Bright," but this was the first time she'd seen artificially lightened hair on a man. A lumpy middle-aged woman stood beside him. "You must be Lulu," she said. "I'm just explaining everything to Rolf here." Her smile, revealing red streaks on her prominent front teeth, was warm and welcoming. "I'm Miss Gravell. You can call me Toni on the weekends. When no one else is around."

One end of the counter was for general circulation, the other for books on reserve. Behind the reserve section was an archway to stacks of books that could not be removed from the library. At two o'clock, Miss Gravell announced she was finished for the day. "I just came in to show you two the ropes," she said, her lipstick glinting against the white enamel. She pulled a large patent leather pocketbook out from under the counter, tucked it under her arm, and walked away.

"So long, Toni-on-the-Weekends," Rolf said when she was barely out of earshot.

A few zealous upperclassmen requested books which they carried into the large reading room that lay beyond the card catalogs. Otherwise, Lulu and Rolf sat on stools behind the reserve desk and Rolf talked. He intended to major in music and go on for a PhD in musicology. Lulu had never heard of musicology. Nor did Rolf look to her like a professor. He looked like a rock and roll singer. She broke into his stream of talk. "They say Ricky Nelson's going to be in our class."

"You don't believe that rumor, do you?"

"Well, why not?" Lulu wasn't sure whether she was protecting Ricky Nelson or Lovejoy — or her own gullible self. "They say he wants a normal college experience after living his whole life in a fishbowl."

"Ricky Nelson doesn't need to go to college, Lulu, and certainly not in an out of the way place like Lovejoy. That guy has it made. He has all the connections he needs in the music world. And plenty of dough. Besides, he's older than we are."

"Well, maybe he wants a strong liberal arts education."

"You sound like Dr. Livingston I. Presume."

"But Dr. Livingston's right, isn't he?" Rolf's joke name for the president was pretty funny, but Lulu didn't feel like giving her talky coworker the satisfaction of a big laugh.

"Hah! Ricky Nelson is getting an education you and I could only dream of. If I had his life, do you think I'd bother with college — or graduate school? Ricky Nelson grew up with music. He's performed it since he was a kid. He's got all those top hits."

"But, Rolf, music isn't everything."

"Music isn't everything? Yes, it is, Lulu. The whole of life, the whole of history, can be seen through music. Pop and rock and roll are just the latest. Before that you have country and western and jazz. You have gospel and folk and protest. You have opera and symphonies. Lyrics and instrumental. Harmony and melody. Music has everything, Lulu." Rolf swung an imaginary guitar over his knee and like someone defying reality in a musical comedy movie began to sing "Hello Mary Lou," his golden curls, stiffer than naturally blonde ones would be, bouncing against his forehead. At song's end, he raised his eyes to Lulu and gave her such a soulful look she blushed.

Rolf set aside his imaginary guitar when several students materialized to take out books. When he and Lulu were once again seated at the stools, he resumed talking about music. Lulu was flattered to be his audience, but after awhile she began to feel sleepy. The thought flitted into through her head that her lack of musical ability could prevent her from full appreciation of Western Civilization. She tried to disguise a yawn. "I'm worn out from orientation."

"Go lie down inside, if you want. I'll man the fort."

Lulu couldn't see herself lying down in the reserve stacks, but she was touched by Rolf's solicitude. Maybe he didn't think only of music and of himself all the time.

After supper, there was a floor meeting where the three short wings of the hall intersected. Elise wore a white silk wrapper. Everyone else had on colorful muumuus. The two doubles on the floor besides Deb and Veronica's were occupied by sophomores. These four coeds, it appeared to Lulu, relished the fact that they were no longer mere freshmen. There was also one single room on the floor, lived in by a junior. A coed had to be at least a junior to request a single, Lulu knew from reading the college handbook, as it was considered anti-social at Lovejoy for an underclassman to live alone. In the senior dorm, on the other hand, there were a number of singles because seniors, especially Senior Scholars who wrote theses, might attain a level of maturity to room alone and still be normal. A junior living alone was in a less than normal situation.

The junior living alone on First Floor Chubbuck was Evie. Over her many-colored muumuu she wore a many-different-colored shawl. Like someone's eccentric great aunt, she sat casting stitches onto a knitting needle from a variegated ball of yarn. Although her smile was friendly enough, she spoke not at all. Her manner suggested to Lulu that she had chosen First Floor Chubbuck as the least objectionable option, that she was on the floor but not of the floor, in Chubbuck but not of Chubbuck, at Lovejoy but not of Lovejoy. In high school Confraternity of Christian Doctrine classes, Lulu had been taught that Catholics, although they may be in the world, should not be of the world. She couldn't remember whether the injunction came from an epistle of St. Paul or the Gospel of John. She could ask Wesley. Catholics knew the Bible filtered through the catechism, the lives of the saints and the Mass, not chapter and verse like the Pentecostals.

As for herself, she hungered to experience the world of Lovejoy in all its aspects, to be of it as well as in it.

Sue, a pixilated sophomore, led the meeting. The main order of business was explaining freshmen initiation, which was to begin the next day and last for one week. Each freshman, she explained, was to make a sign listing her name and hometown and to wear it around her neck anytime she left her room. From a large shopping bag, Susan produced blue and silver beanies, which were to be worn at all times starting right that minute. With the beanies on, Lulu thought all the freshmen looked a bit silly except Kateri, who was more beautiful than ever.

Lulu, Jill and even Elise made their signs before lights out. Lulu hung hers on the back of her chair and climbed into the lower bunk. She lay on her back and blessed herself. Elise paused on her climb to the upper bunk. "Oh, how cute!" she said. "Do that again."

"Do what?"

"You know what I mean. Make the sign of the cross on yourself."

"Leave her alone." Jill's voice came from the other side of the room. "Lulu is a good Catholic." Apparently, Jill had forgotten she wasn't speaking to Elise.

"Oh, but don't take offense, either of you," Elise said. "I love the Catholic Church, especially when she's in mourning. I keep waiting for this Pope to die so the world will once again be treated to the grand spectacles of a papal funeral and another convocation."

"You shouldn't want the Pope to die!" Jill's voice was rising.

"It's not that I want him to die. It's that he's bound to because he's so terribly old." Elise's voice sounded low and dreamy, not a bit argumentative. She completed her climb and Lulu heard her rustling among the covers. "Good night, my dears. God bless us, every one."

Rather self-consciously, Lulu blessed herself again. She felt too confused to examine her conscience. Did Elise set out to be mean or did she hurt her roommates' feelings inadvertently? It made Lulu feel better that Jill, like a true friend — a sister almost — had stood up for her. It was funny how Protestants viewed the Pope. To Catholics, it seemed to Lulu, the Pope was a shadowy figure whose picture hung in the vestibule of the church and whose name came up only in the prayers of the Mass. Pope John XIII with his jolly smile, on the other hand, did seem more like an actual human being than Pope Pius XII ever had. Two charismatic Catholic Johns, President Kennedy and the Pope, were leaders of the free world. Lulu felt proud. She said a prayer for each of them.

After Lulu had been asleep for an hour or so, she was awakened by a banging noise and cries of "Put on your beanies and come out! Put on your beanies and come out!" She and Elise and Jill rolled out of bed, put on their beanies and stepped into the hall. Within minutes, they were in a line with the other freshmen marching behind Sue, who was beating on a saucepan with a wooden spoon. The other sophomores and Deb and Veronica stood in the hall clapping in time to the beat. Sue's roommate threw open the hall door and the line marched out into the lobby where the coeds from the upper floors marched or clapped. The line continued down the hall to the double staircase and descended to the dining room, where the freshmen were handed mimeographed pages of lyrics and instructed to sing the Lovejoy fight song. "Louder!" the onlookers shouted. "Louder!" When the freshmen were bellowing and Lulu's face, for one, was scarlet, the upperclassmen signaled their satisfaction by breaking into applause. "Class dismissed!" someone yelled.

"You're Lovejoy's smartest class yet!" Veronica said to Lulu as they walked back up the stairs. Pretty and petite, Veronica was the brunette version of the feminine ideal.

"I know I'd never have been accepted if I'd applied this year," Deb said.

Lulu glowed to think she might be smarter than these two juniors she so admired.

When Sue threw open the first floor door, Lulu heard a keening sound. Sue pursued the sound down the hall and around the bend, the others following. April was sitting up in bed in a sea of stuffed animals trembling, her eyes red, her nose pink, her cheeks flushed and wet. Dottie sat next to her, her arm around her shoulders. "It's okay," Dottie murmured. "You're all right." The scene must have given Sue pause about the rightness of her mission because she came to a standstill at the threshold. Dottie looked up at her. "She took a sleeping pill."

"And I can't be awakened suddenly like that." The streams from April's eyes and nose threatened to run into her mouth. "Not after I've taken a pill." Like Lulu's four-year-old brother Neil, she heaved shuddering sobs between each sentence. "And I must take the pill….I need my sleep."

"It's all right," Dottie soothed. "You're okay." She slid her arms all the way around April, pulled her close and patted her back. If Dottie was afraid of getting snot and tears all over her nightie, she didn't show it.

As Mimi and Janet hurried into their room to offer comfort and Kleenex and the other coeds drifted back to their own rooms, Lulu remained in the doorway, her feelings mixed. What would be appealing in a four year old was repugnant in an eighteen year old. She felt embarrassed for April and slightly disgusted — and then guilty for feeling embarrassed and disgusted because Dottie's was, no doubt about it, the open-hearted response of a well-formed conscience.

Chapter Five

Monday morning the First Floor Chubbuck freshmen joined the stream of students headed for *Great Thinkers of the Western World*. At Judson, Lulu remembered not to genuflect and sat with Jill near where she had attended Mass the morning before. The auditorium was full. The subject was *Plato's Republic*. The lecturer was Professor Snow, the head of the Classics Department. He was a round-faced, pink-complexioned old man who would have looked completely undistinguished save for his thick white hair. As he made his points and counterpoints, he held out one hand and then the other saying, "on the one hand" and "on the other hand." There is nothing new under the sun, he informed his audience. "Man is a stranger in the world doomed to go on and on in a meaningless way unless he purify his reasoning powers in order to transcend base existence and achieve the ideal, the ideal that exists — on the one hand — way beyond man and — on the other hand — deep within him."

Plato's inner deepness sounded to Lulu like St. Thomas's well-formed conscience — or possibly Wesley and Elijah's still, small voice, whatever that meant. The congruence pleased her. She liked for people to get along with each other. She would like for her roommates to get along — even if they weren't crazy about each other.

Jill had lifted her blond desk arm into the horizontal position and was leaning over it, writing furiously. Lulu couldn't see how it was possible to both write and listen. After awhile, although mesmerized by the rhythms of "on the one hand" and "on the other hand," she no longer followed the line of thought. When Professor Snow folded his notes and left the lectern, she shook off her dreaminess the way she often did at the conclusion of Mass.

"Come on," Jill said when they stood up. "We're going to see the Dean, remember?" Lulu did remember but she'd hoped Jill would let the matter drop. Jill's severe expression, however, showed her determination to lay her case before the Dean and to have Lulu accompany her as witness and fellow sufferer.

In Dean Diller's outer office, Jill dropped her assertive manner and like the best behaved, most charming little girl in the world sweetly asked the secretary if she couldn't please speak with the dean. The door to the inner office was open a crack, through which Lulu could see the dean seated at her desk. The secretary, a grim-faced counterpoint to her smiley boss, said Jill would have to make an appointment. "But why?" Jill asked, her eyes wide. "She's here." She scooted around the secretary's desk.

"You can't…" the secretary cried and put out her hand, but Jill had already pushed open the inner door. Dean Diller looked up from her oak desk, a teacup in her hand, her corkscrew curls and Mamie Eisenhower bangs bobbing. The secretary came scurrying behind Jill.

Dean Diller set her teacup down and smiled at Jill. Her hair, which Lulu recognized as the flat black of a dye job, was stuck all over with bobby pins that failed to keep it neat. She waved her secretary back. "It's all right, Miss Maudlin, I always have time for a student."

"My roommate needs to see you, too." Jill turned to indicate Lulu, who stood on tenterhooks in the outer office.

"Yes, certainly, you may both come in. Do sit down." She gestured to a paisley loveseat. Glancing apologetically at the tea cup and half-eaten muffin on her desk, she said without a trace of annoyance, "So many meetings this morning, I hadn't time to eat my breakfast." She smiled as sweetly as Jill had earlier at Miss Maudlin. "And to what to I owe the pleasure of your visit?"

In the glow of this reception, Jill delivered an impassioned, coherent case for Elise being removed from 104 Chubbuck. The Dean responded true to the form both Deb and Bridey had predicted and that Lulu recognized from the welcoming speech — "Not in her power….If she changed a roommate for one, she'd have to do it for all…. Life is full of adjustments….If only she had a magic wand."

Jill's lower lip thrust out. Then it quivered. A tear rolled down her cheek. Lulu was mortified. Whether by design or because she couldn't help herself, her petite roommate was trying to get her way by crying. Lulu couldn't remember ever breaking down like that when crossed. Her eleven-year-old brother would die before bursting out crying. Her eight-year-old brother's eyes would fill with tears only when his older brother teased him beyond endurance. Only the four year old would cry as openly and unselfconsciously as Jill did now. The Dean stood and came around her desk, her body a solid rectangle without indentation at the waist. "Now, now," she said and looked as though she would have elaborated if Miss Maudlin hadn't appeared at the door.

"Dean Diller, your appointment with the President."

"Oh, yes, thank you, Miss Maudlin, my appointment with the President." She accepted the file folder Miss Maudlin handed her and was gone before either Lulu or Jill stood up. Jill took a hankie from her purse, and, as smoothly as Kateri's Charlie Chaplin routine on Sunday, as she pulled it over her face her expression changed from heartbreak to resignation.

On the pathway outside, the two roommates were about to head off in opposite directions, Lulu to Latin class, Jill to the dorm to type up her lecture notes, when two guys, upperclassmen, spoke to them — or rather to Jill. "How come you wrote 'Mass' on your sign?" one guy asked. "Forget how to spell your home state?"

"Or is 'Fall River, Mass' a new law of physics?" the other guy said.

Lulu wasn't good at looking up adoringly at guys and laughing the way Jill now did as though she'd never shed a tear in her life and the things they said were the funniest she'd ever heard. It helped Jill that she was short; many guys, including these two, weren't tall enough for Lulu to look up at. The men said goodbye rather unceremoniously to Lulu and set off on either side of Jill.

Lulu headed for Latin feeling oddly resentful. Ever since the upperclassmen had arrived, the sense of ownership created by the sing-along and the panty raid had gone as flat as a glass of ginger ale left standing overnight. The campus, she could now see, belonged most particularly to the juniors, who would be running student life. The sophomores, last year's darlings, had already formed friendships and had no reason to love the freshman usurpers. The seniors, as far as she could tell, were keeping mostly to themselves. She mounted the stairs to the arts building.

In the proximity of the classroom, Professor Snow's white hair accentuated the red of his skin and the blue of his eyes. Lulu could see why Deb had referred to him as "Old Red, White and Blue." He went around the seminar table of fourteen students, four men and ten women — April, a tissue held to the pink end of her nose, among them — and asked why they had signed up for Latin. "Because it's the mother of all language," Lulu said immediately, proud to have a ready answer.

"Is that so?" Professor Snow looked amused.

"Yuh, I mean, isn't it?" His amusement disconcerted her.

"You are from northern Maine — Aroostook County."

"Yuh." His non-sequitur confused her further.

"It's your 'yuh' for 'yes' that gives you away." After the other students spoke, Professor Snow picked out a word or phrase with which he could pinpoint their home states. He explained that on the one hand he was a classicist while on the other hand he was a linguist.

Growing up, Lulu had been aware of two accents. As a town dweller, she spoke with what her high school English teachers called the standard accent. These same teachers were forever correcting the speech of the country kids. Until that moment, it had never occurred to Lulu that that there might be more than one standard accent and that hers might not be the most urbane.

Professor Snow leaned forward, his elbows on the table, his hands tented in front of his face. "In this class, we'll leave aside the *agricula* and *puer* stories you read in high school — those of you who took a year. Nor will we undertake *Omnia Gallia in tres partes est*, which you would have undertaken second year. Instead, we will be reading simplified stories from *Ovid's Metamorphses*. In the *Ovid*, we'll be using the names of the Latin gods, which, of course are derived from the Greek. Next year, when you start Greek, you'll become familiar with those names, and those of you who major in Greek will encounter them in all of Greek literature, which is, of course, the foundation of world literature."

A thrill went through Lulu. Professor Snow assumed she'd take not only Latin but also Greek, and Greek, he'd said, was the foundation of world literature. Perhaps she'd become a Greek major.

"And now a word about time." Professor Snow sat up straight and splayed his hands on the table. "*Chronos*, on the one hand…" He lifted one hand. "…is the Greek word for the passage of time like that measured by the library clock and the chapel carillon. *Kairos*, on the other hand…" He lifted his other hand. "… means time in the sense of opportunity or favorable occasion. Your four years at Lovejoy are an example of *kairos*, an opportunity to immerse yourselves in the great works of art and literature. Your use of *chromos* is also important. You must learn to structure your semesters, weeks, days and hours in a way that will serve you as learners. Studying Latin every day will ensure your retaining the material in a way that cramming never will.

"Now let me say a word about Hades…"

It startled Lulu to hear Professor Snow switch to the supernatural.

As though reading her mind, he said, "I'm not talking about the mythological but rather about our own upper circle of hell here at Lovejoy. Don't fall into the habit of squandering time in the snack bar. Time is better spent attending to your studies. And when you do have leisure time, *schole* in Latin, there are more profitable ways of spending it." He raised his bushy white eyebrows. "The trick is to balance the three wisely. To quote Aristotle: *all things in moderation*."

Lulu felt right at home in Professor Snow's class. He reminded her of a gruff old great uncle with a soft heart. Or, except for his thick white hair and bushy eyebrows, of the photograph in the vestibule of Our Lady of Perpetual Help of Pope John XXIII.

At French class the next day Lulu did not feel at home. She wondered if she'd done herself a disservice by performing well enough on the placement test to qualify for a survey of French literature. M. Diderot spoke entirely in French, and Lulu found him hard to follow. When a coed asked a question in English, M. Diderot snapped to attention, his blue eyes flashing as though he had been gravely insulted. *Mademoiselle, en francais, si vous plais. Toujours, en francais en cette classe!*"

After class, the first thing Lulu heard when she returned to First Floor Chubbuck was *"Comment ca va,"* which she recognized as the everyday speech of French people in Meduxnekeag. A pudgy middle-aged woman in a blue uniform dress with the Lovejoy insignia over her ample breast was greeting a younger woman also in uniform. Both smiled shyly at Lulu. "Good morning," the older woman said. "I'm going to clean your room now."

The mother of Lulu's friend Alice was French Canadian. Maybe if Lulu had made a point of practicing with Alice's mother she wouldn't feel so inadequate in M. Diderot's French 201. There were plenty of French speakers in Meduxnekeag, but they spoke it only among themselves. Even Alice didn't know much more than *comment ca va*, although her older sisters could carry on a conversation. French people were expected to speak English, but English people weren't expected to speak French. For the first time, this struck Lulu as odd — and unfair. When French speakers were around English speakers, they switched over, the way these maids did. "Oh, okay, I'll stay out of your way." Lulu wasn't sure how to act around maids. Working as a nurses' aide was the lowest rung on the hospital ladder, equivalent perhaps to being a maid at Lovejoy, but she hadn't felt as awkward waiting on others as she did being the one waited on.

The door from the lobby opened and Dottie came in, her thick glasses misted and her blonde curls awry from the morning's humidity. Her blouse was damp under the armpits and her collar with the circle pin encrusted with brilliants was twisted almost inside out. She wiped her right hand against her skirt, stuck it out to the older of the two maids and laughed her warm, goofy-sounding laugh. "Good morning. I'm Dottie. I guess you've already met Lulu. I'm around the corner in 108." She shook the younger maid's hand too. "I'm afraid I don't know your names." She gave a self-deprecating laugh.

"Alma," the older woman said.

"Claudette."

Pure human decency, Lulu marveled. Dottie knew how to treat anyone — with pure human decency.

That afternoon, Lulu attended her first physical education class. She had signed up for lacrosse. Each student was handed a gym uniform which consisted of a gray cotton tunic over blue bloomers. "Escapees," Bridey hissed. She and Kateri had also signed up for lacrosse. Suited up, the class trotted across campus to a playing field. Lulu had never been one for team sports, but this one, as the teacher explained the rules, sounded remarkably simple. Lulu was chosen for the face-off and found that her height gave her a distinct advantage. She forced the ball in the direction of her team, and Kateri rose straight up into the air like a hummingbird, cradled the ball in her net and, on the run, hurled it a remarkable distance to a teammate who bungled it to cries of, "That's okay, that's all right, get in there and fight, fight, fight."

When Lulu's side won, she felt so happy she didn't know how she could keep herself from gloating over the losers. She'd never thought of majoring in physical education — she wasn't even sure physical education was a major at Lovejoy — but perhaps she had hidden potential and should reconsider. "Great game," she said to Kateri, in order to divert herself. "Have you played this before?"

"No, but it's my people's game." Kateri smiled her faraway smile.

Her people? It took Lulu a moment to catch on. Ah, yes, Kateri was talking about being an Indian. Lulu preferred to think of her floor mate not so much as an Indian as a fellow Catholic, like Venerable Kateri Tekawitha, Lily of the Mohawks.

That evening, Lulu was still aglow from the game when she opened her foot-long, six-inch-deep, hardcover French textbook. She found she could get the gist of the reading as long as she didn't pause at every word but took each column in sweeps across and down the page. She'd catch on to the French spoken in class, she was sure, and she was thrilled at the prospect of completing a survey of all of French literature.

Dottie was in Lulu's English class. So was Rolf, who sat next to the coed who'd danced to his music the first night of Freshman Week, his arm slung over the back of her chair. The teacher, with his baby face, boyish build and brush of strawberry blond hair, looked like a contemporary of Lulu's brother Johnny. Mr. Lunt alternated between drawling at the class with his feet on the desk and leaning forward passionately, his feet squarely on the floor. "Welcome to bucolic Killjoy with its early Howard Johnson architecture."

Lulu pictured the red-brick, white-trimmed Howard Johnson restaurants and motels on Route One in southern Maine. It was pretty funny, she decided, but not very nice for Mr. Lunt to sneer at the Lovejoy campus.

"Poetry," Mr. Lunt said, leaning forward. "Not *what* a poem means but *how* a poem means." He thumped the blue paperback anthology lying on his desk. "Poems should not mean, but be. *Imaginary gardens with real toads in them*. I'm talking Marianne Moore, not that Edna St. Vincent Millay crap you studied in high school. I'm talking about imagery, symbolism and epiphanies — in the course of this year, you might even experience an epiphany of your own. You'll be *writing* poetry too, but not that mealy-mouthed, rhyming stuff you composed in third grade for Mother's Day. As for themes in fiction, we'll be talking about class struggle, racial inequality and the battle of the sexes." He sat back, swung his feet up onto the desk and folded his hands behind his head. He surveyed the class. He grinned. "Welcome, freshmen. You have no idea what's in store for you."

Lulu leaned forward. She was catching his enthusiasm for his subject. She'd probably major in English.

"In two weeks, Greek Rush starts. All the liquor you can drink free of charge. You can go to every open house on campus. Or you can hunker down in one. That's what I do. I'm actually an honorary Brother. Either way, float or soak, you won't have another opportunity like this until the first Big Weekend. Sorry, ladies, the sororities serve tea only, so I'm told." He winked. "And, guys, if you can't wait, you can always pay for drinks downtown at the High Dive, no ID required. There and Hades are where you'll get your real education.

He drew his hands out from behind his head, banged the front feet of his chair to the floor and leaned across the desk. "For next class, you'll write a 500-word essay, which I will read red pen in hand. Try not to embarrass yourselves. Try not to bore me. *We have miles to go before we sleep.*" Mr. Lunt picked up the green cloth book bag at his feet, slung it over one shoulder and strode out of the room ahead of the students as though he had an urgent appointment elsewhere.

Lulu and Jill were in the same math class. Professor Cosmo entered the room after the students were seated, nodded and said, "Welcome to Mathematics 101." He turned his back to the class and began writing on the board. Lulu wondered if he were shy. She couldn't follow his progression across the board or his succinct commentary. The fringe of hair surrounding his bald spot was dry and frizzled. She had a math teacher in high school whose hair was like that. People said that in place of shampoo, he rubbed his head with a bar of soap. She wondered if Professor Cosmo washed his hair with a bar of soap. She wondered if all math teachers substituted bars of soap for shampoo.

She didn't expect to major in math.

After class, Jill seemed to go out of her way to give Professor Cosmo a sunny smile as she and Lulu filed past him, but once outside she frowned. "I couldn't understand a thing he said. Could you, Lulu?"

"Maybe I'll get it when I read the textbook."

"The problem is, Lulu, Professor Cosmo wrote the textbook."

The second time the class met, the professor gave a quiz. Both Lulu and Jill got failing marks. "This is impossible," Jill cried afterwards in Chubbuck 104. She and Lulu had both found Professor Cosmo's textbook as opaque as his classroom demonstrations. Jill went next door to Deb to ask how she could get her math class changed.

"By flunking the course." Deb's answer was as short and neat as her person.

"But I've never flunked anything in my entire life. What would mommy and daddy say?"

"Everyone who flunks Math 101 gets to take it over with Miss Grundy sophomore year."

"Miss Grundy?" Lulu asked. "Like in *Archie Comics*?" She pictured Archie's teacher, straight and skinny as a ruler, bosomless, her white hair pulled into a severe bun, her open mouth twisted to one side from which emanated a speech bubble full of bold-face.

"Yeah, funny, right? But nothing like Archie's Miss Grundy. This one's almost young. And rather pleasant. And she has a reputation as a spoon feeder."

"Well, I, for one," Jill said, "am not going to wait until next year and have to take Math 101 all over again."

"The person to go to for class changes is Dean Diller," Deb said. "And you know what to expect from her."

Jill's expression brightened. "She owes us a favor! Lulu, are you coming with me?"

Maybe Jill's being an only child accounted for her convoluted reasoning that the dean owed them anything. Lulu didn't want to let herself in for another of Jill's tearful, futile demonstrations. "That's okay. I'll catch onto Professor Cosmo's style eventually."

Jill went by herself and came back all smiles. The class sizes had somehow gotten uneven, the Dean explained, and moving one student from Professor Cosmo to Miss Grundy presented no problem. "Besides," Jill said. "She knew darn well she owed me a favor!"

Lulu wrote home that it was going to be hard for her to choose a major when the time came. She was excited about all her classes, although math and French were hard right from the start. The archaic French at the beginning of the survey was a stumbling block. Thank goodness, there were footnotes — too bad they were in French! She'd flipped ahead to the Existentialists — that's what she really looked forward to. And Lovejoy did offer a major in French. The Latin teacher was probably the smartest professor on campus. His class wasn't too hard and actually quite a bit of fun. English was fun too because the teacher had a good sense of humor. She did not add that he joked about drinking and made fun of the campus architecture and of Edna St. Vincent Millay, the Maine poet whom Lulu had indeed studied in high school and who was one of her mother's favorites. There was no chance she'd major in phys ed, she wrote, but it was fun to get outside and run around. When she got home, she'd show her brothers the rudiments of lacrosse.

About her roommates, Lulu wrote that she enjoyed Jill more than she did Elise and spent more time with her. It didn't seem necessary to go into the unpleasantness of Elise vomiting on Jill's bed or the dean turning down Jill's request to have Elise moved.

As Lulu read over what she'd written, her life at Lovejoy sounded good — and promising. She imagined her mother reading the letter to herself as soon as it arrived and later, aloud, at the supper table. She pictured her father and brothers looking up from their American chop suey or baked beans and brown bread. She saw each of her brothers' faces — Neil's flushed baby cheeks, Mickey's bright, splashy freckles, Johnny's intelligent eyes — as they listened attentively to their sister's report on college life.

Lulu felt glad she was not an only child.

Chapter Six

On Wednesday evening, Lulu and Kateri walked across campus to the Newman Club meeting, which was held in a room on the second floor of the library. Fr. Flannery sat in a captain's chair in one corner reading from what Lulu supposed was his breviary. Four students, including the altar boy at Sunday's Mass, sat side by side in the center of a long rectangular table at the head of the room. Everyone else wore a beanie. In fact, there were so many students with beanies that the altar boy got up and muscled open a partition, doubling the size of the room. He asked Fr. Flannery to open the meeting with a prayer. The priest cleared his throat, stuck a thumb into his breviary and stood. The students also stood and, with the priest, made the sign of the cross and recited an "Our Father," "A Hail Mary," and a "Glory Be." Fr. Flannery sat and reopened his breviary.

Like a junior Fr. Flannery, the altar boy began by clearing his throat. He said his name was Bob, he was a sophomore and he was President of the club. His high-pitched voice and his manner of peering through his thick glasses ruled him out, in Lulu's mind, as a dating prospect. He introduced his three tablemates as representatives of the sophomore, junior and senior classes and asked if there was a volunteer for freshman class liaison. Before Lulu took time to think, her hand shot up.

Bob thanked Lulu for volunteering and called for old business. The secretary was one of the two women at the head table. In all her years of schooling, Lulu had yet to encounter a president of anything coeducational who wasn't male or a secretary who wasn't female. Old business concerned the possibility of praying a novena, of visiting a nursing home in downtown Lovejoy and of ordering a Catholic film to show to the entire student body. The freshmen didn't raise their hands to take part in the discussion. They were there, it seemed to

Lulu, to judge whether this particular extracurricular would have a future in their busy schedules. The fact that Bob, the President, was a mere sophomore did not bode well. The officers discussed the points among themselves until one by one each was tabled for future consideration. Lulu had a feeling some of these points may have been tabled before, perhaps many times before.

Bob peered hopefully around the newcomers and asked for new business. Kateri raised her hand. "Yes?"

She stood and smiled her beatific smile. "Dance," she said, her voice an entire octave lower than Bob's. "I would like to have liturgical dance during the Mass. I would be willing to instruct anyone who wanted to dance with me."

Bob sat up straight. "Dance?" he squealed. He looked at the other officers. He turned to look at Fr. Flannery, who had stuck his thumb into his breviary and was looking in the direction of Kateri but who said nothing. "Discussion?" Bob looked all around. None of the freshmen raised a hand. Kateri's suggestion intrigued Lulu, but she herself was too clumsy a dancer to perform at Mass — she'd come up looking like a fool if Kateri expected the entire congregation to join in. A brief discussion ensued among the officers. It was decided to table the point. "Thank you for the suggestion." Bob nodded in Kateri's direction.

"Congratulations," Kateri said later as she and Lulu skipped down the library steps.

"For what?"

"For being freshman liaison."

Lulu glanced sideways at Kateri to see if she was being sarcastic, but her fellow Newman Club member had the same guileless smile as always. "It wasn't as though there was any competition…. I'm sorry about the dance thing. The club doesn't seem interested in new ideas."

"Or any ideas."

Lulu hit the bottom step and turned to face Kateri. Surely, that last remark was sarcastic. But her new friend looked as serene as ever.

***

"Where's Elise?" Jill said, more than a hint of suspicion in her voice. She and Lulu had stripped their beds and stuffed the sheets into the pillow cases.

"Oh, I'm sure she'll get to changing her linens," Lulu said. "She has all afternoon."

As the two roommates descended to the basement, they heard a booming, authoritative voice. "Line up! Show me two sheets, one pillowcase!" Deb's roommate Veronica, in addition to her scholarship job as dining room captain, ran the Gordon Linen concession. Possibly, Lulu thought, Veronica was the one person at Lovejoy with fewer financial resources than herself. Even with her present fierce manner, Veronica, dressed in a pink and white striped shirtwaist dress, still looked the brunette version of the feminine ideal.

Jill turned to Bridey, who was behind her in line. "Why do we need a drill sergeant to exchange our sheets?"

"For the future. This week everyone will turn in the right amount of dirty ones and take the right amount of clean."

"Why wouldn't they?" Lulu asked.

"You'd be surprised all the uses you can put a sheet to — banners, streamers…" She winked. "…escape ropes…"

"Yes, go." Veronica glanced back and forth from the parade of coeds to the pile of fresh linens. "One pillowcase," she barked at Jill as though they were complete strangers.

"But I have two pillows."

Veronica shook her head. "One pillowcase!"

Jill's lower lip thrust out but she dropped the extra pillowcase.

Back in 104, Lulu and Jill made up their beds. "Still no Elise," Jill said.

"I think maybe she had a one o'clock class."

"Do you always give everyone the benefit of the doubt, Lulu?"

"What do you mean?" What Jill said didn't sound like a compliment.

"I mean do you think everyone is basically good? Because I don't. I'm no Pollyanna."

When Lulu was in third grade, the year her father sat all day every day in a wicker rocker by the kitchen window looking lost, she had read *Pollyanna* over and over. In even the hardest circumstances, that heroine found something to be glad about. "What's wrong with being a Pollyanna?"

"Oh, you know what I mean, Lulu. It's not the book, it's the idea — what everyone means by being a Pollyanna."

"Well, okay, I know it's not one of the great books of the Western World, but..."

"Pollyanna was a child, Lulu. Her thinking was childish. Life isn't like that. What are you smiling at?"

Lulu tried to squelch her smile. Jill looked like a child so much of the time. When she was happy, she sang to herself; when she was unhappy, she cried. And, yet, she could be very businesslike and she had a way of taking the best as her due.

When Lulu and Jill returned to the dorm for supper, Elise was lying in her top bunk on her old rumpled sheets smoking a Parliament. "You missed Gordon Linen," Jill said.

"Yes, well, this isn't boarding school, thank God." Elise sounded as world weary as an American Expatriate in Paris.

"You'll have to wait another whole week to get your linens changed."

Elise sat up, swung her feet off the bed and gave Jill an affectionate look. "Jill, dear, you are so middle class, so bourgeois. Lulu, isn't Jill bourgeois?"

Lulu felt her face turning red. She enjoyed friendly arguments but not mean clashes where everyone got their feelings hurt. She made a comical face, held up both hands to signal STOP and shrugged.

"What's so wrong with being middle class?" Jill gave Elise a withering look.

Elise didn't look the least bit withered. She let herself down the ladder and walked to her desk, her nylons whispering against each other. She squashed her Parliament in the ashtray in her hand, placed it on the desk and turned to give Jill an appraising look. "You're cute, Jill. How tall are you?"

Jill stamped her foot. "None of your beeswax!" She pulled open her wardrobe door, yanked her towel off its rack and stalked out of the room slamming the door behind her.

Elise stood still, the elbow of her right arm resting on her left hand. Her glance slid to Lulu and she winked. "Perhaps our dear Jill is expecting her friend."

"Her friend?"

"Her period. You know how on edge we can all get." Elise smiled at Lulu as though the two of them were in cahoots.

Lulu smiled back. She knew she was being disloyal, but she couldn't help herself. Jill had looked so ridiculous stamping her foot and marching out the door and slamming it behind her. Also, "none of your beeswax" was something even Lulu's eleven-year-old brother would feel too grown up to say.

The following Saturday there was another letter from Wesley.

Dear Lulu,

I'm back in Boston and the great thing about living here is that you can find anything you're looking for. I found a theater that was playing Death of a Salesman, *and my friend Dave went to it with me. I know how you felt. I also felt bad when the mother says a man like that deserves respect.*

I don't think your father is anything like Willy Loman. People respect your father. He jokes with everyone who goes into the Five and Dime. He pays just as much attention to kids spending nickels and dimes as he does to grownups spending dollars. (Which, when you think about it, is right considering that the store is a five and dime. Ha ha!)

The movie made me think of my father too. You're right about him owning his own business. That makes him happy. The thing is, though, he wants me to come home and take over the business eventually. That is, if I don't become a minister. The shoe business is fine for him, and living in Meduxnekeag is fine for him, but the thing is I'm not so sure I want to settle down in so small a place even though it was a great place to grow up in — well, maybe not great, maybe just okay. I was always kind of a square peg in a round hole there. Boston has more possibilities. All kinds of folks live here, not just one kind of person. Anyway, if I become a minister, I wouldn't be going into the business anyway. Wade could do that. He's more the salesman type. And maybe his accident has slowed him down a little. If I do become a minister, I want to work in a city. There's plenty of harvest for the Lord right here in Boston. I can see it all around me.

Well, I'd better sign off. By the way, Dave didn't even come close to tears at Death of a Salesman. *So maybe you have to come from Meduxnekeag to really appreciate that movie. Ha!*

I'm reading your letter over again. Elijah is running from Jezebel and others who want to kill him, and he keeps looking for a sign from God. He expects to hear God in thunder or wild winds but instead he hears a still, small voice, like a whisper or a breeze, and that's God talking to him.

I pray for you every day, Lulu. Please pray for me.

Your friend,

Wesley

Under his signature, Wesley had sketched two pictures. One was of a man dressed in a suit, white shirt and tie at a counter waiting on a child at the head of a line of adults. The other was of a man, the sleeves of his dress shirt rolled up, kneeling to fit shoes on an old lady. Lulu smiled. She folded the letter and slid it back into its envelope. She was glad Wesley had a good friend at Nott. In high school, although he wasn't what anyone would call popular, he wasn't exactly friendless either.

She pulled the letter out of the envelope and looked through it again. Wesley's reference to "the harvest for the Lord" and his talk of their praying for each other and, most especially, the fact that he was considering becoming a minister reminded her that they belonged to very different churches. Meduxnekeag's Full Gospel Tabernacle of Our Lord and Savior Jesus Christ was located on Water Street. From its back door, a long wooden staircase descended to the river where teenagers and adults were baptized — the tabernacle didn't hold with infant baptism. Lulu supposed Wesley, at one point, had been fully submerged in the filthy waters of the river. Sunday mornings and Wednesday evenings anyone driving along Water Street could hear singing, stomping and clapping coming from the tabernacle. People said the congregation worked themselves up until they were babbling and rolling on the floor — "holy rollers," people called them behind their backs.

Lulu looked at the "your friend" with which Wesley had signed his letter. She wasn't sure she wanted to pursue a friendship with a member of the Full Gospel Tabernacle. She slipped the letter back into its envelope and held it over the wastebasket. Then she opened a desk drawer and dropped it inside.

Later that afternoon, Lulu and Jill lugged their dirty laundry to the basement where white washers and dryers stood on the cement floor against white sheet-rocked walls. Every half hour or so, they returned to move their loads or plug in more quarters or dimes. "Let's see how many days — or weeks — it takes Miss Upper Class to find the washers and dryers," Jill said, her mouth set in a short prim line.

Saturday evening Lulu went to see *To Catch a Thief* at Hesseltine with some of the first floor Chubbuck freshmen — not including Jill and Bridey, who rode downtown to the High Dive with the two upperclassmen who had spoken to Lulu and Jill outside Dean Diller's office. Lulu figured by rights she should have been part of that foursome, not Bridey, and she would like sooner rather than later to partake of her first alcoholic drink, but she had to admit to herself that neither of those guys interested her all that much. Besides, they were both on the short side.

The sophomore who introduced himself to her after the movie was also on the short side. "Hi," he said. "I'm Ike, like the former President."

To Catch a Thief's happy ending had left Lulu clear-eyed and fresh-faced — and in awe of the sophistication that Grace Kelly and Cary Grant exuded. She saw herself one day proficient enough in the language to make her way around the French Riviera. "I've never met an 'Ike' before," she said. "Or a 'Dwight' either."

"Do you want to go somewhere for a drink?"

The High Dive! Wouldn't Jill and Bridey be surprised to see her walk in with a date. "Well, are you having one?"

Ike narrowed his eyes. "Would this be your first drink?"

"Yes." Lulu blushed.

"I don't want to be the one to buy you your first drink." Ike took a step backwards, then leaned in towards her. "Let's just walk around campus for a while."

Lulu didn't know whether to be annoyed or grateful at Ike's protective attitude.

They walked in the direction of the pond. Ike's hair was trimmed to minimize its curliness, the way Wesley's might be if Wesley had a more up-to-date approach to his appearance. Ike's well-shaped nose was larger on his face than noses Lulu was accustomed to seeing. His lips were full, his five-o'clock shadow evident. She wasn't surprised when he told her he was from New York. He looked like other New Yorkers she saw at Lovejoy, not like the tall, fair New Englanders she was more used to.

At first, they chatted easily about the movie, and she had as many opinions as he did. After awhile, they ran out of things to talk about — at least she did. Ike seemed able to talk indefinitely, and the more he talked the less she did. She had seen current popular films, but he had seen art films. She knew there was an East Germany and a West Germany, but he knew all about the wall that had recently gone up in Berlin. She had read plenty of fiction in high school; he had read not only fiction but also history, philosophy and science fiction. She had hoped so much to become an intellectual at Lovejoy, but ultimately the one-sided conversation on lofty subjects demoralized and — she hated to admit it — bored her. When Ike said goodbye at the door of Chubbuck, he said he'd be in touch, but she knew darn well she'd come off as too much of a hick to interest a New Yorker.

Later, lying in bed examining her conscience, she pictured Bob's near-sighted expression, Wesley's ravaged complexion and Ike's blue jaw. *Dear God, will I spend the rest of my life ruling out one guy after another?* She pictured Keith Sinclair, as handsome and almost as sophisticated as Cary Grant — and with more personality than Wesley, Bob and Ike combined. *Or will the only men I fall in love with be too splendid to fall for me?*

Chapter Seven

Ike came by the next afternoon when Lulu was working at the reserve desk and leaned against the counter. "Yes, may I help you?" Since she wouldn't be dating him, she was determined to be businesslike.

"Oh, I don't need a book. I just wanted to say hi." A speaker was coming to campus to talk about bomb shelters and Ike wanted to know whether Lulu was for or against them. She hadn't given much thought to bomb shelters, but she was willing to listen, and unlike Rolf, who'd been going on and on about musical counterpoint, Ike seemed to care enough about her opinion to give her time to formulate one and to talk. Maybe he realized he'd done too much of the talking the evening before.

She told him about the two elderly sisters who each lived alone next door to each other on Main Street in Meduxnekeag. They were the only people Lulu knew who'd been both scared enough and rich enough to build bomb shelters. People expected them to build one for the two of them, but, no, they built two because their poodles didn't get along. Lulu laughed as she repeated what her father had said, "Bomb shelters are a good idea if you have money to burn."

"I'm completely, 100 percent against bomb shelters," Ike said. "They'd be useless in an atomic attack, and they're a tool of the Republicans to scare the citizenry." Lulu's parents were Republicans, most of Meduxnekeag was Republican, Maine was a Republican state. She wondered if Ike was actually personally acquainted with any Republicans. She wondered what her father would think of his views. "So, shall I call for you at 7 on Thursday?"

Lulu must have lost track of the conversation. "What?"

"The bomb shelter lecture. Shall I call for you at 7?"

"Oh, yes, that would be very nice."

With a wave of the hand, Ike walked off in the direction of the reading room.

"How're you, Miss Dux?" Another guy had come up to the desk.

"Jimmy Taylor!" He'd be a senior now, one of the few in the trickle of Dux grads who went on to Lovejoy and hadn't flunked out. The pearl buttons on his plaid shirt and the sulky expression on his pretty face made Lulu think of James Dean in *Giant*. "I'm fine, Jimmy." No matter the circumstances, "fine" was the standard Meduxnekeag answer to polite inquiries. "How are you?"

"Fine. How's Lovejoy treating you?"

"Fine."

"I'll take a *Samuelson*." Copies of *Samuelson*, apparently the premiere textbook for economics, filled an entire shelf in the reserve stacks. When Lulu placed the raggedy green book on the counter, Jimmy signed the card, pushed it across the desk, and said, "You let me know if you need anything." He flashed a fleeting confidential smile. "We Dux folks have to stick together."

After Jimmy had ambled off, the taps of his leather boots clicking against the hardwood floor, Rolf said, "You're pretty popular around here, Lulu. You'd probably have to throw dice to decide who to invite for Sunday dinner over at Chubbuck."

"I'm not planning on inviting anyone anytime soon." As far as Lulu could see, the guys invited to Sunday dinner were serious boyfriends.

"I hear the women's dining halls are really nice."

"Aren't the men's?"

"Heck, no, we all eat in one big mess hall in Conwell. The food is slop. The walls are whitewashed cinderblock."

"We have early American paintings on the walls."

"We have early airplane-hangar décor."

"Why doesn't the college fix up your dining hall?"

"With what? Early American paintings? Guys would stick gum on the ends of the noses of the drones in those paintings. No appreciation. You gotta understand, Lulu, there are a lot of animals over on the men's side of campus." Rolf broke off as two coeds aproached the reserve desk. After he and Lulu had each fetched a book and reseated themselves on their stools he said, sounding wistful. "It must be nice to eat a served meal in civilized surroundings."

Only that night when she lay in bed making the sign of the cross did it occur to Lulu that Rolf might have been angling for an invitation to Sunday dinner at Chubbuck.

Since it was raining, the physical education class met in the Hesseltine gym where the students threw balls back and forth. Mrs. Johnson took Polaroids of each coed in several postures wearing only panties and a bra. She explained that this project was a national physical fitness program and that she had been trained to spot abnormalities. At the end of class, she called Lulu into her office. She pointed out on one and then another of the pictures that Lulu's right hip was higher than her left. "Can you see it?" she said.

Lulu squinted. "Yes!" No wonder she sometimes felt awkward.

"You need a lift."

Lulu's eyebrows went up. "I feel fine."

"In your shoe, Lulu."

"Oh!" Lulu left Mrs. Johnson's office with a rubber lift in one shoe. She'd get used to it, Mrs. Johnson said. It was the proper precaution to forestall future problems. One minute Lulu felt as though she were walking on the level for the first time in her life. The next minute she felt as though she were pitching from side to side like a toddler.

"Been playing hooky at the High Dive?" Elise asked when Lulu got back to 104 Chubbuck.

Later, preparing to attend the bomb shelter lecture with Ike, Lulu tied a cardigan around her waist in case the evening turned cool. Her hand was on the doorknob when Jill crossed the room, untied the sweater and draped it around Lulu's neck. "That's better, Roomie."

"Agreed." Elise looked up, mascara wand in hand, from where she had been beholding herself in the closet mirror. "You're not in Kansas anymore, Lulu."

"How come you seem taller today?" Ike asked when they walked out of Chubbuck. They had been eye to eye. Now she rose slightly above him.

Lulu kept the lift in her shoe for a week. One morning she couldn't lay her hands on it and went to breakfast without it. She felt like her old self. It didn't turn up and she didn't ask Mrs. Johnson for another. It crossed her mind she might not be taking proper precautions to forestall future problems, but the thought didn't haunt her.

Dottie walked into 104 clutching *Plato's Republic* to her heart. She sat crossed-legged on Jill's bed, her coarse blond curls sticking up like little antennas, her eyes glistening with ardor behind her thick lenses, the book open on her lap. "Listen to this," she said. "*Now in this, as I believe, lies the chief value of wealth, not for everyone, perhaps, but for the right-thinking man. It can do much to save us from going to that other world in fear of having cheated or deceived anyone even unintentionally or of being in debt to some god for sacrifice or to some man for money. Wealth has many other uses, of course; but, taking one with the other, I should regard this as the best use that can be made of it by a man of sense.*" Dottie looked up from the book, her eyes as shiny as though she had been crying. "This is about the meaning of life!"

The meaning of life! Lulu thought of the Parisian cafes where Hemingway and Fitzgerald, Sartre and Camus spent their days and nights discussing the meaning of life. She and Jill went and sat on either side of Dottie and peered at the passage. Lulu cupped her chin in one hand. "I don't think a person could go to hell by *unintentionally* deceiving someone else."

"It's about justice," Dottie exclaimed. "Don't we have an obligation to share what we have with the poor and the downtrodden?"

"I agree with Lulu," Jill said. "No one goes to hell for unintentional mistakes."

"Shouldn't we keep ourselves informed so that we don't hurt others either intentionally or unintentionally?" Dottie's voice took on the calm, kind, authoritative tone Lulu had heard her use with Bridey.

"Well, when I get to the gates of heaven, God will know that I followed my best intentions and He'll let me right in." Jill jumped to her feet and smoothed her skirt.

"I believe God created the world but that was eons ago," Dottie said. "He doesn't know us personally. To Him we're no more than grains of sand. So, how can we leave it up to Him to make the world better?"

Jill walked to her desk and picked up her math book. "I have a quiz tomorrow."

Lulu hoped Dottie wouldn't think Jill was being rude.

"Oh, I'm sorry." Dottie got up and walked to the door. She turned, hugging the open book to her chest. "Isn't Plato wonderful?"

Jill sat and opened her math book. After Dottie's footsteps receded down the hall, she said, "I like Dottie and all but I don't like her practicing the Socratic Method on us — all those questions!" She sniffed. "And that kind of talk about God offends me."

If Lulu had not heard such talk from Keith Sinclair during the summer, she also might have taken offense. It was a point of view that apparently many good people shared. The very idea, however, that God didn't know her, Lulu, as Lulu, was too chilling to entertain.

Elise didn't sit in 104 evenings studying the way Lulu and Jill did, and she slept through breakfast. By the time Lulu and Jill returned, she was up and applying her makeup, her first Parliament of the day aglow in the ashtray. Lulu would often spot her mid morning surrounded by her cadre eating an ice cream cone or a hamburger in Hades. With all her meals provided, Lulu saw no need to go into the snack bar. Elise ate the evening meal at Chubbuck but spent the rest of the evening out, returning just before curfew.

Lulu never saw her studying. And, yet, she could give the appearance of a model student. At the *Great Thinkers* lectures, she either looked intently at the speaker or bent her head to write in her notebook. Once, Lulu ended up sitting behind her and, when Elise leaned to listen to Muffy, saw written in beautiful script all down the page: "Mr. and Mrs. Franklin Samuel Thatcher III."

Lulu and Elise were in the same *Great Thinkers* seminar. Mr. O'Rourke, the young instructor, looked to be what Lulu's father would call a "black Irishman." As dark and intense as Mr. Lunt was fair and flighty, he appeared fascinated with Elise. It seemed sometimes to Lulu as though she and the rest of the class were spectators at a discussion between the teacher and his star pupil.

"I'm a liberal," Elise announced one day in class.

Mr. O'Rourke seized on her remark like a dog with a stick. "And just what is your definition of a liberal, Miss Robinson?"

"A liberal doesn't merely accept what is handed down by authority. A liberal learns through experience and forms his own judgments." The definition, spoken in a drawl with a lisp, rolled right off the tip of her tongue. Lulu wondered how it had gotten there.

"And you find that your fellow students are not liberals?" Mr. O'Rourke favored Elise with a conspiratorial smile.

"They're conservatives." Elise made "conservative" sound like a dirty word.

"Can anyone defend the conservatives?" Mr. O'Rourke looked around the room. The discussion had gone far afield, but apparently this topic interested him more.

Lulu's hand shot up. She didn't know what she was going to say, but she felt as stung as though she'd been personally attacked.

"Miss Delaney will now defend the conservatives." A few people chuckled.

"Conservative," Lulu began. "It means conserve. It means we should keep what has been handed down to us. We should honor traditions. We should obey the law." Lulu stopped, her face scarlet. Her attempted definition sounded childish to her own ears. Still, she felt sure she had a point, even if she couldn't express herself so eloquently and coolly as Elise did. Lulu glanced over at her roommate, who sat with her chin on her fist, her head tilted back, an amused smile on her lips.

"This course is an introduction to liberal education," Mr. O'Rourke said — a little pompously, Lulu thought. "Hopefully, over the course of the year, you will trade in received ideas for original ones. It will behoove you meanwhile to keep an open mind."

"If the course isn't conservative, then why are all the books we're reading from so long ago?" Rolf, who had been lying back in his seat looking bored, spoke up without raising his hand. Was he coming to Lulu's defense? A thrill of appreciation ran up her back and cooled her face. She glanced again at her roommate to see if she had noted Rolf's possible chivalry, but Elise's winner's smile had not altered.

Lulu wished Elise would discuss great ideas in Chubbuck 104 where her comments had been limited so far to her Bass Weejuns and her Parliaments.

The door to Lulu's junior advisor's room stood open, and Deb looked up from where she sat writing at her desk. "Whew," she said. "This always depresses me a bit."

"What?" Lulu stood in the doorway waiting to be invited in.

"Filling out the schedule for the semester — when papers are due, exams, the reading assignments. It always seems like too much." She held up a large sheet of paper that had been ruled into many little boxes, some of them written in.

Lulu nodded. She had known people in high school who approached schoolwork with the same sort of fussy attention to detail, but in the end they hadn't gotten any better grades than she had. Some of those people didn't even get into the National Honor Society. "I'm more intuitive, myself," she said.

"Oh?" Deb looked doubtful, then smiled. "Well, you're lucky then." She bent her head to her work. It didn't look to Lulu as though she were going to be invited in. Regretfully, she moved on to 104.

That night in bed, as she lay reviewing her day, Lulu wondered if she'd be better off with a written down, plotted-out schedule like Deb's. Maybe it would simplify the increasing complexity of her studies. She wouldn't know, however, where to begin such a task.

Although she didn't feel like writing home about it, Latin was becoming less pleasant each session. Professor Snow seemed hell-bent on getting the class through declensions and conjugations even as he launched them into what he called easy reading. Assignments were a tedious combination of memorizing and puzzle solving.

Math was another series of puzzles. Senior year in high school she'd never have done as well as she did in trig if Mr. Mason hadn't been soft on the girls in the class and fed them answers on the tests. Earlier, she'd done well with algebra problems because they were stories and with geometry because it was pictures. Junior year she'd taken the television course in New Math. Wesley's face came to mind and the way he would twirl his open notebook filled with exquisite diagrams and notations so that she could read it. Eventually, New Math made sense.

Math 101 at Lovejoy made no sense. She hadn't done well on the quizzes so far. She hoped it would all become clear as the semester went on.

As for French 201, Lulu wished that she'd bombed on the multiple-choice placement test and had to start all over from the beginning. From the way the other students nodded and laughed or groaned or sighed in class, Lulu assumed they understood every word M. Diderot said.

It was late, and Lulu was still wide awake, lying on her back, her arm under her head. Through the crack between the top of the window and the venetian blinds, a silvery gray moon lighted up a navy blue sky — Lovejoy's colors: blue and silver. The whole world outside her window was blue and silver. Her whole world was now Lovejoy. She was in the right place. She wouldn't have been accepted if she couldn't do the work. She wouldn't have been placed in French 201 if the department didn't believe she'd catch on — the way she'd eventually caught on to New Math. She turned on her side and surrendered to sleep.

Her "friend," Elise happened to remark to Lulu one day, was late. A day or two later, to be pleasant, Lulu asked Elise if her friend had arrived yet. Elise turned the way she had a habit of doing and regarded Lulu over her shoulder. "I prefer not to discuss matters of a personal nature," she lisped. She walked out of the room. Lulu blushed.

A day or two after that, Lulu walked into the bathroom as Elise emerged from the tub stall, a towel around her head, her white silk robe loosely belted. "Wow, look at all that steam!" She blushed and wondered if she had said something of too personal a nature.

Elise didn't appear ruffled. "I felt the need to purify myself."

Lulu thought that if she'd spent as many evenings drinking as Elise did she, too, might feel the need to purify herself. Twice more, Elise had come into 104 at curfew, curled up at the foot of Jill's bed and vomited.

"I'm giving her my bed," Jill said to Lulu after it happened a third time. "I don't want to sleep there anymore after all the puke that's landed on it."

"Good idea."

"Of course, the upper bunk wouldn't be good for me. I'm short and the rungs on that ladder are too widely spaced." Jill cast an appealing look at Lulu.

"You'd probably get used to it."

"I'm scared of heights, too. I'd be afraid every night I was going to turn over and fall out and break my neck."

Lulu pictured Jill pitching out of the top bunk and bouncing off the floor. She turned aside to keep from laughing, and pictured Professor Snow lifting first his left hand and then his right. On the one hand, Jill was overdramatizing in order to get her way — it occurred to Lulu to point out that there was a railing. On the other hand, here was an opportunity to do her generous roommate a kindness that wouldn't cost anything. Lulu took a deep breath. "I'll take the upper bunk."

"Oh, would you, Roomie? Thank you, thank you, thank you, thank you!" Jill stood up and put her arms out for a hug, her consternation sliding away like snow on a pitched roof.

One weekday afternoon when neither the reserve nor the circulation end of the counter was busy, Miss Gravelle sent Lulu to the upper stacks with a cartload of books to reshelve. In Meduxnekeag, Lulu had loved browsing the town library and signing out whatever appealed to her. At Lovejoy, she could barely keep up with assigned reading. Now, by the smoky light coming into the dim stacks through low windows, she paged through a volume of poetry she'd taken from the cart. The poet was a woman, and the poems used language different from anything Lulu had seen in her mother's poems — or in English classes. What Mr. Lunt would call "sensuous imagery" was related to private parts of the poet's body — breasts, for instance, and uterus — a woman singing of herself. From the shelf, Lulu picked out another female poet. She read leaning against the shelves until finally she slid to the floor and sat like a child engrossed in play.

By the time she got back to the desk with the empty cart, things had picked up, and Miss Gravelle's lips were set in a prim, disapproving line, no doubt smearing her teeth. After that, whenever Miss Gravelle sent Lulu to the stacks with a cartload of books, she would frown and say, "Don't get lost up there." Lulu knew, however, from working at Our Lady of Sorrows Hospital that it didn't reflect well on her boss to have an idle helper standing around in plain sight. She couldn't see herself using the time to catch up in assigned reading, but she relished the opportunity to indulge in browsing.

On Sundays, when Rolf and Lulu were the only ones behind the counter there was no opportunity to escape to the stacks. Jimmy Taylor usually came by to pick up a *Samuelson*. He and Lulu never held a long conversation, but he always asked her how things were going. It made her happy to think of him as a link to home. Ike usually came by as well and talked for fifteen minutes or so before moving on to the reading room. "Sundays, I catch up on my reading."

What with Mass, dinner and working at the library, Lulu wasn't able to catch up on much of anything on Sundays. Whenever there was a lull at the counter, Rolf would prattle on about music. One Sunday he made a show of looking left and right, up and down. "I haven't seen Ricky Nelson anywhere."

Lulu blushed.

Rolf laughed. "Anyway, *Elvis Is Back*! That's the name of his latest album — in case you didn't know."

Lulu hadn't known.

Rolf swung out his imaginary guitar. "*Are you sitting alone?*"

"I don't know that one." Lulu frowned.

"Lyrics compliments of Rolf." He bobbed his head. "*Do you wish to atone?*"

"Hey, is your whole song in questions?"

Rolf raised his eyebrows and pursed his lips. "The Socratic I!" He bent to the guitar and crooned, "*Do your thoughts turn to me? Present in all that you see? Do you dine by my empty place? Wishing to caress my sweet face? Oh, my darling, are you sitting alone?*"

Tears came to Lulu's eyes. She pictured the kitchen table at home with all her family around it. She wondered whether her chair was still at the table and who sat in it. Or did it remain empty, waiting for her?

Rolf lay aside his guitar and launched into a history of the ballad form. At first, Lulu was interested, but soon his spiel became too detailed for her to follow — or to want to follow. To keep from nodding off, she interrupted him with questions about himself, even quite personal questions, but he didn't seem to mind. By the end of the afternoon, she'd spent more time on his fractured family life, including stepparents and stepgrandparents, than on *Pascal's Pensees* or *Plato's Republic.*

Chapter Eight

"Greek Rush starts tomorrow!" Deb's smile dimpled her cheeks. Definitely the prettiest of all the junior advisors, she sat at her turned-around desk chair, her feet crossed at the ankles, her hands folded in her lap. She composed her expression to explain, rule-book style, that, in order not to exert undue influence, for the first two weeks of the semester sororities and fraternities had been prohibited from wearing their colors or insignia or from inviting freshmen to their parties.

Monday all that would change. All along, the ninety-plus percent of Lovejoy students who belonged to fraternities or sororities had been looking over the freshmen. Now, active recruiting was about to begin. On Wednesday afternoon, the sororities would hold open teas. At Lovejoy, the sororities, unlike the fraternities, did not live in houses. The Sisters lived in dorms — usually members of the same sorority roomed together. Each of the four sororities had a room under the eaves on the third floor of Hesseltine. Deb urged her advisees to visit all four rooms and to keep an open mind. Veronica, who was sitting in on the meeting looking brimful of a mysterious, delicious secret, leapt to her feet and repeated the admonition, "Keep an open mind!"

At breakfast Monday, nearly everyone except the freshmen had on a blazer that was either true blue, pea green, a deep maroon that brought the word "posh" to mind or the fire engine red of Jill's lipstick. All four colors clashed in the cardigan of variegated yarn worn by Evie, the junior who roomed alone. Deb and Veronica wore red blazers; so did Sue and Yael, the two sophomores from First Floor Chubbuck. All were Alpha Omegas. At once and with all their minds and hearts, Lulu and Jill knew that they wanted to be Alpha Omegas, too. It was the sorority most popular with the guys and that had the most fun, Bridey said. She had pledged Alpha O before her disgrace the year before and in the words of the Ivory soap ads was "ninety-nine and nine tenths percent" certain she'd be reinstated.

Dottie wouldn't be attending any of the rush parties or pledging a sorority. "Do you really think the Greek system is true to the Lovejoy name?" she asked that night when a bunch of freshmen in their muumuus gathered in 104.

"But Lovejoy's always been Greek." Jill was passing around a box of chocolates her mother had sent.

"I mean Elijah Lovejoy himself, not the college." Dottie picked out a soft-center and held it up between forefinger and thumb while she explained that Elijah Lovejoy, for whom the town and college were named, was a nineteenth century newspaper editor, originally from Maine, who had migrated to Illinois, where he was murdered for writing in defense of the abolition of slavery. She bit into the soft-center.

"So what does that have to do with the price of chocolate?" Bridey giggled at her own witticism.

"Don't you agree the Greek system is discriminatory? Did you know that…" Dottie directed a look of mild reproof first at Bridey and then at Kateri and Lulu. "Alpha Omega didn't used to take Catholics?"

"But now it does!" Lulu smiled and threw open her arms.

"It still doesn't take Negroes." Dottie turned her head to one side and frowned.

"So let them join one of the other sororities." Jill said. "We've only got two Negro women in our class anyway."

Lulu could see a flaw in Jill's let-them-eat-cake attitude, but giving in to Dottie's reasoning would mean losing out on a big, big part of what Lovejoy had to offer. "Maybe one day Alpha O will accept Negroes," she said. "Just like it didn't used to take Catholics and now it does."

"Even if a sorority takes all religions and all races, it's exclusive. That's the whole point of a sorority. Some get in; some get left out."

"Well," Jill said in a tone that suggested she was summing up the matter, "we all have to take our chances."

Lulu didn't think Jill was taking much of a chance. Everyone loved her. Everyone thought she was so cute and peppy — everyone except Elise, and Elise had no say over sorority picks.

"I know!" Dottie looked to Lulu as though the Holy Ghost had whispered in her ear — if she even believed in the Holy Ghost. "Does anyone want to attend the Annual Elijah P. Lovejoy Lecture with me on Thursday? For a different perspective?"

"I'll go with you." Now the Holy Ghost was whispering in Kateri's ear. No one else spoke up.

"How about you, Lulu?" Dottie said. Lulu wondered what it was that made her seem likelier than most of the others to attend a lecture that was not a requirement. She blushed. "Actually, I'm going with Ike."

"Ooooh," the room swooned in unison. "Lulu has a boyfriend!"

The box of chocolates finished, the visitors to 104 stood up to leave. At the door, Dottie fixed the others with her characteristic kindly look. "Don't you think you might each want to think long and hard about joining a sorority?"

Lulu did not like to think long and hard about anything. If she thought long and hard, she'd get confused and miss out on the best life had to offer. If she'd thought long and hard, she might have joined a convent instead of coming to Lovejoy. There were things she wouldn't consider doing — heavy petting, for instance, or setting out to get drunk or signing up for Art 101. Nor would she deliberately be mean to anyone or spread ugly rumors. She aimed to steer a middle course. She aimed to go Greek.

Alpha O's discrimination policy was unfortunate, but it wasn't as though Lovejoy were overrun with Negroes or as though there were no sororities to take them. The two Negro women in the freshmen class would be, it seemed to Lulu, perfectly happy as Posh Maroons or True Blues or — even — Pea Greens.

Lulu was telling herself all this as she lay in bed making her examination of conscience. A term and definition from Confraternity of Christian Doctrine classes popped into her head — *Rationalization: the sinner's way of excusing wrongdoing.*

In the morning when Elise was still asleep and Lulu and Jill were dressing, Lulu said, "I've decided not to attend the open teas."

"What? Why not?" Jill stopped with her denim skirt halfway up her legs.

"Sororities are exclusive."

"So's Lovejoy."

"I mean on the basis of race."

"So's Lovejoy. Look around you, Lulu. How many Negroes do you see?"

"That's not the point. The only sorority I want is Alpha O, and Dottie says Alpha O discriminates against Negroes."

"First of all, Lulu, that's like saying you have to eat your spinach because there are starving children in China." Jill pulled up her skirt, fastened it and yanked her brush through her thick wavy hair. "And second of all, you're letting Miss Socratic Method influence you to a ridiculous degree. I'm ready for breakfast."

"Dottie raised some good questions."

"Never mind her, Lulu." Jill laid the brush on her bureau and held the door for Lulu. "We'll go to the open teas together. In the meantime, keep an open mind."

"If your mind's too open, your brains tumble out." Elise's voice drifted from where she lay under the covers.

"Good morning, Elise." Lulu went through the door and Jill pulled it shut.

Jill made a face. "I expect her brains to tumble out any day now."

"If they don't pickle first."

Lulu and Jill stood at the threshold of the Pea Green room. In an unfortunate fashion choice, the Sisters had painted the walls their signature color, which lent a sallow cast to both the room and its inhabitants. Back home pea green was a despised color. Lulu could picture her high school friends wrinkling their noses as they said the words. There was something unformed and unpolished about both the Sisters in the room and their freshmen guests. Jill touched Lulu's arm and they crossed the hall to the Posh Maroons.

The Posh Maroons and their guests looked very polished indeed. Lulu surmised that these were the coeds who, like Elise, were capable of walking right by her without seeing her as though she didn't exist. She wasn't elegant. She wasn't part of a private school clique, like Elise and Muffy and others of their crowd, who were holding china cups and laughing in restrained fashion with the Sisters. When Jill stepped into the room, Lulu moved on to the door of the True Blues. That room reflected the look of the women in it: smart but not show-offish, neat but not fussy, mainly all-around nice and wholesome, a living example of Aristotle's golden mean. April, Mimi and Janet, whom Lulu couldn't help but think of as April, May and June, were in there talking with a couple of Sisters. Janet and Mimi looked as though they fit in. Lulu wasn't so sure about April, whose pink nose and over-eager expression gave off a rabbity look.

Jill reappeared, took Lulu's arm and pulled her towards the tinkle of piano music. Lulu looked into the Alpha O room. Against the wall to her immediate left was the piano, painted Scotch plaid like a gigantic tape dispenser. A breeze lifted the Scotch plaid half curtains on the two dormer windows at one end of the room and blew out the ones on the three dormers straight ahead. The walls were covered with framed awards. A breakfront on the wall to Lulu's right was filled with trophies. Everything about the room and the women in it proclaimed: *We have fun!*

She would have stood by the door a few minutes longer sizing things up if Jill, with the triumphant smile of someone already admitted to the Sisterhood, hadn't taken her by the hand and led her to Veronica, who welcomed them with hugs. Deb crossed the room to hug them as though she hadn't stood next to them that very morning brushing her teeth. She introduced them as her "cherished advisees" to other Sisters, all of whom appeared thrilled to meet them. *Gosh,* Lulu thought, *Deb sounds so proud of us!*

Comfortable-looking couches and easy chairs were gathered around a large red and yellow braided rug, but since there were too many people for everyone to sit, everyone stood. Sue and Yael circulated with brownies mounded onto white china plates and tiny red and yellow. napkins. "Homemade!" Sue kept saying. Two other sophomores — Lulu surmised it was the sophomores who were playing maid and the juniors who were playing hostess — offered trays of crystal glasses of either iced tea or pink lemonade. Lulu would have preferred milk or even coffee with her brownie, but with murmured thanks accepted a sweating glass of lemonade.

After the Lovejoy lecture, Ike bought hot dogs and cokes at Hades, and he and Lulu walked to a bench under a willow on the near side of the pond. "So, did you go to the open teas?" He spoke with his mouth full, and Lulu thought, not for the first time, that although he was nice enough to be with, he was no Adonis.

"I went to the Alpha O one."

"Oh, wow, you're aiming high."

"You think Alpha O's the best?"

"Depends on what you mean by best. Maybe they're not the smartest or the richest, but they're the most popular with the jocks and the party guys." He bit off a too-large piece of hotdog and bun. "Doesn't seem like your style, Lulu."

Lulu stiffened. Was Ike suggesting she wouldn't fit in with the popular crowd? "I like the Alpha Os. I liked their tea."

"The beginning and the end."

"The beginning and the end?"

Ike wiped his mouth with his napkin. She'd almost expected him to use his shirtsleeve — or the back of his hand. "That's what alpha and omega mean. The first and last letters of the Greek alphabet."

Lulu wished she could say she already knew that.

Ike held up the remainder of his bun. "If the ducks were around, I'd feed them this."

"I suppose they've got their heads under their wings over there in the weeds." Lulu pointed towards the wild grasses and cat-o'-nine-tails on the far side of the pond. "Anyway, they don't need my leftovers." She put the end of her hotdog and bun into her mouth.

"You don't worry about the ducks, like Holden Caulfield? About where they go in the winter, for instance?"

"No!" The protagonist of *The Catcher in the Rye* had scared Lulu. Holden Caulfield was all mixed up, maybe the way her father had been the year he sat looking out the kitchen window. Her father didn't do great things but he was cheerful now and every day he got up and went to work at the Five and Dime, whereas Holden worried about all the wrong things, things he had no control over, and not about the things he could do something about, such as staying in school and out of the mental hospital or whatever that place was where he ended up. She swallowed and took a drink. "Where the ducks go in winter isn't up to you or me. It's up to Mother Nature."

"I think Elijah Lovejoy might have worried about the ducks. Before he got to work on abolition, he was depressed. He almost committed suicide."

"Elijah Lovejoy almost committed suicide?" The guest speaker had lambasted everything American, including *Time, Life* and the *Reader's Digest,* the very magazines Lulu's parents subscribed to. He had said nothing about the lecture series' namesake, and Dr. Livingston in his introduction had talked only about journalism and slavery. Lulu felt betrayed. How could Elijah Lovejoy be any kind of moral guide? Even if he was against slavery — and who wouldn't be against slavery anyway? Maybe he purposely carried things to extreme so others would do to him what he was afraid to do himself. Depression was one thing — Lulu's father had had it, might have it again, but at least he didn't commit suicide. She couldn't bear to think he might have contemplated it. It was as bad as shutting a newborn baby up in a trunk. She spoke decisively. "Suicide is a mortal sin!"

"You don't sound very sensitive, Lulu, if you don't mind my saying so."

"I'm certainly not sensitive the way Holden Caulfield was. Or Elijah Lovejoy either." The evening was turning cool. Lulu untied her cardigan from around her neck and pulled it on over her arms. She and Ike stood and made their way back to the paved path. Another couple passed them, he with his arm round her waist, she with his sweater over her shoulders. Lulu hoped one day she'd have a boyfriend she'd be crazy about and who would be crazy about her.

"By going to only one tea, Lulu, you put all your eggs in one basket. But even if you do get in, don't let Alpha O become your beginning and end."

"I don't know what you mean."

"I mean there's lot to do on campus. There're a few guys in my fraternity who spend every evening around the house. If they're not studying, they watch TV in the common room and horse around with other guys. They don't belong to anything else."

"What do you belong to, Ike?"

"Besides the fraternity? The International Relations Club, Tin Can Playhouse — I'm assistant business manager of the Tin Can."

"I'd like to try out for a play."

"You should, Lulu. Tryouts for the fall play are in a couple of weeks, as soon as Rush is over — *Six Characters in Search of an Author*."

"What six characters?"

"*Six Characters in Search of an Author* — that's the name of the play. You should try out, Lulu. You really should. Tin Can would suit you better than Alpha Omega — the…" Ike lowered his voice to the ominous tones of the radio show *The Shadow Knows*. "…beginning and the end."

They had reached the door of Chubbuck. For someone who seemed so much interested in her, Ike never tried to kiss her good night or hold her hand. And she was just as glad he didn't.

Only the women each sorority would consider giving bids to were invited to its closed tea. Lulu was invited to Alpha O's. Maybe if she'd actually walked into the other rooms, she would have been invited to at least one other. She did want to be a part of the Greek system, and now it appeared she had indeed put all her eggs in one basket.

She went to the Alpha O closed tea with Bridey, who she figured must be a shoo-in, and Jill, who had been invited to all four closed teas and planned to go to three of them even though Alpha O was far and away her first choice. They were met at the door by Deb and Veronica, who hugged all three as though they had already been chosen. Once inside, Lulu noticed that each entering freshman was greated equally warmly, which seemed a touch cruel because there were three times the number of guests as there was room for in a pledge class. She composed her features. It was okay for Jill and Bridey to smile as though they already belonged, but that was an attitude Lulu couldn't afford.

Veronica asked everyone to sit. The juniors and seniors took the chairs and the sofas, the sophomores hung around behind the furniture, and the freshmen sat on the red and yellow braided rug. Lulu recognized most of the freshmen from either the dorm or a class or Mass or *Great Thinkers*. She gave a little wave to Wendy, the vivacious blonde who had danced to Rolf's music the first night of orientation and who always sat next to him in English class.

Veronica, who remained standing, told the freshmen that Alpha O was delighted they had accepted the invitation to the closed tea. "And now for a little history." She told how Alpha O had begun as a southern Sisterhood and spread all over the country. Given its origins, it was not surprising that the national organization did not allow Negro women to join. The freshmen were not to worry, however, because the Lovejoy chapter had a bylaw that permitted it to accept Negroes. It was of recent vintage and had never been invoked, but the freshmen could rest assured that should the chapter locate a Negro woman worthy in all other respects it would not hesitate to challenge national policy.

Jill gripped Lulu's arm, turned to face her and widened her eyes as if to say: *You see!* Lulu's conscience eased like a sunburn swabbed with calamine lotion. She no longer had to defend herself, in her mind, against Elijah Lovejoy, who was pretty well compromised himself.

The sticky business of discrimination taken care of, Veronica went on to extol the merits of belonging to Alpha Omega. She pointed to the walls full of framed awards and to the breakfront crammed with trophies. Nine times out of ten, she informed the freshmen, Alpha O came in first in the women's division of Winter Carnival sculptures and of Greek Sing. Alpha O was invited to the most desirable of the fraternity parties. She named the three elite fraternities that had invited Alpha O to a party the Saturday after bids went out. Lulu noted that Ike's fraternity was not one of the three. Veronica ended her speech by urging the guests to put Alpha Omega first on the bid they submitted to the dean. Veronica beamed at her listeners. "Alpha Omega is the best!"

Lulu felt the blood rush to her head. She could be a winner, a winner in an entire Sisterhood of winners, of which she would be one if Alpha O matched her bid. All her life, she had been cautioned not to be too proud or boastful, to give others their due and not to presume. In high school, she had belonged to the debating club and senior year she had been in the one-act play contest. No one expected Dux High to advance very far in competition, and the emphasis was not so much on winning as it was on being good sports. Alpha O, on the other hand, actually expected to win at everything. And, looking around the room at the trophies and citations, Lulu concluded it apparently did.

Bids went out on a cool and breezy Saturday afternoon. Dottie and Kateri carried armloads of reading to the library while the other First Floor Chubbuck freshmen waited nervously in their rooms. Lulu opened her Latin textbook and stared at a vocabulary list. Jill sat at her desk writing a letter. She was dressed in her usual red denim skirt and a white blouse with a yellow scarf around her neck — Lulu had not presumed to wear either red or yellow. Elise, looking like a model out of Vogue Magazine, smoked one Parliament after another. One would never guess from the look of her that weeks' worth of laundry lay in a heap on her side of the closet and that she hadn't changed her sheets since she'd arrived at Lovejoy.

Two juniors in maroon jackets appeared at the door and walked to Elise, who had stood, and, Lulu was surprised to see, was trembling. "Congratulations, Elise," one said handing her a small white envelope. "Our Sisterhood loves you." She embraced Elise, who had tears running down her cheeks smearing her makeup. The other coed hugged Elise also, and the three walked out of the room their arms around each other.

Tears came to Lulu's eyes. Elise had always acted so blasé about everything that Lulu had assumed she didn't care whether she got into a sorority or not, and Lulu was surprised to find she felt happy for her aloof roommate.

Veronica and another Alpha O junior appeared in the doorway, both wearing red blazers with yellow insignias. Lulu and Jill half rose from their seats and sat down again. "Two bids!" Veronica sang out and Lulu and Jill rose again. Jill ran across the room and hugged Veronica, then the other junior. Lulu stood awkwardly at her place, unsure of whether to hug or put on her jacket. Jill turned to her and hugged her, a white envelope in her hand, tears in her eyes. Lulu felt numb and embarrassed. Veronica pressed a white envelope into her hand. "Aren't you happy, Lulu?"

"Come on!" Jill grabbed Lulu's hand and, jacketless, they ran alongside their soon-to-be Sisters to the Alpha O room where someone was thumping out a tune on the plaid piano and women in red blazers sang and clapped and stomped. Lulu and the other freshmen were pushed through a gauntlet of hugs, at the end of which the freshmen all hugged each other. Bridey was there, her flushed, wet face twisted into such a zany smile that to Lulu she looked on the point of a breakdown. Rolf's friend Wendy was there. Alpha O had gotten a full class.

Alpha O always got a full class, the new pledges were informed. They were given the sofas and chairs, while the Sisters sat on the rug serenading them, first with rousing, slightly naughty lyrics and then with sweet tunes resembling love songs. Saturday evening Alpha O would attend a mixer given by Lambda Rho, one of the three fraternities that had vied for them.

Before supper, the women returned to their dorms, each freshman drunk with enthusiasm and wearing a borrowed blazer that had been thrust upon her, an Alpha Omega pledge pin on the lapel. When Elise came into Room 104, the understated maroon of her borrowed blazer matching her nail polish and her Bass Weejuns, all three roommates congratulated each other as though they were the best of friends. At supper, freshman pledges sat with their new Sisters, creating distinct geographies of red, maroon, true blue and pea green. Lulu spotted Janet and Mimi, but not April, among the True Blues.

Later that evening, when Lulu walked down the hall past the telephones, a terrible sound came from one of the booths, a great intake of breath and an exhale as powerful as a dog's howl followed by shuddering sobs. Lulu stopped mid-stride as though she had stepped on a live wire that sent an electric shock up her body and exited through the top of the head. April was huddled in a booth pleading between sobs, "I…Want…To…Come…Home."

Only afterwards when she lay in bed reviewing her day, did it occur to Lulu that instead of walking on by after her brief electrified moment she could have pushed open the bi-fold door of the booth and put her arms around her floor mate. Her high spirits teetered on the edge of an abyss of guilt. And Ike had accused her of not being sensitive! Suddenly, she felt furious with him and with April, who — on Professor Snow's metaphorical one hand — deserved sympathy, but who, on the other hand, was ruining the happy mood of Bidding Day. Then she thought of Dottie and Kateri, non-Greek by choice and both so principled and kind. Surely, they would enfold April in an unofficial Sisterhood. Lulu was rationalizing, she felt sure, but her mind eased and she settled herself for sleep.

Chapter Nine

"Congratulations." Ike leaned against the reserve desk and glanced at Lulu's pledge pin. "Alpha Omega, that's impressive." He straightened up. "I don't suppose you'd be interested in coming to my lowly fraternity house Saturday evening."

Lulu reddened. "Actually, all us Alpha Os are invited to Lambda Rho on Saturday."

"The Lamb Chops."

"Yuh, does your house have a nickname like that?" Lulu didn't really have time to chat. Rolf had not shown up for his Sunday shift, and she was alone at the desk.

"If it did, it would probably be Chopped Liver." As though he sensed he was getting a brush off, Ike said goodbye and walked off in the direction of the reading room.

Lulu watched him go with a pang. She didn't like feeling mean.

After supper on Saturday, the Sisters and pledges gathered in the Alpha O room. The Sisters sang the snappiest of the songs from Bidding Day. The pledges clapped along and in some cases were able to sing the words. Lulu's singing and clapping were never what she wished they were in any circumstances, but the mood was so joyous and the music-making so loud that she dared to join in — softly.

The singing stopped when they left the Alpha O room and they lowered their voices to a joyous but lady-like volume. Lulu walked beside Wendy, who smelled as Jill did of cinnamon and soap. Wearing a tailored jacket over a flowery shift, she looked the most sophisticated of the pledges. She had the clear, bright complexion that can come from an expert use of makeup. Her eyes were shadowed, her lashes darkened, her bright hair the same true blonde it must have been from childhood. She reminded Lulu of Elise except that Wendy was cheerful and friendly with everyone and never ironic.

"Do you know what fraternity Rolf got into?" When Lulu worked alone at the reserve desk on Sunday, she was surprised to realize she missed his patter.

"Poor Rolf! He didn't get into any."

"Not any?"

"He aimed too high. If he'd gone further down the list, he'd have stood a chance."

Lulu pictured Rolf, Rolf with his confident air and slightly artificial but magazine-model good looks. "I thought he'd get in anywhere he wanted."

"Rolf? Guys can't stand him. Even women find him hard to take. With Rolf, a little goes a long way. Haven't you noticed he only talks about himself?"

"Yuh….but I never see him alone. He has so many friends."

"Women, not guys. Women will put up with a guy who's all wrapped up in himself."

"But, Wendy, aren't you practically his girlfriend?"

"Girlfriend? No, I'm his friend, and, don't get me wrong, I like Rolf, I really do, but he isn't mature enough to be a boyfriend."

Lulu shuddered. Only by the grace of God had she been considered mature enough — or popular enough or good-looking enough or smart enough or friendly enough or interesting enough, whatever the criteria might be — to become a Sister in the only sorority she had aspired to.

The Lambda Rho Brothers and pledges, dressed in neat khakis and open-necked buttoned-down shirts, stood around outside their house to greet the Alpha Os and usher them to the basement where soft lighting, soft, throbbing music, soft sofas and big soft floor pillows created an atmosphere that was a cross between a child's clubhouse and the womb.

"May I get you a drink?" The speaker, a Brother she recognized from Mass, had the freckled cheeks and big blue eyes of a Christmas card choirboy. His tousled hair would have resembled Wesley's if Wesley were to towel his dry and let it fall forward.

"Why yes, thank you." She anticipated that the next question would be what she wished to drink and she wasn't sure how to reply. Instead, she was immediately presented with the one drink everyone was holding. It was some kind of punch scooped from a wide ceramic bowl into a paper cup.

In high school, Lulu had been warned about punch. You never knew what had gone into it. One night when she was working at Sorrows Hospital, six Indians had been brought in who had drunk punch made of Koolaid and Sterno Canned Heat, a denatured alcohol meant for fueling camp stoves. The victims were well-thought of in the Indian community and were the parents of young children. Two died. White high school boys had also been known to experiment with Sterno as a beverage.

Lulu felt sure the Lambda Rhos had not spiked their punch with Sterno. On the other hand, you never knew how much alcohol of any kind might be in a cupful of punch. She'd drink just the one cup. She took a sip. It was sweet and easy going down. As far as she could tell, it didn't even taste like alcohol.

The music switched to "Let's Go to the Hop" with the volume turned up. Wendy had taken off her jacket and was dancing, free form, in a cleared space with one of the Brothers. "Want to dance?" The Brother who had presented Lulu with her drink had to yell and gesture to make himself understood.

Lulu pointed to her drink. The Brother took it from her, set it on a high windowsill along with his own, reached for her hand and led her to the cleared space. She dreaded the moment he would put his arm around her to lead her in a dance step. She knew she was a terrible dancer. Instead, he faced her and danced without touching, the way Wendy was dancing. Lulu moved to the music as best she could. She mirrored her partner's movements as best she could. The space filled up with gyrating bodies. Nobody could see whether anyone else was a great dancer or not. Sweat poured off Lulu, but she didn't care. Her partner leaned so close to her ear she thought he might kiss it. "I'm Tim," he yelled.

When the music stopped, Tim reached for her hand, led her to the windowsill and handed down her drink. It was still cold and she realized she was very thirsty. She took more than a sip this time, but she didn't drain the cup.

Tim drained his cup. "You want another?" He was enough taller than Lulu that she had to lift her head to look into his eyes, more Wesley's height than Ike's.

"No, no, I'm fine." Lulu clutched her cup to her chest.

"Nice dancing with you." Tim sauntered off in the direction of the punch bowl.

Lulu hoped it really was nice dancing with her.

She danced off and on the rest of the evening. Wendy, Jill and Bridey danced the entire time. During a lull, Lulu looked around. The Alpha O pledges were more in demand as dancing partners than the Sisters were. Two Alpha O seniors sat side by side on a couch, like tulips painted on a wall. Although nice enough — very, very nice, in fact — they were rather dull in appearance and personality, and Lulu wondered what had recommended them to Alpha O in the first place. Deb danced exclusively with her boyfriend Ed. Some of the other Sisters also had boyfriends among the Lambda Rhos, and three were "pinned," which meant they were wearing their boyfriends' fraternity pins. It was like going steady in high school, Lulu deduced, except on a more mature level. Veronica, who had no steady boyfriend, danced all evening long with one Brother or pledge after another and drained many a cup of punch. Lulu glanced over at the two wallflowers. She would hate to think she could ever end up as a senior discard.

As the evening went on, Tim and Wendy performed every dance together. Their moves became so intricate others cleared a space and stood in a circle to watch and applaud. During the final slow number when the floor filled up again, the two merely swayed in a tight embrace as Elvis pleaded about his insistent love. Lulu was dancing with a very nice freshman, but she couldn't help but envy the coeds who were in the arms of real boyfriends — and Wendy and Tim, who looked like an honest-to-goodness, albeit hastily-constructed, couple.

The mixer was a success. Two pledges asked Jill and Bridey out for the following weekend, and Tim made a date with Wendy. The Lamb Chops who'd danced with Lulu said hello when they saw her on campus.

She was asked out not by one of them, however, but by an Omega Kappa pledge from her math class and the following weekend by an OK pledge in her *Great Thinkers* seminar. OK was Jimmy Taylor's fraternity.

Although Ike continued to visit her at the reserve desk, he stopped asking her out and that suited Lulu just fine. There were so many guys to get to know and so many women who were about to become her Sisters that, for the first time in her life, she felt full up in the dating and friendship departments.

Lulu walked alone past the men's side of campus and along a pine needle path through a mixed-growth wood that wasn't landscaped like the rest of the campus but tangled and gnarled like the woods she grew up playing in. Up ahead she could see the lights of the Tin Can Playhouse, a Quonset hut which bore no relation to Lovejoy's prevailing Federalist style. She'd asked Jill and Bridey if they wanted to try out for the fall production. They'd said they were much too busy with classes and studying and Alpha O and dating to consider taking on anything else but that it would be nice for Lulu and that they'd come see the show if she got a part.

The door shrieked on its hinges like a cat in heat. Inside, Lulu spotted Evie sitting on the edge of the stage. In her peasant dress and varicolored vest, she looked more at home in the Tin Can than she ever did on First Floor Chubbuck. She looked pleased to see Lulu. "So you're a Thesbian!"

"I thought I'd try out for the play." Lulu was uncertain of the meaning of "Thesbian."

"Evie, your choice of words is frightening the dear girl." A tall skinny man with stringy black hair and a five o'clock shadow stood on stage gesticulating with a cigarette. He had on a filthy tan trench coat with turned-up collar over a blue shirt and black pants. "Don't worry, my dear," he said to Lulu. "All we are concerned with here is talent. Marc, scripts please."

"Yes, Mr. Wilson." An upperclassman, whom Lulu recognized from Mass, handed out booklets. "Everyone take a seat, please." Marc had ice-blue eyes, a pitted complexion and an authoritative manner.

"Women will be reading the part of Stepdaughter, men the part of Father." Perhaps Wesley's bad complexion would not have counted against him in high school had he possessed Marc's savoir faire.

"Don't, *for God's sake*, all think you're being considered for the leads." Mr. Wilson jumped from the stage and strode to a seat in the middle of the theater. "If you try out for a part tonight, you will accept whatever role I assign you. Understood?" He peeled off his trench coat, sat down, and crossed his long legs. "Marc, let the games begin."

The next day, Lulu read the cast list posted outside Hades and shivered with pleasure to see her name next to "Madame Pace."

"A minor part, but it's a start." Ike had come up behind her. "Congratulations, Lulu. I'm coming at the end of rehearsal tonight."

"Thanks, Ike." She found herself slightly irritated that he pointed out her part was small.

That evening, the players seated themselves in chairs arranged in a circle on stage while Marc passed out scripts. Only three seats remained when Mr. Wilson strode in, threw his coat over a chair and sat. He looked at his watch. "Six forty-five sharp. Let us begin. I'm sure you are all familiar with this play, if only by reputation. *Six Characters in Search of an Author* is the most important play in the history of world literature. As you no doubt know, Pirandello went in for the dreamlike, the expressive and the symbolic to reveal the inner lives of his characters. As he has the father say — with an unacknowledged nod to Aristotle — fictional characters, because they are fixed eternally, are more real than actual human beings. Marc here, for instance," Mr. Wilson pointed with his cigarette, "is less real than Odysseus or Hamlet because those characters are fixed in our minds, millenia in the case of one, centuries in the case of the other, while our own Marc, approaching the zenith of his college career, has been constantly changing and will continue to change and what he will be ultimately, *je ne sais pas*. And now, let us begin by reading the play."

When the door of the Quonset hut shrieked, Lulu turned to see two guys enter and make their way softly to the empty chairs, where they sat and opened their scripts on their laps.

Mr. Wilson smiled at them. "Welcome, gentlemen. Everyone is entitled to one mistake. You have had yours. Rehearsals begin at six forty-five sharp. I do not expect you to be late ever again. Understood?"

"Yes, Mr. Wilson. Sorry, Mr. Wilson."

Lulu made a mental note never to be late.

As the group read through their parts, she couldn't see what the play was about, what the plot was or whether there was a plot. But none of that mattered. Nor the fact that Madame Pace had very few lines. Lulu was glad to have a part at all. Until two weeks ago, she'd never heard of the play or of the playwright. In *Great Thinkers*, Aristotle was a classifier of knowledge, not a drama critic.

As they finished reading, Lulu heard the theater door shriek open again, and Mr. Wilson called out, "Welcome, Isaac, my good man!"

Lulu turned in her seat. *Isaac? Ike was Jewish*!

"Ike, you're Jewish," she said to him as soon as they left the Tin Can and began walking through the woods.

"No kidding!"

Ike had suddenly become exotic, fascinating — and definitely off-limits for serious dating. "If I'd known, I'd never have let you eat a hotdog. I think maybe they have pork in them."

"My family eats pork all the time, Lulu. We're not religious."

The fact, if it were true, that Ike's family wasn't religious was more shocking than the fact that they were Jewish. In Meduxnekeag, people belonged to all different kinds of churches, but Lulu couldn't think of anyone she'd grown up with who wasn't at least a nominal member somewhere. Catholics, in Lulu's mind, were admired by non-Catholics for their strict and observable behavior — abstaining from meat on Friday, going to Mass every single Sunday and holy day of obligation, not taking off in the summer the way some of the more lax Protestant churches did. And Jews, she'd always thought, were even stricter than Catholics. "How can you be Jewish and not be religious? Judaism's a religion, isn't it?"

"We're liberals, Lulu."

"That isn't a religion!" The only other professed liberal Lulu knew was Elise. Ike didn't seem mixed-up like Elise. But they both were critical of the middle class way of life, a way of life Lulu aspired to. And maybe, as the Byronic Mr. O'Rouke had said in the *Great Thinkers* seminar, they were more open to new ideas. "I'm a conservative," she told Ike. It felt good to declare her new-found allegiance.

"Yeah, I've noticed." Ike gave her a sideways glance. "But I've got hopes for you, Lulu. You could expand your philosophy."

"Plato says you shouldn't study philosophy until age thirty."

"So why come here at eighteen and take *Great Thinkers*?"

"Good question." But it wasn't a good question. Endless questioning was as confusing as thinking long and hard.

Lulu and Ike emerged from the woods where the path forked, and with a wave of the hand Ike set off in the direction of the men's quad. Before she'd declined his fraternity party invitation, he'd have walked her to her dorm. She lengthened her stride to catch up with Evie.

On Christ the King Sunday, Bob, in his capacity as Newman Club President, enlisted Lulu and the other officers and class reps to pass out shiny cards with a prayer on one side and a robed and crowned Jesus on the other. In his sermon, Fr. Flannery explained that Pope Pius XI had instituted the Feast of Christ the King in 1925 when competing philosophies of Communism, socialism, secularism and nationalism roiled Europe. "The Feast of Christ the King reminds us to rise above our automatic, self-protective, warring natures. Nor should any earthly government or political party be our highest authority. Nor should our egos rule. In *The Book of Proverbs* we meet Wisdom, whom Jesus Christ personified, crying aloud in the street, pouring out her spirit to all who will listen. It is Wisdom that should rule us."

Lulu loved it when Fr. Flannery worked himself up to a dramatic, flush-faced pitch. She decided he must be a conservative.

Fr. Flannery shifted his weight, paused, looked searchingly at his congregation and continued in a softer tone. "As you know, Pope John XXIII has called for a council of the Church to open next year."

Lulu knew no such thing.

"This council, Vatican II, will address issues left unfinished over one hundred years ago during the First Vatican Council. The

Feast of Christ the King was a stand against the perceived evils of modernity. The Second Vatican Council will be an effort to relate the teachings of the Church to the good in modern times and to open a dialogue with all men of good will and most especially with our fellow Christians; for we Catholics are, at base, Christians."

Lulu thought of Wesley as a Christian. She had always thought of herself as a Catholic. Also, Fr. Flannery's talk about the coming council made him sound more like a liberal than a conservative.

Before the final blessing, Fr. Flannery invited the congregation to join him in reading the prayer card aloud. "Be King of those who are deceived by erroneous opinions or whom discord keeps aloof… call them back to the harbor of truth…so that soon there may be one flock and one Shepherd…"

It occurred to Lulu that Mr. Lunt would find the metaphors horribly — ludicrously, actually — mixed. She turned the card over and studied the crowned and robed figure. Where in this royal depiction was Wesley's — Elijah's, rather — still, small voice?

"Coming to breakfast now?"

Jill shook her head without looking up. Sitting cross-legged on her bed, surrounded by books and index cards, her notebook on her lap, she mumbled through the pen between her teeth. "*Great Thinkers.*"

Lulu had an hour exam in her *Great Thinkers* section as well, but she didn't think it wise to skip breakfast. Or to work so hard at the last minute. "A good night's sleep and a good breakfast are the best preparation for taking a test," she said. Jill didn't look up again, and Lulu went to breakfast by herself.

When Lulu returned to 104, Jill had thrown on her clothes, and, without having bothered to run a brush through her hair, was leaving for class. "Wish me luck, Lulu — and good luck to you."

"You'll do well!" The one thing Lulu considered she had in common with Holden Caulfield was that she never wished anyone good luck. It felt irreligious, superstitious even.

Jill did do well. Her exam came back with an A minus. Lulu was taken aback to get a C minus.

In Math 101, a C minus would have been a relief. With each quiz, her mark was lower until finally, on the first hour exam, she got an F. Alone, back in her dorm room, she took Wesley's letters out of her desk drawer and read through them. Although she hadn't planned to write back, she took out her stationery.

Dear Wesley,

Thank you for your last letter. I'm sorry to take so long to respond. Things have been very busy here at Lovejoy. Besides working in the library, going to classes and studying, there are the extracurriculars. For one thing, I've joined a sorority, and we have late afternoon pledge meetings. Also, I've tried out for a play and rehearsals are almost every evening. They run late, but the director wrote a letter to my housemother asking special permission for me to come in after freshman curfew. Weekends, there are always parties at the fraternity houses, and naturally, we freshmen coeds get lots of invitations!

Lulu's invitations were always to the OK house on a date with one or another of the pledges, but she would feel awkward including this bit of information in a letter to Wesley.

Do you remember what a time I had catching onto New Math? Well, I seem to have the same difficulty with Math 101 at Lovejoy. But I'm sure it will all work out for the best the way it did at Dux High.

I look forward to seeing you at home over Thanksgiving vacation.

Your friend,

Lulu

Reading through the letter made Lulu feel better. She really was taking full advantage of what Lovejoy had to offer. No wonder she found it hard to keep up in every single little thing. Addressing the envelope and sticking on a stamp from one of two in her desk, she felt as though she had taken firm action to solve her problems in Math 101.

Wesley's next letter came in the return mail. Lulu sat at her desk chair reading it while Jill put away laundry.

Dear Lulu,

Congratulations on joining a sorority. We don't have the Greek system here at Nott, needless to say, and we hear awful things about what goes on at fraternity parties, but I'm sure it's greatly exaggerated. I think it's a good idea to take advantage of whatever your school has to offer — and to always walk with Jesus. For me, Boston is an important part of what Nott has to offer and I'm taking full advantage.

Congratulations, too, on being in a play. I would go see a performance if Boston weren't so far from Lovejoy.

I'm sorry you are finding math hard. Remember that you did well in New Math once you got on the right track. All math is like that. If I'm having trouble nailing something down, I go over it with Dave or John, who love math as much as I do. You might try looking for a study buddy.

Speaking of Dave, he and I have both applied to go to Mexico to preach the Word second trimester. That means we would be away for both Thanksgiving and Christmas. It's part of the plan of the program to wean us from spending all our holidays with our folks instead of reaching out to God's little ones. I hope I get into the program — it's harder to get in as a sophomore than as a junior — but I feel ready. My only regret would be that I wouldn't see you back home.

Please pray for me, Lulu. You are always in my prayers.

Your Friend,

Wesley

Lulu remained at her desk with the letter in her hand, waves of emotion washing over her. The first was disappointment that Wesley might not be in Meduxnekeag for Thanksgiving, then relief that he wouldn't be showing up for a performance of *Six Characters in Search of an Author* — not that she had ever expected him to do that, but should he on the off chance come she couldn't imagine him fitting in with her Lovejoy friends — then jealousy that he was experiencing so much, Boston and perhaps Mexico, even though he was at a backward Bible college and she was at the pride of Maine, and, finally, irritation with his references to walking with Jesus and their praying for each other. Was he, with his Pentecostal zeal, portraying himself as the real Christian and her Catholicism as some kind of sham?

Besides, she'd always thought of Mexico as a Catholic country, home of Our Lady of Guadaloupe. What were the Pentecostals doing there? On the other hand, she'd never heard of a group of Catholic students going there. Maybe Catholic students from Catholic colleges did that sort of thing. She opened the desk drawer that contained nothing but letters from Wesley and dropped the latest one in.

At the window, Jill was watering her spider plant and singing "A Boy Like That" from her memorized trove of *West Side Story* songs.

That night when she got to Wesley's letter in her examination of conscience, Lulu regretted her bristling reaction. She felt a surge of gratitude to him for bolstering her confidence in math. She could use bolstering in her other classes as well. Jill's papers rolled right out of her pink typewriter as slickly as letters to Ronnie. Elise merely retyped old papers from boarding school at the last minute. Lulu didn't have essays from high school, and even if she had she had a feeling they wouldn't come up to the Lovejoy standard. She could usually think of a thesis sentence and some idea of how she wanted to conclude. Everything in between, however, took an excruciating amount of time and her middles were as muddled as her math equations. English and *Great Thinkers* were more forgiving than math, however, and although her papers got returned hemorrhaging red ink, she got B's. For French assignments, it being French and not her native language, she was settling for C's.

She was still awake. So she began going over her lines for the play. Slowly, Madame Pace's words, and those of other characters, filled her mind. For all its demands, Lovejoy was a lovely place and she was, as Dr. Livingstone had advised, taking full advantage of what it had to offer.

Chapter Ten

In the shower and on her way around campus, Lulu rehearsed her meager lines for *Six Characters*. She also kept repeating the playwright's name. She would find herself smiling and almost talking out loud — she especially liked the feel of "Luigi Pirandello" rolling off her tongue — and would have to rein herself in so people wouldn't think her crazy. As opening night approached and rehearsals were longer and more frequent, Mr. Wilson required all cast members to attend for the entire time. She would sit in the theater, math book or French anthology open on her lap, listening to everyone's lines. By day, there was much that was new in what the professors said and in what she was studying. But after nightfall at the Tin Can, the play was becoming more and more deeply the same. To know what each character was going to say and how that character would move had created a kind of intimacy among the actors.

On the evening of dress rehearsal, after she left Lovejoy's landscaped grounds and neat paths and was walking the woodsy trail, she felt herself rising out of her mind and looking down on herself, Lulu, walking through the woods, and she knew, in spite of the waves of homesickness that still occasionally swept her, that she was very, very happy, a condition she'd never before experienced so consciously.

Marc stood in the open door of the Tin Can tapping the tapered end of a pot of oil onto the hinges so that they wouldn't yowl like a cat. His flannel shirt had been washed so many times the colors had blurred and faded, like those of the more countrified boys Lulu had gone to high school with. Unlike the countrified boys, however, Marc wore the sleeves of his flannel shirts rolled to the elbows, which made him look manly. As stage manager, he was involved in all aspects of the production. Evie, too, worked on whatever needed to be done — often in concert with Marc. Lulu didn't see how she herself could spare the time to do more than perform her role. Besides, she didn't think she had much aptitude for designing or mending costumes, painting sets or working ticket sales.

"*It's Madame Pace...Here she is!*" Marc spoke the lines that greeted Madame Pace's entrance on stage. The silver of his chunky expansion bracelet contrasted against the thick, dark hairs of his forearm. His pitted complexion didn't make him less handsome the way Wesley's pimples did, and the deep vee of his receding hairline gave him a mature look. To him, Lulu was never Lulu, always Madame Pace. As a member of a popular fraternity, a star on the hockey team, and a major in philosophy, he couldn't be expected to remember the name of a freshman with a minor part.

"*It does not seem to me — how you say it — good manners that you laugh of me.*" Lulu quoted one of her few lines in Madame Pace's bizarre accent and speech pattern.

The dress rehearsal was the first time the play was performed in one, straight, uninterrupted run. Evie had a quick change which she executed in the wings, one hand on Marc's arm. If he or anyone else was surprised to see her in her underwear, no one let on. It was artistic license, Lulu thought, bohemian, like Evie.

Later, walking back to Chubbuck with Evie, Lulu still felt the glow of her earlier, conscious happiness. "I feel so close to the cast," she said. "We're like family."

"Yes, for the time being."

For the time being? Lulu's glow dimmed briefly at the thought of rehearsals coming to an end. "I had such a good time tonight I wouldn't care if we never performed for an audience."

"Oh, no, Lulu!" Bohemian Evie sounded as shocked as a Victorian maiden hearing an indecency. "The applause is everything."

The next night, at the first of four performances, Lulu stood in the wings awaiting her cue. The sickening waves that passed through her weren't homesickness this time but fear. She promised herself she would never again try out for a play.

Marc appeared at her side and handed her an open fan. He lighted a cigarette, took a puff and transferred it to two fingers of her other hand. "Break a leg, Lulu." *He did know her name!*

"*Now watch! Watch!*" On cue, Lulu waddled onto the stage brandishing cigarette and fan. As the other players scattered at the approach of Madame Pace, the shaky feeling fell away like a dropped cloak. At the curtain call, when she took her bow at one end of the line of actors, the applause hit like a declaration of love. Evie was right.

Sunday, after the last performance, while Lulu tissued the goop off her face with hunks of cold cream and changed out of her heavy padding and costume, the crew struck the set. She emerged as the party was starting. The pizza tasted different than her mother's homemade Bisquick, Velvetta cheese and stewed tomatoes version, but there was a similar comfortable feeling of being among family. She sipped her cup of cold foamy beer. She'd stick to her policy of one drink an hour and no more than two total.

"You were wonderful, Lulu!" Ike was repeating what everyone was saying to the actors and what they were saying to each other. "I didn't know you had it in you."

"*Each one of us is lots and lots of people,*" Lulu quoted, "*…because of all the countless possibilities of being that exist within us.*"

"*Life is like that; it's made up of absurdities, things which don't make sense…*" Ike had attended so many rehearsals that he, too, knew many of the lines.

"*…and which, like it or not, don't need to be credible because they are true.*" Lulu concluded his quote.

"*How can we ever hope to understand each other if I put into the words I use the meaning and value that things have for me in my interior world, while the person I'm talking to is bound to receive them with the meaning and value those words have for him*"

"*We think we understand each other. In fact we never do.*" Lulu was enjoying the canned repartee as much as though she and Ike were making it up as they went along.

"*Pretense! Reality! What the hell! I've had enough! Lights!*"

"*Le coeur a ses raisons que la raison ne sait pas.*"

"Beg pardon?"

"The heart has its reasons which reason does not know. Pascal." She was pleased to say, for once, something intellectual which Ike didn't already know.

"Wow, Lulu! You really are lots and lots of people!" He was nursing his beer the way she was hers. "Will you try out for *Guys and Dolls* next semester?" They sat on the edge of the stage, their feet dangling. Long strings of cheese dripped from his pizza slice and draped one hand.

"I'm not musical, Ike. Sorry to say."

"You know the background of *Guys and Dolls*, don't you?" Ike licked the cheese off his hand. He related the play's synopsis and production history, digressing into sidelights on crime in Detroit and other American cities, stopping from time to time to ask Lulu's opinion, which he considered with his customary attentiveness before building on it or tearing it down.

Lulu only half listened. She was both grateful for Ike's companionship and at the same time sorry to be having such a staid conversation while all around her the party was heating up and her own glow was fading. Evie had shed her quiet, slightly out-of-it manner and laughed boisterously and traded risqué jokes with the crew. Marc stayed close by Evie, watching her. After awhile she got quiet and sat on his lap kissing him. Other members of the cast and crew paired off and there was a lot of kissing and fondling going on — sometimes between people who up to then had seemed only to tolerate each other.

Ike talked for awhile of the finances of the Tin Can Playhouse and then fell silent. Lulu sensed he felt as awkward as she did. One late afternoon in seventh grade, when her house was empty, Alice invited a bunch of girls and boys into her living room. Soon all but Lulu had paired off and were making out on the sofa and arm chairs and even the rug. She felt as out of place at the cast party as she had that day in Alice's living room.

"Actually, Ike, I need to get back to the dorm." Actually, she had special permission to stay out past curfew.

"I'll walk you back." Ike jumped down from the stage and put his hand out to guide her.

As Lulu was gathering her things, Evie looked up from Marc's lap. His chunky silver bracelet dangled from her wrist. "Oh, Lulu! You can get back all right on your own, can't you?"

"Oh, sure. Ike's going to walk me."

Marc looked up at Evie's upraised face. Then he lowered his head against her bosom; she looked down and with her index finger traced the vee of his receding hairline.

Ike walked Lulu all the way to Chubbuck. As he talked about the upcoming guest lecture, she mentally framed a diplomatic refusal to attend with him, but when at the door of Chubbuck he gave a wave of the hand and said, "Good night, Lulu," she didn't know whether to feel disappointed or relieved.

In the next day's mail, she got a business-size envelope with the Lovejoy seal in the upper left hand corner. When she unfolded the enclosed letter, her insides pitched and crashed like parfaits on a tipped tray. She had gotten a warning in math.

In class, Lulu mostly saw the back of Professor Cosmo's freckled, bald head with its fringe of frizzy skin-colored hair. Face to face in his office, she felt uneasy. His kind expression and the family photos smiling up at her from his desk invited her to explain herself, something she wasn't sure how to do. "Is anything worrying you?" he asked.

"No, nothing." To say that what worried her was the prospect of failing math struck her as tautological.

"Because you seem preoccupied. Everything all right at home?"

Lulu nodded. "Yuh."

"You know, Lulu..."

Lulu was surprised to be addressed by her first name. In class she was "Miss Delaney."

"...mathematics is as sure a path to truth as anything you freshmen take up in *Great Thinkers* — Plato, Aristotole..."

Aristotle again. Aristotle was all over the curriculum and the extra-curriculars.

"...the thread runs through history. It's Aristotle's conception of logic and Pythagoras's faith in the proportions that underlie all relationships. More will be coming in your lifetime, a whole new way of perceiving and accounting for reality, as beautiful and elegant as philosophy and literature and history — and much clearer and more precise." His voice had taken on an excitement Lulu had never heard in the drone that accompanied his progress across the blackboard during class. He sat up straighter and lowered his voice. "I offered to give a lecture or two for *Great Thinkers*, but the humanities fellows thought math lay outside the syllabus." He laced his fingers over his tweed-covered gut. "Lulu, you do see how true mathematics is, don't you?"

"I thought I did until I took New Math in high school." She was warming up to this talk with Professor Cosmo. "That's when I learned that two and two are not always four."

"Aha!" Professor Cosmo slapped his hands on his thighs. "A good beginning, Lulu!" As he went on to talk about Sputnik and the space age, binary operations and computers, the twenty-first century and the higher, sharper math skills it would demand, Lulu felt her own enthusiasm rising. Alone with her in his cozy office, Professor Cosmo seemed to care about her as warmly as her high school teachers and the principal and guidance counselor had. She could see herself as a math and science person. If she gave Math 101 her full attention, as Professor Cosmo advised, surely she'd catch on.

Professor Cosmo rose and offered his hand. Lulu stood and put out hers. The desk photos smiled their approval. She bounded down the steps of Math & Science onto the sidewalk where curly yellow leaves like giant cornflakes whispered at her feet. Through bare black tree limbs, the steeples of the library and chapel stood tall against the sky. Saplings were still in red leaf, and green-leafed whips turned their silver backs to the breeze. In the distance, pale yellow wheat grass rose above the low undergrowth and shimmered in the shafts of sun that had been denied it when the leaves were on the tallest trees. The carillon rang the half hour. Maybe she'd become a math major.

"*It's happening now! It's happening all the time!*" Lulu ran into Evie in the hall on the way to breakfast and greeted her with one of Evie's lines from the play.

Evie made a solemn expression. "*The eternal moment!*" She dropped the pose and smiled almost shyly.

"How's Marc?" Lulu glanced at Evie's arm but the silver bracelet was no longer there.

"I really don't know. I've barely seen him since the cast party."

"But that was two weeks ago, Evie."

Evie laughed — not the rich loud laughter of the cast party but her gentle, everyday laugh. "Oh, Lulu, plays are artificial and the friendships are temporary. They're only real while they last."

"*I would ask you not to speak of illusion!*" This time the quote sounded stale to Lulu. She wondered if Evie and Marc had been "going steady," as it was called in high school, and, if so, if they had "broken up" and if that would explain why Marc's bracelet was no longer around Evie's wrist. But she didn't want to be rude.

They arrived at the head of the line and selected their breakfasts. Evie went ahead of Lulu and sat at one of the smaller tables by herself near a window. She had a sheaf of papers under one arm and a pencil behind her ear. Like Lulu's mother, she was a poet. No doubt she wanted to go over submissions for *Eleusis*, the student poetry magazine she edited. Lulu headed for a table of freshmen women. She wasn't sure she had much in common with Evie anymore.

Or with any of the cast and crew of *Six Characters*. These days they exchanged greetings as they hurried by each other, the intimacy and excitement of the production having dissolved in the urgency of course work. The Lamb Chops, too, were brief in their greetings. The OK pledges, on the other hand, continued to seek Lulu out and invariably one would ask her out for Saturday night. Weekday evenings, she had AO pledge meetings to attend. She was finding it hard to stick to her resolve to keep up with math.

"Dottie's gone home for her coming-out party." Bridey was sitting on a desk chair, a towel around her neck, while Jill cut her hair. Since Bridey and Jill had started dating fraternity brothers, they spent more and more time together.

"Her coming-out party?" Lulu was sitting at her desk studying math but couldn't resist the suppressed excitement in Bridey's voice.

"Yeah, her debutante ball!" Bridey dropped her head so Jill could clip the nape of her neck.

"But she's not part of the boarding school crowd." Based on her experience with Elise, Lulu had decided that the products of boarding school were all wild as the result of having been locked up for four years. They didn't need to study first semester because they'd already covered the material. Appearances were everything although a studied nonchalance was obligatory. They were tribal, having regard only for one another. Not only did they like to drink, they were prone to drunkenness. They cared very much for high quality and labels — Bass Weejun shoes, for instance. As "liberals," they empathized with the down and out. That concern did not extend to the middle class, the "bourgeoisie," whom they held responsible for the down and outs or to blue collar workers such as the maids, whom they ignored or treated imperiously. They were capable of viewing the faculty as hired help and would have treated them as such if they thought they could get away with it. They were impressed by wealth, prestige and famous names and whispered among themselves about who was who. Their obsessions kept them from entering into friendships with people outside their tribe. "That bunch isn't anything like Dottie."

"Maybe not, but you can bet she did go to boarding school. Dottie is Main Line."

"Main Line?"

Jill, her lips pursed in concentration, held the scissors vertically to feather Bridey's bangs.

"Philadelphia," Bridey said, "Like Grace Kelly."

"Oh, Grace Kelly!" In seventh grade, Lulu had gone to the movies with Alice and Lenore to see Grace Kelly in *High Society*, Lulu and Alice feeling a little superior to Lenore because Grace Kelly — and Bing Crosby, too, for that matter — was Catholic. And then Grace Kelly married Prince Rainier of Monaco, who also was Catholic, in a fairy tale wedding, went on a honeymoon cruise — like the one in the movie where the newlyweds sang "True Love" to each other — and nine months and four days later gave birth to her first child.

"Dottie doesn't actually remind me of Grace Kelly." Jill gave Bridey a hand mirror and lay her head to one side to examine her efforts. "Cute, Bridey!"

"She's so much more…down to earth." Lulu couldn't summon up an image of Dottie in makeup and a ball gown, and "homely" was much too unkind a word to apply. Besides, she was beautiful on the inside where it counted. "Everything about her is so plain and simple."

"Not her jewelry — her bracelets, her rings, her circle pin — that's not run-of-the-mill stuff."

Except for her circle pin, Lulu hadn't noticed Dottie's jewelry. Everyone had a circle pin. "Her circle pin has brilliants."

"Brilliants! Lulu, those are diamond chips. The green stones in her scarab bracelet are real emeralds. The red stones are real rubies." Bridey set the mirror down and lifted the towel full of swaths of black hair off from around her neck. "Now Kateri and I won't be twins anymore. I told her she should get you to cut her hair, Jill. She said she'd think about it. How about you, Lulu? Want to get your hair cut?"

"Lulu wouldn't look good in a pixie. She's got the height for long hair — like Wendy's."

Lulu felt her color rising. It was embarrassing to be talked about as though she weren't there. At the same time, she was pleased by the attention and flattered to be compared favorably with Wendy.

After Bridey and Jill left and as Lulu tried to apply herself to math, she kept picturing how she would look with long hair.

Elise spent three evenings in a row in 104, polishing her nails or paging through *Glamour Magazine* or *Cosmopolitan*. She neither studied nor wrote letters. Communication with her parents appeared to be conducted entirely by long distance calls from the phones in the hall — an expense Lulu wouldn't have considered.

On the third evening, when the three roommates were at their desks, Jill swiveled in her chair towards Elise. "How's Sammy?"

Elise took a drag and blew smoke towards the ceiling. "Sammy is dead."

"What?" Lulu also turned to face Elise.

"Dead to me. And I'd appreciate it if you didn't speak of him to me ever again."

"What happened?" Jill wasn't so easily deterred.

Elise fixed Jill with a deadpan look. Then she dropped her gaze to the article she'd been reading. The room was quiet for the next half hour when Jill stood and spoke in her best little-girl manner.

"Excuse me, please, I have to go to the bathroom." Lulu and Elise looked up as Jill took her towel and left the room. Elise winked at Lulu, and Lulu betrayed her favorite roommate by laughing out loud. When Jill returned and hung up her towel and sat at her desk, Elise again winked at Lulu. Lulu put a hand over her mouth, but a burst of laughter escaped. Jill looked around at the others. "What's so funny?"

"Jill, dear," Elise said. "This is not study hall. And you are not at home with mother and dad."

"So?"

"So, we don't need to be informed every time you respond to a call from nature." Elise smirked.

Jill looked full in the face first at Elise, then at Lulu. Sufficiently impressed to feel the humor ebb out of her, Lulu returned Jill's sober expression. "I know who my friends are." Jill stood, picked up her book and walked to the door. Elise shot an amused look at Lulu, who ducked her head to the letter she was writing home. The door slammed. No doubt, Jill was on her way to Bridey's room. Although in letters home, Lulu fretted a bit about her studies, she thought it would sound too much like tattling to write something like: *Jill just left in a huff and now she won't be speaking to Elise for the next few days.* She signed and folded the letter. Maybe she hadn't missed out in not having sisters.

Elise was sitting sideways to her desk filing her nails, one nylon-stockinged foot draped over the other, her loafers at her feet. "Your front teeth are so even and straight, Lulu. Judging from them, anyone might think you'd had braces."

In spite of how mean Elise had been to Jill, Lulu smiled at the compliment. She did think her teeth were her best feature. She didn't know what her parents would have done if she'd needed orthodontia, the way Lenore had. If she'd been as buck-toothed as a bunny, they might have come up with the money somehow, but if the flaw had been minor, she'd just have had to live with it. "How do you know I didn't have braces?" Acting slightly contrary made her feel less disloyal to Jill.

"My dear, if you'd had the very best dental care, your back teeth wouldn't resemble a veritable silver mine."

Lulu ducked her head to address the envelope. She licked a stamp, stuck it on and licked and sealed the flap. She felt her face burning but she was darn sure she wasn't going to let anyone kick her out of her own room. "A letter to my folks," she said pointlessly — and a little too loudly.

"You like your parents, don't you, Lulu?" Elise sounded as though she were making a philosophical observation in Mr. O'Rourke's *Great Thinkers* seminar.

"Of course. Don't you like yours?"

"And do your parents like each other?"

"Sure."

"Love each other?"

"Well…" Lulu looked at the letter in her hand — *Mr. and Mrs. Harold Delaney and Family.* "…They're not mushy about it, but, yes, they love each other." This declaration, brought about by Elise's persistent questioning, felt like a happy discovery.

"My parents don't love each other."

"Really! Why don't they get a divorce?" Divorce was as rare among the parents of Lulu's hometown friends as it was for the subjects of the *Ladies Home Journal's* "Can This Marriage Be Saved?" Still, for Protestants, it was a possibility.

"I'm afraid they will — any day now." Elise's mother was a descendent of Boston Brahmans; her father's folks were blue collar. Both families had opposed the marriage; so, to begin with, it must have been true love — or rebellion. Elise's father didn't own the restaurant he managed, and it wasn't five star. "He can't support her, quote, in the manner to which she was accustomed, unquote." Elise held up one hand and studied her nails.

"But he sent you to boarding school…" Lulu pictured Elise's self-assured, well-mannered father from their first day in Chubbuck, his hair expertly cut, his sports clothes casually elegant. Maybe such high-class manners came from running a restaurant. In comparison, her own father might have come off as a hick. "…and he's sending you to Lovejoy."

"It isn't his money. There's an educational trust on my mother's side of the family." Elise studied her other hand. "The thing is, my dad's always at the restaurant and he sleeps in the guest bedroom. This year my little brother went away to school. So now they're free to get divorced."

"Maybe that wouldn't be the worst thing in the world."

"Easy for you to say! Elise picked up a bottle of maroon polish and shook it like a terrier with a rat. "How would you like to go home at Thanksgiving and find out your parents have moved into separate apartments and your house is up for sale?"

"Sorry, Elise, you're right. I wouldn't like that."

"Well, it will never happen to you because your parents love each other." Coolly, Elise splayed her fingers on her knee and began meticulously spreading polish.

"I'm afraid my parents will get a divorce." This time, it was Jill speaking. After her three evenings in 104, Elise had apparently gotten over the breakup with Sammy. She had picked up with her boarding school crowd again and came into the room only minutes before curfew.

Lulu pictured short, erect Mr. Stassi, who had kissed her cheek, and short, plump Mrs. Stassi with her enveloping arms. She saw them standing with Jill in a huddle in the middle of 104. "But your parents are so affectionate."

"They fight all the time."

"About what?"

"My Nonna. She lives with us, and she can be bossy. My mother says it's like the house isn't hers; it's her mother-in-law's. My father says he'd never turn away his own mother. So now they're free to get a divorce."

"Why now?" Lulu had learned enough not to say a divorce might not be the worst thing in the world.

"Because I was the only thing holding them together. I love them both — and Nonna, too — but they don't exactly all love each other. If they do get divorced, it will be my fault."

"How could it be your fault?"

"I could have gone to junior college and lived at home. But, in the end, I decided coming to Lovejoy was the best thing for me."

Jill's decision struck Lulu as a little self centered — but maybe not in a bad way. In her prayers that night, she thanked God her parents loved each other and would never get a divorce. The one worry she'd had about them was that her father might suffer another nervous breakdown. How had her mother coped with his previous periods of despondency? When there were just the two of them, Lulu and her mother before the boys were born, had her mother considered leaving her father and going back to her own parents? Lulu knew unhappy marriages existed — Meduxnekeag, especially the hospital, was full of such stories. She wasn't used to thinking about whether her parents were happy, and the thought that they might be either not happy or not happy with each other was ruining her prayerful mood. During Thanksgiving vacation, she'd make it her business to see whether they were happy.

Chapter Eleven

On the Tuesday afternoon before Thanksgiving, Jimmy Taylor pulled up to Chubbuck in a car with the most exuberant fins Lulu had ever seen. She'd written her parents she'd be home on Wednesday's bus — students were forbidden to skip Tuesday classes — but in class on Saturday morning Mr. Lunt had said, "I certainly hope none of you are planning to be here Tuesday. I know I won't be." He winked and put a forefinger to his lips. "Don't tell!" Sunday at the library Jimmy, who had no Tuesday afternoon classes, had offered her a ride. The change of plans hadn't warranted a long distance phone call home.

Jimmy was wearing a sheepskin-lined black and red lumberman's jacket and a black cowboy hat pushed to the back of his head. At Lovejoy, he played up being a country boy. In high school, Lulu was pretty sure he wore blue wool Air Force pants from the Army Navy surplus store, same as all the other boys. He probably wore white bucks or brown oxfords from Dux Shoes. At Lovejoy he wore narrow blue jeans and scuffed boots — Frye boots, Bridey had informed her, too expensive a line for a small–town store.

"This rain is supposed to turn to sleet." He squinted into the steady downpour and patted the steering wheel. "This baby is a '58 DeSoto. It can handle just about anything. You feel okay traveling in this weather?"

"Oh, sure." Lulu settled herself on the passenger side of the plush front seat. She knew that Jimmy, like all farm boys, had grown up handling all sorts of vehicles in all weathers.

"Mind if I smoke?" Jimmy's request was pro forma.

"Oh, no, not at all." Lulu's answer was equally pro forma. Actually, she didn't mind cigarette or cigar smoke. She associated it with a sense of well-being, just as the smokers no doubt did. She thought, in fact, after she graduated and was working full-time at a good job, she would take up the habit.

Jimmy pulled the smoke deep into his lungs and let it out in a smooth blue stream. "That Dean Dithers is built like a brick shit house, isn't she? Oh, sorry, Lu, I should watch my language."

"That's okay. I don't mind." Lulu knew that for certain Meduxnekeag men using vulgar language conferred the strength Samson had derived from his hair.

"You getting along all right with old Mrs. Drag Ass?" As they dropped down the hill to town, Jimmy leaned forward to peer into the rain.

"I don't see much of her now the semester is underway."

"You probably never saw much of old Harding or Cyr in high school either." Jimmy slid his gaze her way, then back to the rain.

"No, did you?" Lulu was being polite. She knew the answer. When she was a freshman, Jimmy was one of the senior boys often paged to go to the office. People couldn't believe it when he got accepted to Lovejoy. They were even more surprised he didn't flunk out.

"They were always nipping at my ass about one thing or another." He gave a quick laugh. "Not that I blame them. They did right by me in the end — better than right." He glanced at her again. "You deserve to be at Lovejoy, Lulu. I'll bet nobody had to clean up your record."

She didn't feel like telling him about the warning in math. If she passed the course in the end, that warning would remain her little secret.

"The thing about college is I figured out right off the bat what you could get away with and what you couldn't." They were on the road to Bangor now. The rain had eased. Jimmy sat back and drummed his fingers lightly on the wheel. "I had to learn to study, Lu, really study. At Dux you could get away with bullshitting or looking over stuff at the last minute. I work my tail off from Sunday afternoon through Saturday noon time." He grinned. "That gives me the rest of Saturday to have fun and Sunday morning to sleep it off."

It struck Lulu that Jimmy's study habits sounded a lot like Wesley's, even though one guy had the reputation as a playboy and the other as a straight arrow. "I didn't realize college would be so much harder than high school." It was the closest Lulu had come to admitting that the course work at Lovejoy was beginning to frighten her.

"In college the main thing is not to flunk out. In high school, the main thing is not to get a girl knocked up. That could lead to a shotgun marriage and ruin your life — like my old friend Donny."

Lulu's stomach dropped. She didn't like to think her friend Alice had ruined anyone's life. Nor could she bear to let her mind linger on the possibility of flunking out of Lovejoy. "I don't think Donny's life is ruined."

"Maybe not. But he'll be stuck on his father's farm the rest of his life. Also, they're Catholics and, pardon my saying so, Lu, but you know what that means — babies, lots and lots of babies."

By Bangor the rain had turned to sleet. Jimmy leaned forward and pulled his hat low over his forehead. "Do you think this will turn to snow?" Lulu asked.

"Do bears shit in the woods?" The strain of peering through the window had turned Jimmy's voice to a growl. "Oh, sorry, Lu. I should watch my language."

"That's okay." The sleet lashed the windshield and pinged against the car. She certainly didn't want Jimmy to become distracted by watching his language. In Meduxnekeag there were two kinds of men: those who employed vulgar, blasphemous language and those whose expletives consisted of *gosh, golly, darn* and *gee whiz*. Most rough talkers knew to curb their language in polite company and at least some of the smooth talkers, Lulu surmised, lowered their standards in certain circumstances — plus, barnyard terms were common to both groups — and so, expressed as a Venn diagram, the two circles would have a broad overlap.

In Lincoln, Jimmy pulled into an Esso station. When he went inside to pay, she followed, tired of the sitting position despite the luxurious plush seat. He picked two submarine sandwiches wrapped in waxed paper and two Cokes from the cooler and laid them on the counter with a twenty dollar bill. When Lulu offered to pay for hers, he waved her away. They ate in the parked car with the engine turned on for warmth. It was almost like being on a date.

"Think we should continue, Lu?" Jimmy balled up his waxed paper and shifted himself into the driving position. It was getting dark and snowing fat lazy flakes.

"Oh, I'm sure we'll be all right." She had complete confidence in his driving. And they'd done fine so far. Besides, where would they stay? A motel would be awkward — and expensive. Better to soldier on. Jimmy turned the key in the ignition. By Mattawamkeag, the snowflakes were tiny and so driven the windshield wipers strained to keep pace. Twice, he stopped and got out to swipe his forearm over the glass. At the bottom of Santa Claus Hill, the solid '58 De Soto slewed wildly.

"Jesus H. Christ!" Jimmy eased up on the accelerator and geared down, and the car began grinding upward. Lulu bent her head as she was in the habit of doing whenever the name of the Lord was spoken either with reverence or in vain. All the little towns fell behind as they drove into swirling snow through a tunnel of trees. They passed through forest townships with no centers and no names, just numbers and letters to designate a spot on the map. There were no motels or even gas stations. And no other cars on the road. Jimmy switched off the radio when the only station that would come in got too staticky to make out what Rolf had referred to as Johnny Cash's "chickaboom-boom-freight train" delivery of "I Walk the Line." Lulu and Jimmy were quiet except for his occasional muttering. Her head bobbed three times whenever she made out "Jesus, Jesus, Jesus." She'd have offered to take a turn at the wheel if she thought he would accept her help.

When Lulu was little, she had thought the empty stretches between built-up areas were nowhere — nowhere and nothing. Was nowhere and nothing what she would be if she flunked math and got too low an average to keep her scholarship? Was the awful feeling that was taking hold of her what Emily Dickenson meant by, "I'm nobody, who are you?" Was it how April felt about not being in a sorority? Usually, Lulu was so busy with sorority and classes and the library and dating, she had little time for such wintry thoughts. She sighed.

Jimmy looked over. "Almost there. We're going to make it, after all, Lu."

"Oh, I have no doubt." This drive was nothing compared with the prospect of flunking out of Lovejoy.

When finally he pulled the De Soto alongside her driveway — there was too much accumulation for him to drive in — Jimmy said, "I wouldn't have kept going if it hadn't been for you, Lu. I was some scared." Lulu was surprised. She hadn't thought continuing the drive was any more her idea than his.

She thanked him and let the De Soto's door thud shut behind her. A plow had been by at least once, and the long white hillock it had created came to the tops of her boots. Falling snow cleansed the air and muffled all sound. It felt like home.

Lulu let herself into the unlocked front door, and, careful not to rouse the sleeping house, crept up to her bedroom at the top of the stairs where she quickly fell asleep. She awoke when her mother wrapped her arms around her and leaned in close "Oh, Lulu, you're home early!" Her mother's tears wet Lulu's cheeks.

"English got canceled and I got a ride with Jimmy Taylor."

Her mother drew back. "Oh, Lulu, I was afraid you'd given up on college."

So, although her mother had not alluded to it in her letters, Lovejoy must have sent home a copy of the math warning.

Her mother wiped her eyes. Her face was older than Lulu remembered it, the circles under her eyes making her look as haggard as photos of Depression-era Appalachian women. Lulu felt like putting her arms around her and telling her everything would be all right, but her mother had composed herself and the moment for being demonstrative had passed.

At breakfast, ready for the day in an old wool sweater and skirt — Lulu could count on the fingers of one hand the number of times she'd seen her mother wear pants — and with an application of lipstick, her mother looked more the way Lulu remembered her. Lulu's brothers were dressed in the striped jerseys and wide-wale corduroy pants little boys had worn to school for as far back as she could remember. Their jackets and snow pants hung by the kitchen door; their green gum rubber boots stood underneath, glistening with melted snow. There was the faint odor of wet wool and feet. All three boys had flaming cheeks from being outside. Johnny had delivered his papers and shoveled the front walk. Mickey had been sliding with other neighborhood children, and Neil had constructed a snow creature, a lumpy mess Lulu spied outside the kitchen window. "It's a bunny, Lulu," he said. "You can help me finish it."

Her father held out to Lulu a concoction he had fixed for himself. "Honey and vinegar plus a few secret ingredients, Lu. For a long and healthy life." His looks had not changed. His normally cheerful appearance retained something of the perennial boy. She declined the offer. The health drink was a new development, but not a surprising one. With her father, there were always new developments. Laughing, he held his glass up to the sunlight streaming across the kitchen table and heaved a great sigh. He gestured with the glass to his wife standing at the stove. "You want some, Mumma?"

"You are so notional, Hal." Lulu took note of her mother's tone. It wasn't indulgent; neither was it mean.

"It will keep you living longer in good health, Mumma." Her father sounded neither surprised nor annoyed nor offended. He had his peculiarities and his wife had hers. He didn't expect her to drink honey and vinegar each morning for however long his enthusiasm for it lasted, but he liked teasing her a little. He gestured with the glass in turn to Johnny, Mickey and Neil, and each boy made a face and shook his head. Neil giggled. They were amused by their father, Lulu thought, maybe even a little pleased to be offered his drink, to be taken into account by him. She felt better seeing them together and knowing her worries about the boys despising their father the way Biff despised Willy Loman were too much of an illusion to ever become reality.

Her father took a drink, screwed up his face — it must taste awful, Lulu thought — swallowed, said, "Ahhhh!" and belched.

"Hal," said his wife, just to the exasperated side of matter of fact.

"Sorry, Mumma." Lulu's father didn't look sorry. He put his glass down, his eyes shining, smarting probably from the vinegar, and sat smiling at his little world. His wife put a plate of scrambled eggs and toast in front of him and he began to eat.

As was Dux High tradition, Lulu spent a good part of the day, along with other '61 graduates, at her alma mater, being invited into classes to regale the seniors with tales of college. Wade Carmichael limped up to her in the hall, his red hair and freckles gleaming, his grin confident as ever. Throughout high school, he'd conducted himself as best friend to everyone from the president of student council to the freshman farm boys to Norrie the cook. Too short to be a star on the basketball team, he was a valued and peppy second stringer, even in this, his senior year and in spite of his accident. He threw his arm over Lulu's shoulders and walked her to the door of his next class. "How's things at the country club?"

"Fine." Lulu laughed at his little joke. Her senior year she'd been teased plenty about going to a campus as well groomed as a golf course and with a reputation for heavy drinking. Lovejoy had turned out to be a whole lot harder than belonging to a country club, but she didn't feel like saying that to Wade.

"Wesley didn't come home. He's in Mexico!"

So Wesley hadn't told his family he was corresponding with her. On the other hand, she hadn't told anyone in Meduxnekeag either. "You must miss him."

"Yuh, hard to keep them down on the farm once they've seen the big city." Wade chuckled and gave Lulu's shoulders a little shake. "Speaking of seeing the big city, when's Lenore expecting?" Lenore and her husband were living out of the purview of Meduxnekeag on an Army base down south.

"Who says she's expecting, anyway?" Lulu hoped her tone was light but she didn't like it when people assumed Lenore had "had" to get married. Some people had no appreciation for true love.

"Oh, sorry, Lu, I guess I was thinking of Alice. Speaking of Alice, did you hear the one about the truck driver who pulled out to avoid a child?"

Lulu smiled. "No, Wade, I didn't hear about the truck driver who pulled out to avoid a child."

He pulled her close and spoke into her ear. "He fell off the couch."

Lulu pulled away. "Wade!"

"Hey, Lu, just kidding." He gave her shoulders a squeeze, then sauntered into his classroom. It was amazing how two brothers could be so different from one another.

"Lulu, how are you making out at Lovejoy?" Mr. Cyr had come up behind her in the hallway that was emptying of students.

So her high school had not been informed of her warning in math — or of any other academic struggles she was encountering. Lulu gave the automatic response. "Fine, thank you, Mr. Cyr, just fine."

At home that evening, Johnny showed her his latest comics, Mickey asked her three new riddles, and Neil said he wouldn't take a bath unless she gave it to him. Later, under the patchwork quilt her Nana had made for her, she lay in bed looking out at the same moon that shone through the windows of Room 104 Chubbuck. She hoped Jill and Elise's homecomings were as happy and harmonious as hers. She offered a prayer that neither set of parents would announce a divorce. She thought to add a petition for Rolf's family, in which divorce was rampant, that they be spared another.

The next morning, Lulu set the table with her parents' wedding present silver and the crystal and Wedgwood that had been her Nana's. By noon, the house filled up with aunts, uncles, cousins, and the aroma of roasting turkey and pumpkin pie. The relatives' innocent queries made it apparent that her parents had not told of the math warning.

At 2:30, Lulu excused herself from the table and went upstairs to change into her nurses' aide uniform. Our Lady of Sorrows had called the day before and lined her up for the three-to-eleven shift Thursday, Friday and Saturday. "Don't know how we got along without you," Sister Timothy had said over the phone.

Lulu walked through the front door of Sorrows feeling like Florence Nightingale reporting to the front. Within ten minutes, a doctor had looked right through her when she greeted him in the hall, a nurse had expressed disappointment in having Lulu assigned to her rather than an LPN, and an orderly had barked at her to hurry up with the lunch trays that hadn't all been collected on the previous shift. She reminded herself that she was at the bottom of the ladder —

an aide who took temperatures, spoon-fed the feeble, and shoved bedpans into place, eased them out and emptied them. Unlike at Lovejoy, her opinion was not sought nor even tolerated. At Sorrows, the main thing was that she show up on time and do as she was told.

With the patients, her age and station were advantages. The old guys in the Men's Ward teased and flattered her. The gynecological patients asked her about her studies and her social life at Lovejoy. The children in Pediatrics, if they were well enough, wanted her to play with them or, if they weren't, to hold them. Lulu realized she had missed seeing children — and old people. At Lovejoy she lived and studied exclusively with people her own age. Everyone else — the professors, instructors, administrators and staff — was somewhere along a continuum she thought of as "middle-aged."

Lovejoy and Sorrows were each a whole world in itself. Each had a pecking order; each had its good and bad features, its *on the one hand* and *on the other hand*.

On Saturday morning, Lulu asked her father if she could borrow the family car to drive out to Alice's. Instead of his usual hemming and hawing and haranguing, he handed her the keys to Old Nelly with a smile. He was treating her like a grownup. Or maybe he felt sorry for her.

She drove past Wesley's church, the Full Gospel Tabernacle of Our Lord and Savior Jesus Christ. When she was a freshman in high school, her friend Helen had dated a senior who was regarded as a bit of an oddball. Both attended the meetings of the tabernacle's Wednesday evening youth group. One Thursday morning, Helen arrived at school with Casper's class ring on a chain around her neck. Made reckless by love, she confided to her friends that she and Casper had prayed together. Prayed together! The other girls couldn't have been more shocked — and then amused — if Helen had admitted to going all the way. And yet…

…and yet, such intimacy both repelled and attracted Lulu. In her experience, people didn't pray together except in the case of a Mass or school assembly or a mother teaching her child or a family — not hers but Alice's, for instance — kneeling in the living room after supper to recite the rosary. She pictured Helen and Casper kneeling alone together to pray. Although it was a ridiculous image, Lulu felt oddly jealous all over again. She was sorry Wesley wasn't home for Thanksgiving. After their friendly correspondence and all the good advice he'd given, she would like to see him again, face to face.

She eased into the one-way traffic around Market Square and past the shops and banks and law offices that kept the downtown humming. Dux Shoes had a "help wanted" sign in the window. Perhaps her mother might get a job next year when Neil started kindergarten. Even if it didn't pay much, her father could replace Old Nelly with a more reliable vehicle. She got so busy imagining the new car — maybe a used DeSoto in good condition — she almost missed the turn off Route 1 just beyond the Whoa Daddy Restaurant. She passed three abandoned farmhouses and several cars left to rust away, one stripped of tires and hood through which a sapling shot straight up. Central Maine didn't look like this. On the other hand, she wasn't familiar with the back roads in Central Maine — or anywhere else.

She passed a pasture where she and Alice used to pick potatoes. The fall she was ten, her mother had told her and Johnny that soon they would have a new baby brother or sister. She explained quite a bit about the developing baby — no stories of storks and cabbages — and about the projected birth at Our Lady of Sorrows Hospital. Just how it got started inside her, however, was left for Lulu to piece together on her own. One morning soon after her mother's revelation, Lulu was on her knees scooping potatoes into a basket when she heard a bellow from the adjoining pasture. A bull had reared himself up onto the hind quarters of a cow and was ramming her. It looked to Lulu as though the cow, if so minded, could have gotten away, but she stood stock still withstanding what must have been a tremendous weight and a powerful jolting with an inscrutable expression that could have been either resignation or bliss.

It took Lulu a couple of wrong turns before she reached the old farmhouse. At the time Alice and Donny got married, it had recently become vacant, his grandmother having died and his grandfather having moved into Donny's parents' big modern home closer to Route 1. Lulu felt a little guilty about not seeing much of Alice since she'd gotten married. Senior year, Lulu had been so caught up with school and school friends and Alice with being a farmwife it was almost as though they spoke different languages. Alice had even begun to talk like a middle-aged country woman, and her new best pal appeared to be her mother-in-law Marlene.

Alice was in the kitchen rolling out pie dough when Lulu opened the door, rapped once on the doorpost and walked in. The blonde of Alice's hair was of the dishwater variety and there was nothing spectacular about the blue of her eyes. She possessed, however, the sort of sparkling personality that passed for beautiful, especially with boys. She possessed also a sense of style and was wonderfully good-natured. Possibly, she would not have been offended by Wade's joke. Possibly, she would have smacked him on the arm and said, "Oh, you!" News of her pregnancy, however, had been received by her family as no joke, and the young couple had gone about at first with a sheepish air. Alice's parents had not entertained the idea of her going to college — she was enrolled in the general course — but they had expected her to graduate from high school. Gradually, Alice and Donny lifted their heads, and by the time Little Donny was born, they were as readily accepted as any other married pair, their circumstances, it had dawned on Lulu, not so unusual as the older generation would have the younger believe.

Little Donny was sitting in a high chair next to his mother poking dry Cheerios into his mouth one by one. Curls of his mother's fair hair in a lighter brighter shade circled his head and his eyes were his father's striking blue. The kitchen was one of those big square farm rooms full of modern appliances scattered all over with no thought to efficiency. It looked cleaner than the last time Lulu visited. She pulled out a chair and sat at the table. She and Alice knew each other too well to hug and carry on the way Jill would be doing with her friends down in Fall River, Massachusetts. "Look at you, making a pie!"

"It took me all last spring to get good at this, Lulu. My land, I made a pie every day."

"You and Donny ate a pie every day?" Lulu didn't imagine Little Donny would be much help consuming a pie.

"I made them at Marlene's." Alice hadn't been prepared to fix a main meal for Donny every single day. Lulu could have surmised that. Growing up as the youngest, Alice had shirked her way through childhood leaving the acquisition of the womanly arts to her older sisters. When she got married, she couldn't do much more than fix peanut butter and jelly sandwiches and heat up a can of tomato soup with milk. And that's what she did for Donny when he came in at noon from working with his father on the farm. And worse. The day after she served popcorn and Koolaid, he went to his mother's for his noon dinner. That night, Alice figured Marlene was probably mad at her, but the next morning early, her mother-in-law phoned to say, "Oh, honey, I told Donny he should have brought you with him. You come over here this morning after you get straightened around and help me fix the noon meal."

After that, every morning about ten o'clock Alice drove over in the '55 Chevrolet dedicated to her use and let Marlene teach her how to cook what Donny liked to eat. At first, Alice slept until just before it was time to leave for Marlene's. As the pregnancy advanced and she began to feel better in the mornings and paid attention to how Marlene accomplished her housework, she actually did straighten up before leaving the house. Donny complimented her on her housekeeping and her cooking and, after Little Donny came, her mothering. No doubt about it, Alice was a natural-born mother. She lifted Little Donny out of his high chair and placed him on Lulu's lap.

"Hello, little man," Lulu crooned. She looked up at Alice. "I suppose you didn't pick potatoes this fall." She was kidding.

"No, and I don't go over to Marlene's every day the way I used to, but I did during picking. There were so many extra people at the table. There's something different to do here every season. I cut seed in the potato house with Fred, Donnie's grandfather. He's so interesting, God love him, and he just loves Little Donny. And Marlene is showing me how to help with the books. I was always pretty good at math, you remember, and addition and subtraction is all it is. There's so much to learn on a farm, Lu. Sometimes I feel my life didn't get started until I moved here." Her pie in the oven, Alice brought a mixing bowl containing a chicken carcass to the table and picked off bits of meat to drop into a smaller bowl. Little Donny wriggled off Lulu's lap and crawled in the direction of the cats' bowl. "Stay for dinner, Lu.

Donny would love to see you." Alice stood, wiped her hands on her apron and lifted the cats' bowl to the counter. Little Donny sat back on his heels.

"Okay, thanks." Lulu tried to make her voice sound casual. "Do you remember Wesley Carmichael?"

"Wesley — Wade's brother. Sure. Not like Wade though. No personality."

"It comes out in his letters."

"Wesley Carmichael writes to you, Lu? My land!"

Lulu felt herself blushing. She wondered if Alice thought she had no personality either.

"Oh, Lu, I didn't mean anything bad about Wesley. I'm sure he's just shy. But he's smart, Lu, like you, and now that I think about it, not bad looking. 'Course he's a holy roller, and doesn't he go to a Bible college?"

"They don't just study the Bible there, Alice. Nott's a real college like any other college." Lulu never thought she'd find herself defending Nott, but she was struck for the first time by the truth of what she was saying. "Besides, Pentecostals and Catholics are all Christians, after all."

"Good for you, Lu! I agree. True love beats all!"

Lulu was about to protest that she wasn't in love when the door opened and Donny came in. He had the hulking good looks of the comic strip Lil' Abner, right down to the curl of blue-black hair over his forehead. Instead of Lil' Abner's single-strap denim overalls, he wore dark green Dickies pants and a matching green work shirt. "Hi there, Lu. How're things at Lovejoy Country Club?"

Lulu was almost surprised Donny remembered her name, let alone where she attended college. "Fine, thank you, Donny."

"You ever run into Jimmy Taylor down there?"

"Actually, he gave me a ride home."

"Last time I saw him he was dressed like a cowboy." When Donny laughed, Lulu glimpsed the carefree, slightly reckless senior boy she remembered from when she was a high school freshman. "Old Jimmy and I used to have some good times." He scooped up Little Donny and hugged him until the child laughed and squealed.

He hoisted him into the air three times and yelled, "Whoopsie daisy!" He held him sideways and aimed him at Lulu like a battering ram. He put the baby down and kissed his wife on the cheek — a nice, comfortable kiss. He rolled up his sleeves, strode to the sink, turned on both faucets, splashed water on his face and scrubbed his hands and arms up to the elbows like a surgeon preparing to operate. Then he sat in a captain's chair, picked up Little Donny who'd crawled to him and waited for his dinner to be put in front of him.

After Donny had returned to work, Lulu fed Little Donny a bottle while Alice loaded the dishwasher. "Isn't Little Donny precious, God love him?" She turned on the dishwasher, which made a low contented murmur, as though in fellow-feeling with the baby. "I wouldn't mind if another rabbit had to die soon."

"They really do that, the way we learned in biology?"

"Yuh, the rabbit gets an injection and if you're expecting it dies."

"The poor rabbit!"

"Life's unfair, Lu. That's one thing I've learned living on a farm."

Driving back through the countryside, Lulu still felt Little Donny's imprint on her lap, his head in the crook of her arm. She pictured Donny's kiss on Alice's cheek. She pictured the kitchen full of modern appliances. Alice had it good, better than Lulu's mother in some ways. If her mother got a job, maybe in addition to replacing Old Nelly her parents could buy an automatic washer, dryer and dishwasher. Lulu wouldn't want Alice's life, not yet anyway, but it certainly suited Alice, possibly better than Lovejoy suited Lulu.

Lulu's father was home from his Saturday half day at the Five and Dime. He sat in one of the two wooden rockers on the glassed-in porch, polishing the boys' shoes. The sun that was rapidly melting the snow warmed the porch like a greenhouse. "How's Alice, Lu?"

"She's fine, Dad."

Her father stopped polishing, both hands in the air, his left with a shoe on it, and fixed her with a look that could have been either deadly serious or dryly humorous. "The parents are always the last to know." He was referring, Lulu realized, to Alice's pre-marital condition. His remark was by no means idle but intended as a caution to Lulu not to follow her friend's bad example. His message delivered, he swiped at the shoe again. "I'm trying out a new invention, Lu. After these shoes are polished, I'll coat them with a vegetable and silicone formula that will permanently waterproof them. Dux Shoes need never again lay in a supply of rubbers."

Lulu felt insulted by her father's roundabout warning not to get pregnant, touched by his protectiveness towards her and frustrated that, although he would throw out *bon mots*, he would never actually engage in a discussion on anything of a personal nature. Conversation with him had to be on an impersonal topic that captured his imagination. She sat in the other rocker and watched him polish another shoe, the sun through the windows warming her clear through to the cockles of her heart. "What about all the abandoned farmhouses, Dad? Where do those people go?"

"Connecticut." He slid his left hand into a shoe.

People had been leaving Meduxnekeag for Connecticut for as long as Lulu could remember, but she'd never given much thought to it before. "Why?"

"Economics." He rubbed polish over the front of the shoe. "Donny McDowell's father has enough acres to make a good living potato farming, same as Jimmy Taylor's, but, gee whiz, there's no room for the little guy any more. So those fellers give up and head for the factories in Connecticut. They sell their souls to a union. 'Course, they're no more compromised than the feller who goes to work for a huge corporation. The banks here are bad enough. They'll squeeze a feller and squeeze and squeeze, but corporations! Corporations chew a feller up and when they're done with him they spit him out. The men who run those companies — where you and I have hearts…" Her father set the shoe down and laid his hand over his breastbone. "…they have gizzards." He picked up another shoe. "At least, a union member has some protections, in spite of the fact that the leaders are gangsters."

"So only the big farmers are safe?" A green reserve-desk *Samuelson* flashed into Lulu's mind. "Economically speaking?"

"They're not safe either. Gosh, Lu, The County conducts itself like a banana republic — all potatoes all the time. The big farmers need to diversify — broccoli maybe or a hybrid of some sort. As it is, they're exhausting the soil. Also, they're completely at the mercy of the market. But you can't get them to understand that. All they understand, all they want to understand, is growing potatoes."

"Dad, why are we a Republican state?"

"Business, Lu. A farmer is a small businessman. Maine's economy runs on small business. The Democrats don't understand why someone like the McDowells and the Taylors can't pay higher taxes. After all, their assets are high. But, gee, if one of them has to sell a field or equipment to pay taxes, then he loses his means of production and has to operate at a standard lower and lower…" Her father let his shoe-encased hand drop. "…until what he's left with isn't worth a pee hole in the snow."

"Pee hole in the snow" was one of her father's barnyard expressions. Another was "cat in heat," which he had applied to Alice when she and Lulu were juniors — "that girl runs after the McDowell boy like a cat in heat" — and which, for all Lulu's disavowal, proved apt. He gazed approvingly at the lineup of polished shoes. "Course, Dux Shoes will still do business in overshoes and boots, but rubbers, Lu, will become a thing of the past. Hold this bucket steady, will you, while I pour in the formula."

Lulu was struck by how smart her father sounded given the simple nature of his job and how happy it made him to be caught up in one of his projects. She didn't think he was headed for another breakdown any time soon.

"Too bad you didn't get a chance to get your hair cut, Lulu. The time went so fast. But in less than a month you'll be back for a longer stay." Lulu's mother was standing at the ironing board and Lulu, dressed for her shift at Sorrows, sat facing her.

"I'm thinking of letting it grow out….Mum, next year you could get a job." Growing up, ironing was Lulu's favorite time for talking with her mother. Unlike her father, her mother willingly discussed personal matters — up to a point.

"Oh, I don't think so, Lulu." Her mother nosed the iron along the collar of a white shirt. She put down the iron, flipped the shirt, picked up the iron and slid it along the yoke. "For one thing, the boys come home for lunch."

"They could take lunchboxes to school like I did." That was when Lulu first went to school and her father was not well, the period Lulu remembered as his Sad Days.

"Did you, Lulu? Oh, yes, I suppose you did. For a short time. Well, I think it's better for the boys to come home at noon. And you know how your father counts on my being here for for the noon meal." Her lowered eyes and the pressure she applied to the sleeve she was working on signaled the topic closed. It occurred to Lulu that her mother had something in common with Evie — a private part of their minds where they preferred to be to themselves. Maybe it had to do with their being poets.

"Mum," Lulu switched to a neutral topic. "Do you remember hearing about a Lovejoy coed who had a baby and put it into her suitcase. It was in all the papers."

"Oh, yes, that poor girl!" Her mother looked up and handed the shirt to Lulu.

"The baby was a girl?" Lulu hung the shirt on a wire hanger.

"Oh, I don't know what the baby was. I'm speaking of the mother." Her mother ran the iron over the collar of a second white shirt. Her voice was comfortable again and sad.

"Mum, she killed her baby."

"I know. Think how desperate she must have felt."

Lulu hadn't thought of the coed's desperation before, only of that baby shut up alive in a suitcase. "Maybe her parents wouldn't have accepted the baby."

"Oh, they would have, Lulu. People feel awful about that sort of thing. It almost kills them sometimes, but they get over it, and almost always they love the baby when it arrives. In the newspaper it said the baby's father married her after she got out of jail. He'd had no idea. He would have married her before. That baby could have lived. The poor girl was too upset to think straight." Her mother set down the iron and gazed out the window at the sun on the dormant garden and the icy river and bare woods beyond. "Of course, it was terrible publicity for Lovejoy. Some people questioned the whole idea of sending their daughters there."

At Sorrows that evening when Lulu was dressing a fat-cheeked, black-eyed Indian baby for discharge, she looked up to see Kateri and a second, older Indian woman. In another instant, Lulu realized it wasn't Kateri at all but the mother of the infant. The older woman put out her arms for the baby while the young mother, whether shy or inept, stood by.

Kateri, Lulu thought, would have known how to handle her own baby. Kateri, on the other hand, wouldn't have become a teenage mother.

"Gosh, Lulu, you don't have to go back." Her father turned to her at the foot of the stairs, his hand on the banister, as though what he was saying had occurred to him on the spur of the moment.

It was early Sunday afternoon. The family had been to Mass and eaten a scaled-down version of Thanksgiving dinner. Lulu was standing by her suitcase at the front door waiting for Jimmy. All weekend, until this oblique remark, nothing had been said about the warning in math. "What?"

"If it's too hard for you, Lovejoy. You don't have to go back. You could get a job at the Five and Dime."

Her father must have mentally rehearsed what he was saying. She was touched that he felt sorry for her. He meant what he said. She didn't have to go back and be afraid all the time that she might lose her scholarship or flunk out — which amounted to the same thing. "Thanks, Dad, but I want to go back." The thought of a clerk's job in Meduxnekag for the rest of her life frightened her more than the possibility of flunking out of Lovejoy. She wouldn't complain any more in her letters.

A pair of car fins swooped into the driveway. A horn sounded. Jimmy Taylor had arrived.

Chapter Twelve

"***Write a poem*** based on your own experience and your own observations," Mr. Lunt had said, his feet stretched out onto his desk, his hands clasped behind his head. "And whatever you do, don't give me flowery language." Lulu felt more confident of her result than of any other Lovejoy assignment so far. The following class, Mr. Lunt passed out mimeographed copies.

> *Economics*
>   *by Lulu Delaney*
>
> *On country roads abandoned farmhouses*
> *Ghosted elms guarding the driveways*
> *Tiger lilies stalking the dooryards*
> *Cannibalized cars and stove-in well houses*
> *Mourning their dead*
> *"Gone to Connecticut," my father said.*
>
> *In town an abandoned house*
> *Kids sneak into*
> *Furniture in place*
> *Clothes hanging in closets*
> *A half-eaten pan of peanut butter fudge*
> *On the drop-leaf table in the kitchen*
> *As though the family had*
> *Stepped out, looked at the stars*
> *Piled into the second-hand Ford*
> *To pick up milk and a pack of Lucky Strikes*
> *And — what the heck —*
> *Kept on driving to Connecticut.*

"Comments?" Mr. Lunt asked the class; then, as was his wont, he forestalled discussion by doing all the talking himself. "Nice details, nice imagery," he pronounced. He pointed out that the abstract title paired well with the closely observed details of the stanzas. Although he was basically opposed to rhyme in student poetry, "dead" and "said" being typically awful examples, he gave near praise to the near rhyme of "what the heck" and "Connecticut."

Lulu blushed with pride.

"Of course, the whole poem captures the desperate situation of a depressed part of the country. It's as sad as it is amusing."

Lulu's flush deepened. She had betrayed Meduxnekeag. Maybe all of Aroostook County.

After finishing the poetry and short story paperbacks, the class read a novel that had been out for less than a year, a find on the part of Mr. Lunt. *To Kill a Mockingbird* was like what Lulu had read in high school for book reports or for pure entertainment. Feet up on his desk, Mr. Lunt read aloud from the part where Jem explains to his little sister Scout that in their small town there are four kinds of folks. The best folks, the ones who had once been large landowners, are still treated with deference. Then there are the low-class whites, the respectable Negroes and the disreputable ones. Scout says she thinks there's just one kind of folks: "folks."

Mr. Lunt tossed the open book onto his desk. "What about in your hometowns," he asked. "Are there levels of folks or just *folks?*

In a pensive tone, as though she were thinking out loud, Dottie said, "In my town, there are two kinds of folks. One kind lives in the houses and the other cleans them."

"In Portland, there's a hundred kinds of folks." One of three OK pledges who always sat together spoke up — not Tony, the OK who'd asked Lulu out the last two Saturday nights and who almost never talked in class, but one of the other two.

"That's because it's a city. The people who clean the houses in my town don't live there. They live in Philly." Behind her thick misty glasses, Dottie's eyes looked pained.

"Sounds as though Jem's lowest class of people never make it into your leafy suburb, Miss Van Dame," Mr. Lunt said. "They never make it out of the city."

For the first time, it occurred to Lulu that Meduxnekeag was not all one kind of folks, that there was an upper level that didn't include her and her family. That would be the people who lived in big white or brick houses on Main Street, the people whose forefathers, like those of Atticus Finch in *Mockingbird*, had settled the town and made fortunes in lumber or land. Even if some of those families appeared to live modestly now, there was money squirreled away for their children to go to college and into the professions. Keith Sinclair and his twin brother were the perfect examples, one a medical student, the other a lawyer.

"And Negroes?" Mr. Lunt was saying. "Who are the Negroes in your hometown?"

"Not many Negroes in Portland. But poor white trash — we've got that."

Everyone laughed except Dottie, who flushed and spoke in a voice that had risen an octave. "A person is never garbage!"

If Lulu's family wasn't of the highest class, at least they weren't poor white trash. And Dottie was right about people not being garbage — even though she looked and sounded slightly ridiculous.

"But you must agree…" Obviously enjoying the stir his ideas were causing, Mr. Lunt dropped his feet to the floor and leaned across his desk, "…everyone needs someone to look down on, right? So, who do the 'white trash' — if you'll pardon the expression, Miss Van Dame — look down on?"

Lulu raised her hand. "No one. We don't have Negroes in my hometown."

"The question, Miss Delaney, is not whether you have Negroes in your hometown. The question is: *who* are the Negroes in your hometown?" Mr. Lunt fixed her with a smug smile.

Blood pounded into Lulu's cheeks as she pictured the unpaved street leading to the dump where the Indians, Meduxnekeag's lowest kind of folks, lived. She remained silent. She didn't feel like giving Mr. Lunt the satisfaction of the answer that had just occurred to her.

The second novel was *The Sound and the Fury*. Lulu had read *Macbeth* the year before and remembered the soliloquy that began, "Life is a tale told by an idiot full of sound and fury signifying nothing." Still, she had trouble appreciating why William Faulkner would begin his novel from the point of view of someone mentally retarded. When Mr. Lunt said that Benjy, who celebrated his thirty-third birthday on Easter Sunday, was a Christ figure, she was too amazed to argue the point, even in her own head. That idea made her want to read more Faulkner novels.

This one, according to Mr. Lunt, had all the same themes and sorts of epiphanies, a phenomenon not limited to poetry, as *To Kill a Mockingbird*. No doubt Harper Lee had borrowed, but that was okay. It wasn't plagiarism, the terrible "ism" all the freshmen had been warned against, because by making the material her own, she had crafted an original work of art.

All the talk about the different kinds of "folks" stayed in Lulu's mind and she went over and over the subject of family the way she used to mentally rehearse her lines in the play. Her parents would never divorce, of that she felt sure. Neither of her roommates' parents were about to get a divorce any time soon either. Jill's mother had taken a job as a bank teller. Her father didn't like it — people might think him not capable of supporting his own family — but it got her mother a break from Nonna.

"So everything's turned out for the best," Lulu had said.

"Oh, Lulu, you're such a Pollyanna!" What Jill said didn't sound like a compliment.

Neither had Elise's comment — "How bourgeois" — when Lulu asked if she'd had a nice Thanksgiving. "We don't go in for *Little House on the Prairie* types of holiday. We went to my *pater's* restaurant and had a jolly time with French cuisine and mucho wine. You'll be happy to hear, dear Lulu, that my parents, after a long hiatus, are once again sleeping in the same bed." This bit of information was delivered as coolly as though Elise were summarizing a subplot of *To Kill a Mockingbird* or *The Sound and the Fury*.

Lulu was glad she was a member of her own family and not Elise's — or Jill's. And yet, there was something disturbing about her family that no one at Lovejoy would understand. She briefly considered confiding in Tony. Like Wesley, Tony wasn't much of a talker. Like Wesley, he was good looking — not in Wesley's solid, fair-haired, geometrical way, but with dark hair and a lithe build. When they went out to the Saturday night movie at the Women's Union — there were restrictions against pledges and their dates spending every Saturday night of the month at the fraternity house — Lulu did most of the talking. She had dragged from Tony the information that his parents were not religious and that he had grown up without any connection to a church, although one set of grandparents was Catholic. It wasn't as though Tony had lapsed, Lulu thought, since he'd never even been baptized. Talk of religion didn't hold his interest. He seemed to like listening to Lulu's accounts of incidents of dorm life and home life. More than once, she had recreated the scene of Elise throwing up on Jill's bed, rendering amusing what had initially appalled her. Tony laughed so hard at the story of Janet dropping the tray of parfaits that she retold it acting out the reactions of everyone else at the table — April and Mimi jumping up to hug Janet, Dottie and Kateri fishing glass off people's plates, Jill stealing glances at the kitchen, hoping substitute desserts would appear.

    What marked Tony as different from the other OK pledges Lulu had gone out with was what happened the second time he took her back to the dorm and every time thereafter. He walked her to a tree that stood to one side of the door. He put his arms around her and kissed her lips. Then he nuzzled her cheeks and neck. It was wintery cold and both were bundled in parkas. It struck Lulu that they might look a little ridiculous. But the longer he kept his arms around her and breathed his sweet, moist, Good and Plenty-scented breath onto her face and neck and kissed her lips, the more she lost track of how they might look and gave herself up to the pleasure of his skin against hers. When the warning bell sounded, he took her hand and led her to the door. "Next Saturday, same time?"

    "Yes, thank you, Tony. Good night."

    Except for English class, they seldom saw each other during the week. When they did happen to meet it was almost awkward, Lulu — and she thought Tony, too — eager to continue on by. Jill and Bridey teased her about Tony being her boyfriend, but Lulu knew she didn't want to spend all her free time with him, the way those with true boyfriends did. Tony was for Saturday nights. That was his slot, like the drawer where she kept Wesley's letters. She was happy keeping all her friendships separate — her dorm mates to begin and end the day and eat meals with, the other AO pledges at their weekly meetings, Rolf on Sundays at the library, Ike whenever he stopped by the reserve desk. She liked greeting the Lambda Rho and OK pledges and the members of the Tin Can and the Newman Club. And then moving on. She knew enough friendly faces on campus to feel at home.

No one in her array of friends and acquaintances at Lovejoy, however, would understand what disturbed Lulu about her family. Nor would anyone at home. In this matter, she stood alone between two worlds. She was Faulkner's Benjy, distraught at finding herself going against traffic around Meduxnekeag's Square, trapped in a moment both past and present, an eternal now.

Dear Wesley,

I've been thinking about the fact that my parents don't seem to care about getting ahead. Next year when Neil starts kindergarten, my mother could get a job of some sort — even working with my father as a clerk in the Five and Dime. The thing is she won't do that even though my family could use the money. I know your mother doesn't work either even though there are no little kids in your family, but your father makes a good enough living so that she doesn't need to. I would be interested in your thoughts on this subject.

On another topic, everyone here has just chosen January Plans. That's a month of independent study. (It's not exactly independent for freshmen because we have been given topics to choose from.) Instead of letter grades, we'll get either "honors," "pass" or "fail." I have signed up for Tragedy. Mimi, who lives on my floor, has also signed up for Tragedy. She's from New York.

Lulu paused, her pen above the paper. She had been about to add that Mimi was Jewish and that like Ike, who was also Jewish and from New York, she was more cultured than the average Lovejoy student, but Lulu didn't exactly know how she wanted to characterize Ike to Wesley. Besides, it didn't seem respectful to harp on other people's religions.

My friend Dottie has signed up for a sort of current events class. It will be taught by Professor Goddard. He was a conscientious objector in

World War Two, and last spring he rode a bus to the South to protest the treatment of Negroes there. He's much admired here at Lovejoy, especially by the government majors…

Lulu stopped herself from writing that the majors referred to Professor Goddard as "God." She was pretty sure Wesley would be scandalized. She was somewhat scandalized herself and she didn't attend a Bible college.

…and by Dottie, who comes into our room and reads out loud to us from a book called Growing up Absurd. The author gave a lecture here a while back. All the boarding school crowd, for some reason, bought the book and attended the lecture.

Lulu stopped herself from writing that, for effect, Elise sat in Hades reading *Growing up Absurd* when she was supposed to be in class. She didn't want to come across to Wesley as snide.

This book is very critical of what it calls "the system."

My friend Kateri has signed up for Anthropology. That's a subject that isn't offered at Lovejoy. The course description says it will be about "excavating one's personal, social and cultural identity." That sounds scary to me. You could go in one person and come out someone entirely different. Jill is taking Beginning Italian. That's another course not taught here. But her family speaks it at home. I said it sounded a little like cheating, but she said she had worked hard all semester (that's true, by the way) and that she deserved a break and a chance to devote more time to her love life. She was sort of kidding, but I do think she wants to see more of Brad. (He's her boyfriend here at Lovejoy. She has another one back in Fall River.) Bridey is taking Italian because Jill is. I guess she figures she can practice with Jill and not have to work too, too hard.

Elise has signed up for "Questing," which is about "man's search for God." A lot of her friends signed up for it, too, because the professor has a big interest in nature, including ski trips to Sugar Bowl. That crowd likes to drink after a day on the slopes. So Jill and I think Questing is made in heaven for Elise. (I hope you don't think I'm being too catty, Wesley, or blasphemous.)

Speaking of skiing, everyone here assume I'm a skier because I'm from Maine. (and also because Jimmy Taylor is a skier.) Does that happen to you? I don't feel like explaining to everyone in the world that downhill skiing is too expensive for most people from Maine, including me. I'm talking about the kind of skiing that involves special boots and expensive skis and T bars and prepared hills, not shuffling through potato fields on any old wooden skis you find in your grandparents' barn. Come to think of it, I think Wade may be a downhill skier, but I don't think you are. It's a moot point for me anyway because I can barely keep up with everything going on here at Lovejoy without spending time and money on skiing.

Well, Wesley, I got off the track asking about skiing, which is really neither here nor there, and on the Jan Plan, which isn't a matter of opinion. I would like your opinion, however, on what it is about my parents that keeps them from wanting to get ahead (as I see it.) I've been enjoying your letters from Mexico and look forward to the next one.

Love,
Lulu

Writing — or writing to Wesley — made Lulu feel like herself again. She looked through the letter picturing Wesley reading it, his eyes crinkling as his geometrically perfect face broke into a smile. With a start, she realized she'd automatically signed "love" the way she did with letters home. Her eraser hovered above the paper and then she put it down. You couldn't erase ink without leaving a smear, maybe even a hole. Besides, a lot of people signed their letters "love." It was standard.

Also, in the largest meaning of the word, she did love Wesley.

Sue and Yael, the sophomore AOs on First Floor Chubbuck, each received a package from home each day for eight days. Sue's was always a pair of new shoes from her father's store. Yael's packages contained specialties from a gourmet food shop. "Hanukkah presents," Jill explained.

"Hanukkah?" Lulu had never heard of such a thing.

"The Jewish festival of lights." Bridey was in 104 discussing with Jill what they would wear that evening to the fraternity house. "It lasts for eight days and you get a present each day. Almost better than Christmas in a way."

"Sue and Yael are Jewish?"

"With a last name like Stein and a first name like Yael, what would you think?"

Lulu wouldn't think anything, but she didn't like to get caught looking ignorant.

"It seems that somebody once wrote to St. Thomas Aquinas asking whether it was true, as he had been led to believe, that the names of the faithful are written on a scroll in heaven. Aquinas replied to the effect that so far as he could see, that was not the case, but that there was no harm in saying so." Fr. Flannery leaned on his lectern/pulpit and paused for the laughter.

"What age will we be in heaven, my dear people — those of us who do not, through the everlasting horror and disgrace of mortal sin, descend into hell?" He paused again for laughter, a little tentative sounding this time. "Will a baby remain a baby? Will an old person be old or will he be a younger, more attractive, healthier age?" He paused, although it didn't seem to Lulu this was a laugh line. "According to St. Augustine, all souls in heaven will be thirty-three years old — because Jesus was thirty-three when he died."

Lulu wasn't sure whether Fr. Flannery was trying to make a joke. In an earlier sermon, he had quoted St. Augustine to the effect that a person had to know himself in order to know God. Was God, then, inside a person, not out there? If so, heaven would also be inside a person and each person's heaven would be unique. The same for hell. If all the souls in heaven were thirty-three, then Lulu hadn't lived long enough to know what she would be like in heaven. Thirty-three was close to Plato's thirty, the age before which a person should not attempt to study philosophy. Lulu hoped that by the time she reached her thirties she'd have become a bona fide adult, that she would have found a meaningful, well-paying job, bought a car, traveled in the United States and Europe, found and married her soul mate and left the meaningful, well-paying job to start a family.

With Bridey and Kateri, Lulu walked out of Judson into winter sunshine. Fresh snow magnified the light; across campus the white spire of the chapel shone like the snow-capped peak of a needle mountain. Suddenly, heaven was a place she didn't believe in anymore. The heaven of her childhood, at least. She didn't feel troubled. Matters of religion could sit on a back shelf of the mind until such a time when they might be taken down and put into use — or discarded or put back on the shelf. With religion, you could take until you were thirty-three or one hundred, if you lived that long. Each college year, on the other hand, was broken down into two semesters separated by final exams, and each semester was marked by semi-finals, and each half semester was chopped up by assignments, quizzes, hour exams and papers until you were like a wild horse leaping hurdles in the direction of an unseen point — possibly a grassy meadow, possibly a sheer drop. Lulu's mind was too taken up with the here and now to allow thought for the hereafter.

Under consideration were *The Song of Bernadette* and *The Sound of Music*. The Newman Club had some money in its treasury, and rather than mail it off for the souls of pagan babies in Africa as Lulu's Sunday school classes used to do, the officers and the handful of others who attended the December meeting had decided to show a movie during the January Plan. Lulu had liked *The Nun's Story* but hadn't recommended it because she thought it possibly more anti-Catholic than Catholic. She glanced at Fr. Flannery lost in his breviary and wished he would give some direction to the discussion.

"I have two suggestions for films. Sorry I'm late." Marc from *Six Characters* came into the room and eased into a chair. His pock-marked face and five-o'clock shadow had the strange effect of making him more rather than less handsome, and his athletic carriage and assured manner made him seem a natural leader, especially in contrast to Bob and the other officers. He pushed on the rolled-up sleeves of his flannel shirt as though he were about to delve into a laborious task. "*Nights of Caberia* and *Wild Strawberries*."

Fr. Flannery looked up from his reading.

"What're they about?" With his index finger, Bob pushed his glasses up onto the bridge of his nose.

"*Nights of Cabiria* is about a girl of the streets who wants to be good and to be loved, but she's taken advantage of by evil people."

"She's redeemed in the end?"

"She suffers and dies in the end."

Fr. Flannery leaned forward in his seat and began to speak in the hesitant manner he had outside the pulpit. "*Nights of Cabiria* attacks the Church, the class system, the movie star culture and everything else that has the potential to destroy the lives of ordinary people."

"It's anti-Catholic?" Bob's glasses had slid back down his nose.

"It's deeply Catholic — but anti-Church." The priest's voice was taking on its confident preaching tones. "The Church, as we know, is in constant need of correction. This Vatican Council the Pope has called for is part of that correction process. The art of film is another."

Lulu had never before heard a distinction made between Catholicism and Church. Nor had she heard of the movies described as art. Maybe only what Fr. Flannery and Marc called "films" were art.

"And your other suggestion?" Bob peered at Marc over the top of his glasses.

"*Wild Strawberries*. It's about a Protestant doctor in Sweden who takes a car trip. In meeting an assortment of other characters, he learns a lot about himself."

"It's about a Protestant?"

"*Wild Strawberries*," Fr. Flannery said in his lofty preaching tones, "is both an outward and an inward journey and, although the main character is Protestant, the themes are thoroughly Catholic. Look, my dear people, since at this point the club has more money than it knows what to do with, I propose we order both."

The Newman Club voted unanimously to rent both *Nights of Caberia* and *Wild Strawberries*.

Chapter Thirteen

When Lulu walked into 104 Chubbuck after the Newman Club meeting, Jill held up her hand in the stop signal, typed a few more words on her pink portable typewriter, yanked the paper from the rollers and stood up. "*Finis!*"

"Maybe I should have skipped the meeting and written my paper for *Great Thinkers*." The semester was coming to a close, and between papers and finals Lulu had so many deadlines she didn't know how she was going to fit everything in.

"Write first, play later — that's what my journalism teacher used to say."

"You took journalism in high school?"

"It was an elective. We learned to get the whole article down in one try — no cross-outs, no rewriting. You just follow the formula: who, what, where, when and how. It's a little different for college papers. Still, it's a formula."

"But writing shouldn't be according to a formula." Lulu hung up her coat and started to undress. "Writing should be creative."

"First, you need a formula. Then you can get creative." Jill was already in her baby doll pajamas and ready for bed. Early in the day of a deadline or even the day before, she would sit at her typewriter with her books and notebooks and a ream of corrasible bond — she hadn't completely mastered getting a whole essay down without correction — and type until she'd achieved the required number of pages. Typing was another subject Jill had taken in high school.

Lulu had not taken typing. That was a subject for girls planning to be secretaries, not college preparatory students. She slipped into her muumuu and picked up her pen, notebook and thesis paper, ready to depart for the lounge.

"Hi ho, fellow students." Elise came into the room throwing

off her coat just as the warning bell sounded. "I see you've finished all your little assignments," she said to Jill, who didn't respond. "Another night in the cold dark dungeon for you, Lulu?" Elise changed into a long tee shirt and got into bed. At night she didn't bother to wash her face or brush her teeth. In the morning, when the others were at breakfast, she'd redo her face. Miraculously, at the *Great Thinkers* class she'd produce a paper to pass in. "*Farewell! Live long, drink deep, be jolly,/Ye most illustrious votaries of Folly!*"

Lulu recognized the epilogue from *In Praise of Folly*. Either Elise had actually read the book recently or, more likely, she was reciting one of the many memorizations Bittersweet Hall imposed upon its students.

Veronica was in the lounge, a cigarette in the corner of her mouth, her fingers flying over Deb's portable typewriter. Typing someone else's longhand into an impressive manuscript at the rate of twenty-five cents a page was another of Veronica's sidelines. She nodded briefly at Lulu without breaking stride. Bridey and Mimi were also there, Bridey because, like Lulu, she wrote her papers at the last minute and Mimi because she was either working on something due the following week or reading for pleasure — something Lulu hadn't done, except sneakily in the library stacks when she was supposed to be working, since arriving at Lovejoy.

Lulu began by looking through her notes, which she found to be sketchy. She opened to page one of *In Praise of Folly* and read the underlined inscription: *An oration, of feigned matter, spoken by Folly in her own person.* Because it had been ingrained in her not to write in library books or school textbooks, Lulu hadn't, at first, marked up her college books. "For heaven's sake," Jill had said to her one evening in 104, "That book belongs to you Lulu. You paid for it. Underline the important parts." After that, Lulu read with a pen or pencil in hand. Unfortunately, she had found so many parts of Erasmus's text important that there was very little that wasn't marked up.

She flipped through, glancing at the under-linings. On the last page she had both underlined and starred the sentence: *I hate a hearer that will carry anything away with him.* Lulu smiled. If only her professors took that attitude! If only they let their words and all the words they assigned wash over the students without demanding written responses. But, she reminded herself, the epilogue was Dame Folly talking, not Erasmus himself, who, since he'd been a professor, had no doubt assigned essays.

Lulu closed her eyes and tried to summon up anything she might have carried away from lectures and class discussions. Erasmus deplored the state of the Church: the promotion of superstition and intercessory prayer by the clergy in order to sell indulgences. Is that how Protestants still viewed the Catholic Church? Her Protestant friends? Wesley? The thing was, Erasmus, for all his criticism, remained a Catholic. Lulu gave her head a shake. None of this was fodder for an essay. Maybe if she started writing, a thesis would present itself. That's what happened in a lively conversation. She would get more and more enthused, her thinking would sharpen and others would turn to her and say with respect, "Wow, Lulu, I never thought of it that way. You're so smart!" The trouble with writing was that there was no warm-up.

"Good luck, Lulu." Veronica stood up and bundled her papers under one arm. "You going to be much longer?"

"Hope not." What Lulu really hoped was that she didn't appear to Veronica like Dame Folly in person. She hated the thought that, while others slept, she would have to repeat previous experiences of writing, wandering the halls, writing some more, chatting with Bridey and Mimi and any other laggards or geniuses who showed up, and finally in a burst of speed brought on by exhaustion conclude her tottery essay — or bring it to an inconclusive halt — and haul herself and her books and papers back to her room, hoping a scant night's sleep would suffice, with coffee, to get her through the following day.

One Sunday morning when Lulu stepped out of her room to cross to the bathroom she caught sight of a small Christmas tree at the end of the hall decorated with what looked like miniature snowballs. She was rinsing her face when Bridey burst in. "It's a sacrilege!"

"What?" Lulu wrung out her washcloth.

"They have their own holidays. They don't have to make fun of ours."

"What are you talking about?"

"That Christmas tree outside Sue and Yael's room." Bridey pointed in the direction of the hall.

Lulu laid her head to one side. "But it looks so pretty."

"Take a closer look, Lulu."

When Lulu left the bathroom, she walked towards the tree. It did look pretty — symmetrical and all decorated in white. Suddenly, her hand flew to her mouth and she gasped like the heroine in a melodrama. The "snowballs" were fluffed tampons hanging from their strings.

In his sermon later that morning Fr. Flannery said, "We are an Incarnation people. Through that baby in the manger, God has been born into history." He went on to quote Chesterton to the effect that by resorting to reason and to knowledge obtained by the senses, St. Thomas Aquinas had "baptized Aristotle."

Aristotle again! Lulu thought, sitting between Bridey and Kateri. *Aristotle is everywhere.*

"Christ experienced the full range of human life," Fr. Flannery continued, "And then He ascended into heaven, where, fully human and fully divine, He, in traditional imagery, sits at the right hand of the Father.

Imagery? Was "The Apostle's Creed" mere poetry? Or was poetry a kind of prayer?

"In other words, what unites us with God is our humanity. That's the Incarnation. And so, when we say, 'God only knows' about a dire situation we find ourselves in — or a joyous or comical one — we are correct. Even if no one else knows, God knows and God cares because in and through Christ He has entered directly into the sensuous human experience, and we are, all of us, children of the Incarnation. Grace is everywhere."

"What was that sermon all about?" Bridey said on the walk back to Chubbuck.

"The Incarnation," Lulu said. "I'm not sure what the word means."

"Incarnate: in the flesh. The same root as carnival," Kateri put a hand on one hip and twisted her other hand in the air like a drum majorette at the head of a circus parade. "It means the spirit of God lives on earth."

"In human beings?"

"In human beings, animals, plants, and the sun, the moon and the stars." Kateri dropped her imaginary baton and lifted both hands to the heavens.

"That's pantheism!" Bridey sounded indignant.

"I don't mean many gods." Kateri's voice had taken on its dreamy quality. "I mean the spirit of the one God in everything."

"Well, I don't think the spirit of God is in everything. I certainly don't think it's in tampons on a Christmas tree!" Bridey sounded even more indignant.

"Oh, I don't know," Kateri said. "Maybe God finds it pretty funny."

Lulu smiled. She liked Kateri's image of an amused God.

Dear Lulu,

I'll address your family concerns first and then tell you what I've discovered about myself in Mexico.

First of all, we are not our parents. That may sound obvious, but it took me going first to Boston and then to Mexico to realize that fact. Our parents have their lives and we have ours. When we were children, honoring them meant obeying them, but, as St. Paul says, when we become adults we put away childish things. I love my parents very much and because they are paying for my college I still owe them a certain amount of obedience, but honoring them as a full-fledged adult is different from obeying them as a child. Of course, I would never want to do anything to dishonor them, but it is up to me to discern what Jesus has in mind for me, not what they imagine is best for me.

So I say don't worry about whether your mother will go to work or whether they want to get ahead. Just as you are not them, they are not you, if you get what I mean. Maybe you can tell that this is something I have given a lot of thought to and have prayed about, especially since arriving in Mexico. There's one thing I have found out for sure and that is that God is not calling me to be a preacher. Dave and Hazel and some of the others can preach anywhere at the drop of a hat and people crowd around and are moved by the Spirit. I do not have their gift. And that's all right. My father would be just as happy because to him that would mean I'd come home and enter the business.

But I feel sure God is not calling me to be a shoe salesman either. I want to design simple homes. I look around here and see that's what's needed. And that's something I'd love to do. Nott doesn't have a major in architecture. For that I'll have to go to graduate school. I'm changing my undergraduate major to Economics. That way I can combine my knack for math with some business training. (Nott doesn't have a business major either.) What do you think, Lulu?

Your January Plan sounds like a chance for growth in the knowledge of God's plan for you. That's what Mexico is doing for me. Please remember me in your prayers as I do you in mine.

Love,
Wesley

In signing "love," was Wesley following Lulu's lead? Did he deliberate, or had he, without giving it thought, merely written what was conventional? Talk of God's plan for her was so Pentecostal! Was that what predestination was all about? It didn't sound Catholic. She pictured him praying and working with Dave — and with Hazel. She thought of Helen and Casper praying together and remembered what mixed feelings she'd had at the time. A funny sensation came over her. More mixed feelings.

Classes ended in mid-December, the week before finals. When she wasn't taking an exam, Jill spent most of her time sitting up in bed surrounded with books and notebooks, her hair in thick unwashed ringlets, her breakfast forsaken. Sunday at the library, students Lulu and Rolf had hardly ever seen before lined up for *Samuelson* and the other texts on reserve. Rolf stopped talking and spent every spare minute hunched over his books. When Lulu passed through the reading room at the end of her shift, she saw Jimmy Taylor scanning his notes, his booted legs stretched straight out under the table. Outside, when she looked back in the late afternoon dusk, she saw lights burning in every one of the many windows like an industrial henhouse that kept its occupants laying day and night.

When she walked into 104 Chubbuck and switched on the light, what first caught her eye was the spider plant Jill had given her. It hung in its basket by the window, shriveled and sere. She went to stick her hand into the soil and found it rock hard. When had she last watered it? For quite some time, she'd been too busy to pay it any mind. She looked over at the next window where Jill's plant hung, bright green and dripping with healthy scions.

Had Jill noticed Lulu's plant was dying and said nothing? Or had it been doing fine and suddenly keeled over like an overweight, out-of-shape, middle-aged man might after shoveling wet snow? She lifted the basket off its hook and carried it into the bathroom and set it in a sink. She turned on the water and let it run until the soil softened. She yanked it out of the sink and gave it a few good shakes. Then she hung it back on its hook. Its few baby spiders had snapped off during the resuscitation attempt, and overall it looked more noticeably neglected than before.

Lulu couldn't think what to say to Jill when she came in just before supper. She would feel awkward apologizing — and maybe, with its liberal dousing, the plant would revive after all. If Jill noticed the plant, she said nothing about it. Elise came in at curfew, walked to the middle of the room and stood stock still, one hand on her hip. "I don't think I can have that pathetic thing hanging over my desk." She walked to the basket and lifted it off its hook. "Do you mind?" She deposited it in Lulu's wastebasket. Lulu couldn't think of an objection to make. Jill said nothing. Lulu was afraid Jill was mad at her.

Two days before they were to leave for home, Lulu found on her desk a package wrapped in shiny red and green Christmas paper. The card read, "To the best Roomie ever with love from your Roomie." The message was tautological but very sweet, like Jill, and it gave Lulu a crummy feeling. She hadn't counted on buying presents for anyone outside her family. "Should you open it right now or wait until tomorrow?" Jill said when she came into the room. Her finals were finished and she once again looked her well-groomed self, her hair ironed flat.

"Let's wait until closer to Christmas." The year wasn't half over and Lulu had spent more than half the money she had in the bank.

She'd replenish some working Christmas and Easter at Sorrows. But Alpha O had an initiation fee, and also she wanted to buy a red blazer with the gold AO insignia. Maybe Jill had to be careful about what she spent, too. Maybe the gift was merely a token. That afternoon at the bookstore Lulu bought three colorful pencils that said Lovejoy on them and wrapped them in second-hand tissue paper she'd smoothed and kept folded in a bureau drawer.

Jill's present to Lulu was a bottle of the cinnamon-and-soap perfume Jill herself wore. It was expensive, Lulu was sure. And she might have known it would be because in addition to the sweetness of her nature, there were two other facts about Jill: she always had money to spend and she was generous.

Jill unwrapped the pencils. "Thank you, Lulu. I didn't have any Lovejoy pencils. What pretty colors!" Jill carried off Lulu's gaffe.

But Lulu could tell she was hurt.

One day towards the end of Christmas vacation. Lulu arrived home after the early shift at Sorrows to find on the hall table an unopened letter with the official Lovejoy seal. She slipped it into her uniform pocket. Her father was at work, her brothers were playing outside as they did every day whether it was sunny or snowing, merely chilly or frigid. Her mother was sitting at the dining room table writing either a letter or a poem. She looked up and smiled. "You want something to eat, Lu?" *Was there worry in that smile? Or pity perhaps?*

"No, thanks, Mum. I'm going for a walk." Lulu changed into a turtleneck sweater and wool slacks. She transferred the letter into her slacks pocket. The envelope was addressed to her parents, not to her, but she thought she should be the first to see her grades, and apparently her mother agreed.

Lulu was a little worried about all her grades, and she didn't feel at all good about Math 101. On the final, she had worked as far as she could starting at the top of a problem and when she got stuck worked from the bottom up, hoping the fudged middle steps would meet with Professor Cosmo's satisfaction or, failing that, that he'd have the mercy to permit a little license, knowing in her heart, of course, that he wouldn't. Math, after all, wasn't poetry.

She put on her boots and coat and walked out into the cold air. She followed the slope behind her house to the river, which due to the frothy chunks of starch floating from the factory upstream never froze over completely, and into the nearby woods where she had grown up playing with other neighborhood children. She used to think of it as *her* woods, a world away from home and school, a wild, enchanted place. *Hard by a deep wood, there lived...*

There wasn't much accumulation of snow and she followed a familiar path until she came to a log that lay across it. She brushed off a spot, sat and looked around. The prominent evergreens, crowded and twisted by the denuded maples and poplars, weren't the perfectly shaped specimens of a Christmas tree farm or a college campus.

She drew the envelope out of her pocket and held it on her lap. During Finals she'd been thunderstruck by how much she didn't know. Beforehand, there hadn't been time to go over all her books and notes and during tests there wasn't nearly enough time for thinking or writing. Not one exam did she walk out of feeling she'd done a credible job. The year before, when Mr. Cyr had cautioned her that she wasn't prepared for Lovejoy, she'd felt betrayed and insulted. She loved to read and talk. She was a member of the National Honor Society. She'd certainly never flunked anything; it wasn't who she was. She had thought herself smart enough to thrive anywhere — one of the Seven Sisters, if she'd had the opportunity, Lovejoy because it was made available to her.

As it turned out, she wasn't one of the smartest at Lovejoy. She wasn't even middle of the pack. It wasn't because of superior intelligence that Lovejoy gave her a scholarship. It was because she was from the same state of the Union Lovejoy was in, a backward part of that state, and because her parents couldn't possibly afford to send her there — or anywhere. She was a charity case, plain and simple.

Deb, as her junior advisor, and Veronica, as AO pledge captain, had each taken her aside after she got the warning in math. Veronica suggested she ask one of the AO Sisters for help, Deb that she emulate Jill's study habits. She'd assured them both that her little talk with Professor Cosmo had gotten her back on track. She realized now she'd been too proud to ask for help, too self-reliant, too foolish.

She didn't want to come back to Meduxnekeag and work at Sorrows or the Five and Dime for the rest of her life. She wanted to return to Lovejoy and stay there until she graduated. *Please, please, please.* She vowed, if the letter in her hand revealed a grade average sufficient to retain her scholarship, she would wise up, starting with asking Jill to help her learn to study better.

She shivered. The log was radiating cold through her buttocks and up through her stomach and into her chest. She pulled off her mittens, tore open the envelope and lifted out the paper. Her insides leaped up and came down again like Janet's tray of parfaits that tipped and slid and crashed. *Thank you, thank you, thank you.* She had an F in Math 101 — how could she not? She'd have to take it again as a sophomore and fill in with an elective second semester. She had passed everything else, however, and her grade average was good enough — barely — for her to retain her scholarship. Tears stung her eyes and iced her cheeks. She took a deep, shuddering breath of the evergreen, Christmasy air.

Chapter Fourteen

The first gathering of Lulu's January Plan took place in the parlor on the second floor of the Women's Union. Fifteen freshmen milled about a sideboard, helping themselves to scones from a silver tray and coffee from a silver tea service. Once they were seated, china cups and saucers balanced on their knees, the chairman of the English Department, who sat in an armchair on one side of the marble fireplace, welcomed them in paragraph-long sentences.

Professor J. Harrison Villers, referred to by the student body due to his premature baldness and freakish lack of eyebrows or eyelashes as "Hairy Jay," was a familiar figure on campus. Tall and loosely strung together, he had a way of tipping his head back and talking to the world at large rather than the person in front of him. He spoke in a Latinate sort of English, long periodic sentences packed with argument, counter-argument, illustration and digression, delivered with a great range of expression and bursts of laughter. Lulu thought maybe the many classroom lectures he'd given had rendered him incapable of mere small talk.

Professor Snow occupied the matching armchair opposite Professor Villers, who turned to the older man with a look of boyish admiration and introduced him as the true expert on tragedy. Lulu felt proud of her venerable white-haired, blue-eyed Latin professor — and also relieved that for the next few weeks she wouldn't have to struggle with translation.

"I will begin," Professor Snow said in his grandfatherly manner, "as all things begin, with Aristotle."

That figures!

Theater, according to Aristotle — according to Professor Snow — had arisen out of the practice of dancing and singing hymns to the gods. The original Greek liturgy celebrated the dying and rebirth of Dionysus, aka Bacchus, god of revelry, wine and free love. He was the son of Zeus and a human woman and so half god, half human. Each spring, during the worship known as the Eleusinian Mysteries, Dionysus was torn apart and consumed by his devotees, thus being brought back to life in them. Professor Snow sipped his coffee.

Professor Villers, who had leaned back in his chair smiling at his colleague as though Professor Snow were a national treasure, did a comical double take, then fixed his eyes on the middle distance. "Is there perhaps, in those details, something familiar-sounding to our Christian ears?"

It occurred to Lulu that the Bishop of Portland, were he apprised, might well deem seminars on tragedy near occasions of sin.

Professor Snow set his cup back into its saucer. "I ask myself how one can understand *Oedipus Rex* without reading it in the Greek. Even if one does read it in the original, however, how can one really understand it without immersing oneself in ancient Greek history and culture? And how can one immerse oneself when that world has been dead for thousands of years? One can, on the one hand, devote years — indeed a lifetime — to study and travel. Still, one only *approximates* the experience of a Greek living in ancient times. Not only other cultures, on the other hand, are mysterious. Even our own is a mystery to us. The human person is a mystery. We are mysteries to ourselves."

With his talk of mystery, Professor Snow sounded a lot like Fr. Flannery. Was there, Lulu wondered, a point like the top of a pyramid where the wise of the world found agreement, leaving lesser minds separated at the base?

People were initiated into the Greek mystery religions, Professor Snow explained, not by regurgitating facts but by submitting to an experience that stirred certain emotions and brought about a particular frame of mind. The catharsis of the emotions of terror and pity amounted to an experience of rebirth.

Was rebirth like an epiphany? If we are wise, Lulu had heard Fr. Flannery preach the day before on the Feast of the Epiphany, we, too, follow an inner or outer star that leads us to truth.

When Old Red White and Blue had spoken in Latin class or lectured in *Great Thinkers*, Lulu had sometimes lost the train of thought and gotten caught up with the rhythms of his speech, his "on the one hand" and "on the other hand," which, afterwards, she would imitate for the amusement of her dorm mates or Tony, substituting nonsense words. Today, she followed his every word and could hardly wait to go back to the dorm and start reading *Oedipus Rex* and *Aristotle's Poetics*.

On the second day the group gathered, Professor Snow explained that *Oedipus Rex* met Aristotle's ideal of tragedy. The ending, hard as it was for the students to appreciate — since marrying his own mother had never been Oedipus's intention and he had gone to great lengths to avoid it — was the necessary conclusion for one who thought he could outwit his destiny. A *deus ex machina* would have ruined the play.

Professor Villers performed a double take. *Deus ex machina*, Professor Snow? I'm not sure we understand what you are talking about."

Lulu was sure Professor Villers knew what Professor Snow was talking about and that the "we" was for the benefit of the freshmen.

"Ah, yes," said Professor Snow. "*Deus ex machina*. In the comedic plays of the ancient world, happy endings were sometimes supplied by the sudden appearance of a god, who arose from a trapdoor." Professor Snow lifted the cup from his saucer. "And was lowered by crane onto the stage." He lowered his cup to the saucer. "Clever but improbable."

Professor Villers lifted his head and addressed the ceiling as though searching it for a crane. "Not unlike the actions of our own God, one might say."

On the last day of the first week, Professor Villers led a discussion of *Macbeth*. Addressing a point high on the opposite wall, he said, "What colors would the play be staged in?"

To Lulu, this was like asking how old everyone in heaven would be.

"Red and black." Mimi sounded sure of her answer.

Professor Villers lowered his gaze and raised that part of his forehead where eyebrows would be if he had eyebrows. "You've seen *Macbeth* performed." It was a statement, not a question.

"Twice. In New York."

Was it her Jewishness or her being from New York that set Mimi intellectually above the other freshmen in the seminar? Lulu had never seen *Macbeth* or any other professional production except for a summer theater performance of Gilbert and Sullivan's *Mikado*, which an aunt and uncle had taken her to when she visited them on the coast when she was fourteen. It must be much easier to read *Macbeth* or any other play, especially Shakespeare, if you could at the same time picture in your mind a particular performance.

That night in bed, after examining her conscience, Lulu promised herself that when she got out of college and was earning a living she'd visit New York and go to plays. As she faded into sleep, an imagined *deus ex machina* confused itself with an image of the Babe in the Manger.

Dear Wesley,

Last week was my best so far at Lovejoy. The Jan Plan is exactly what I had hoped college would be. Aristotle has turned up again. In Great Thinkers of the Western World, *he and Plato were the fathers of reason and science. In* Tragedy, *he's a lover of poetry and plays.*

Last week, we met every morning for two hours and discussed one tragedy a day. (We called our meetings "trage-teas!") I'm a sucker for happy endings, I have to say, but I've enjoyed everything we read even though every single one ended unhappily. Oh, and we also had to read a book called The Tragic Sense of Life *by Miguel de Unamuno. Professor Villers keeps quoting from it, things like,* "Against values of the heart, reasons do not avail" *and* "Out of fancy springs reason" *and his favorite*: "Happiness demands delight."

Every evening I'm free to take part in whatever is going on. Last Wednesday, I attended the film sponsored by the Newman Club. The Newman Club is for Catholic students. It's named for Cardinal Newman who taught in a British university about a hundred years ago. He started out Anglican but converted to Catholicism.

Lulu stopped, pen poised above the paper. Maybe it wasn't nice to write to Wesley about a Protestant converting to Catholicism. She didn't want to start the letter over, however. Better to say no more about Cardinal Newman and keep going.

The film was Wild Strawberries. *It's sad like* Death of a Salesman, *but in the end the old doctor who is the main character is more at peace than Willy Loman is because he has the epiphany that he needs to be more loving towards the other people in his life. The Newman Club took a chance with this film, but it turned out to be very successful. Many students came and also a lot of the faculty, including Mr. Lunt, my English professor. He must have loved all the symbolism! Next week the Newman Club will show* Nights of Cabiria.

For the rest of Jan Plan, each of us in Tragedy *is reading independently. I am reading the novels of William Faulkner (thirteen books in all. And not a happy ending in the bunch, I fear!) Our group meets once a week now. Mostly, the professors lead us in a discussion about the discrepancy between appearance and reality in the various books we're reading. (I do miss the daily trage-teas!) Meantime, all we have to do is read. There are no exams and no papers. I just have to keep a notebook with my reactions. So far, all I've written in it are the words I don't know, and there are several of those on each page. William Faulkner's vocabulary is humungous and prodigious, not to mention fecund and prolix!*

It must be nice for you to be back in Boston and able to walk around the city and see art films etc. (Although, maybe you miss Mexico!) I was sorry not to see you back home over Christmas vacation. I look forward to seeing you at Easter.

Love,
Lulu

Lulu woke up refreshed each morning. Except for Mass and dinner on Sunday, working in the library and the Wednesday morning tragedy tea, she could wear slacks instead of a skirt and knee highs. Outside, the air was crisp and just as the grounds got dingy looking, fresh snow would fall. Each morning she walked to the library and sat at a long oak table in the bright, high-ceilinged reading room, going through Faulkner's novels in chronological order. Since she wasn't required to write a paper at the end, she had no need to underline. Besides, she was reading library copies.

Each day, as she worked her way deeper and deeper into the lives of the inhabitants of Yoknopataupha County, she lost track of herself and of the passing of time. There was such an intricate weave of different kinds of folks from the likes of Colonel Sutpen to Ike McCaslin to Montgomery Ward Snopes that what she learned wasn't chronological but unfolded over time as her understanding grew and as new information and fresh points of view emerged. Faulkner's metaphor of ripples on water after a pebble sinks, ripples that spread to the edge of a pool and spill over to disturb surrounding pools, could just as well have applied to families in Meduxnekeag.

Lulu's mother, who loved to tell stories, put everything in the best light, giving people what she termed "the benefit of the doubt." Lenore's mother, on the other hand, was chatty and frank. The patients in the hospital were equally gossipy, especially in the wards, and there were more of them, a revolving chorus of comment on the town. The nurses were privy to key information, which, especially during down time on the night shift and regardless of a lowly aide in their midst, they talked about in low, comfortable tones, getting to the heart of a matter. The more Lulu read of the Compsons, the Sartorises and the Snopeses the more she felt she was getting to the bottom of things — the way she might one day get to the bottom of a myriad of stories from Meduxnekeag, including and especially, what had happened to her father the year he spent sitting in a kitchen rocker looking out the window.

By four in the afternoon, Lulu would close her book and wend her way under a violet sky, between lavender snow banks — black evergreens in the distance fringing the snow-covered lawns — to Chubbuck, where she'd nap before supper and whatever was scheduled for the evening. She had different friends for each of her pursuits. Saturday evening was a movie with Tony and the tingle afterwards of his lips and breath on her face and neck as they embraced in their bulky parkas. She was happy as a child.

Dear Lulu,

It's good to be back in Boston, although I miss the heat and colors and exotic sounds of Mexico. Mexico is a warm place in every sense of the word. By contrast, I find Nott and Boston itself rather chilly, if you get what I mean. Still, it's good to be back in the good old USA. At first, it seemed funny to understand easily everything everyone around me was saying.

I haven't seen the film you mentioned, but last weekend a bunch of us went to see The Seventh Seal. That's a film I'd recommend for your Newman Club. There's plenty of symbolism in that film too. You know how your church uses wine for communion and mine uses grape juice? Well, in this film one of the characters is with a bunch of people, and he holds a bowl of strawberries and milk up in both hands and says he'll carry the memory of their time together as carefully as though it were a bowl of strawberries filled to the brim with milk.

I have to tell, you Lulu, that what came to mind for me was the way we sat together outside the emergency room when it was touch and go with Wade. That's a memory I hold carefully.

I look forward to seeing you over Easter. Meanwhile, walk and talk with our brother Jesus and pray for me as I do for you.

Love,

Wesley

In a rush, Lulu was once again in Wesley's embrace at Our Lady of Sorrows Hospital, feeling all over again the solid moist flesh of his cheek and arms and the pounding of his heart through his lightweight summer shirt. Although they had never kissed, they had merged more completely than she ever did with Tony.

As she read the letter a second time, Wesley's talk about walking and talking with Jesus made her uncomfortable. When she prayed, it was to God the Father or to Mary, the Mother of God. She pictured the statue of the Blessed Mother at Our Lady of Perpetual Help, her plaster clothes painted blue and white, her plaster hands folded in prayer, her plaster face molded into a sweet and welcoming smile. Perhaps Wesley would think it wrong that she would rather pray to Mary than to either Jesus or God the Father. A father, in Lulu's experience, hadn't the patience to listen to every little thing without turning the discussion to his own interests. Jesus, she supposed, could be viewed as a brother, but brothers — though she loved hers deeply and they her — had a limited interest in her concerns.

That night before getting into bed to say her prayers, she took Wesley's letter out and read it again. This time her thrill had a nagging undertone. Before Mexico, Wesley's excursions were carried out only with Dave. She wondered if "the bunch" who went to see *The Seventh Seal* included Hazel.

Lulu had just awoken from her nap one late afternoon when Dottie knocked once and sailed in through the open door, her wiry blond curls askew, her eyes shining. She flopped into Jill's desk chair and fixed her gaze on Lulu, who was descending from the upper bunk. "Lulu, reading the *New York Times* every day and discussing the news with Professor Goddard is making me into a different person."

"But I like the person you already are, Dottie!' Lulu stretched, yawned and sat side-saddle in her own desk chair.

"That's not good enough, Lulu. I have to get involved in politics. We all have to. Do you realize that the South has what are called Jim Crow laws that make things just as bad for the Negroes as it was when they were slaves? Do you realize that our government has stolen the Indians' land and forced them onto reservations?" Dottie was fixing Lulu with a look very different from her usual benevolent one.

Was she suggesting it was somehow Lulu's fault that Negroes and Indians had been — were being — mistreated? "The Indians in my home town don't live on reservations."

"Do they live in nice houses with large lawns and new cars like the white people?"

Lulu's own family didn't live in a particularly nice house or have a large lawn or a new car, but they did have a house and a lawn and a car, whereas the Indian families on the road to the dump lived in shacks surrounded by bare ground. "Well, no, but…"

"That's my point, Lulu. Generations of white people have created this unfairness, and it's up to our generation to right the wrongs."

Lulu threw open her hands. "How can you or I possibly make a difference?"

"By starting small. Just think what a difference one person could make on this campus if every single student could be made aware of the problems in our country. Next semester I intend to run for intradorm council. By junior year I want to be on Women's Judiciary. You should take my place on the dorm council, Lulu."

"Why me?"

"Because you're a good judge of people and because you have a sense of justice."

Lulu's face reddened with pleasure. She'd had no idea Dottie thought so highly of her. The council met in the housemother's quarters for an hour after supper every other Thursday. Lulu partially blamed *Six Characters in Search of an Author,* although it was a wonderful experience, for her failure in math, but she wouldn't be trying out for the spring musical. Surely, she had time for so small a commitment as the dorm council. "Okay," she said. "I'll do it."

Afterwards, it occurred to her that perhaps Dottie had come into 104 that afternoon with the express purpose of getting her to volunteer for the dorm council, that Lulu had become, in fact, Dottie's first political success.

To Lulu, Kateri's final project, a miniature paper mache totem, looked like a cat's head on top of a dog's. "Get it?" Kateri said. "Wildcat from my first name, wolf from my last." They were in her room, where the totem sat on her desk next to a library copy of *A Short Account of the Destruction of the Indies.*

In eighth grade, Lulu's Sunday school class had made shrines to the Blessed Virgin Mary. Lulu's still stood on her bureau at home. This totem of Kateri's looked like a shrine, too — a sort of pagan shrine. "But the cat in your name isn't from the animal. It's from Blessed Kateri Tekawitha, Lily of the Mohawks!"

"Yes, of course. It's pure serendipity."

"You don't worship wildcats, do you?" Lulu was aware of an edge in her voice. She liked Catholics to stick to Catholicism.

"That depends on what you mean by 'worship' and anyway Catholics don't worship saints either. We venerate them."

Lulu made an effort to keep an open mind. "So, what's the point of an animal totem?"

"It's for inspiration, like what Machiavelli says about the fox and the lion." Kateri smiled her beatific smile. "The wolf-dog is loyalty to my people, the wildcat is freedom from everything else."

"Well, it looks interesting. I'll bet you'll get Honors, Kateri."

"Call me Kat, Lulu. From now on I'm Kat."

"It's like those high school vocabulary lists," Jill said, glancing at the open notebook on Lulu's desk.

"What high school vocabulary lists?"

"Didn't you have to memorize lists of vocabulary?"

"No."

"What did you study in English, Lulu?"

"Grammar, mostly."

Jill stood over the notebook and frowned. "You don't give the meanings, Lulu. This is only the first half of a vocabulary list."

Looking up all the words would have slowed Lulu down. She had signed up for *Tragedy* in the first place because it involved only reading, not writing, and second because the reading had either been written in English to begin with or had been translated into English. Furthermore, she wouldn't be expected to justify her beliefs. It seemed that in history and philosophy and political science, the majors *Great Thinkers* was preparing the freshmen for, students had to take stands and defend their positions. Probably a religion or psychology or sociology major would be the same. Certainly that was true of the hard sciences, the real sciences where there was a right and a wrong, a true and a false. In literature courses, on the other hand, a student could believe in anything — fairies, witches, made-up places and fictional characters. Imagination had free rein. This past month, all she'd had to do was read, not make a written case for whether a story was verifiably true or whether it even made sense, *Six Characters in Search of an Author* being a perfect example of one that didn't.

After Jill's reaction to the notebook, however, Lulu felt hesitant about her final one-on-one meeting with Professor Villers. Ascending the stairs to his second floor office in the library, she was seized with the fear that she might flunk Jan Plan.

He swiveled his chair when she appeared in his door and smiled down his nose at her. "Ah, yes, the Faulkner peruser!" He raised his gaze to the ceiling. "Did you delight in his oeuvre, Miss Delaney? Did you enjoy your month in Yoknapatawpha County? Did you lose yourself in Faulkner's world?"

"Oh, yes, Professor Villers!"

"*Happinesss demands delight.* What did you make of his neologisms?"

Neologisms from neo meaning new and logos meaning word. "I didn't understand all his vocabulary, but I just kept going through the stories trying to get them."

"And did you indeed *get* them?"

"I didn't try to understand everything as I went along. Sometimes things got clearer later in a book — or in a later book."

"Ah, yes, the work of memory and reconstruction, past and present, rendered in a stream of consciousness. *Maybe nothing ever happens once and is finished.*"

Lulu noted the quote from *Absalom, Absalom.*

"So you kept moving forward, Miss Delaney, the way we perforce must do in life?" He fixed her with a look, smiled at her nod, lifted his gaze to the far wall and launched into a sort of lecture designed especially for her, the Faulkner peruser. He pronounced the novels from *Go Down Moses* to *The Hamlet* as Faulkner's "major phase." He touched on the Christian symbols, motifs and images, on the Christ figures — Joe Christmas, for instance, lynched at the age of thirty-three — and on epiphanies and recurring patterns and the difference between appearance and reality. Little of what he said had occurred to Lulu as she made her way through the novels, but everything he said clicked as perfectly as a key turning in a lock. She was at ease now. This was what she'd imagined college would be — a genuine intellectual exchange. She would definitely become an English major. *Real toads in imaginary gardens.* She'd take every course Professor Villers offered.

He stopped mid-sentence and with the look on his face of a child about to open a box of chocolates put out his hand for her notebook. He riffled through the pages, frowned, then threw back his head and gave one of those short sharp barks of laughter he was known for. He turned back to the first page, scrawled a red "Pass" on the top and handed the notebook back to Lulu. "*Better to be burdened with wisdom than with knowledge,* Miss Delaney."

Lulu recognized the quote from Unamuno. She descended the stairs embarrassed to think Professor Villers had been laughing at her, thankful she had passed Jan Plan, elated to have come to know herself as a born English major. It would take awhile to get good at writing the many required essays, but with so much practice, she'd eventually get the hang of it. Maybe she'd get to the point where she enjoyed writing as much as she did reading.

In bed that night, Kateri's totem popped into her head. Inspiration could come from so many directions, from shrines and prayers and Mass but also from books and films and objects — not only religious articles but also photos and artwork and nature. And creatures. Lulu wasn't particularly fond of animals but people were creatures, too, and some of them she found very inspiring. The world was suffused with inspiration.

Jan Plan was as close to heaven on earth as Lulu ever expected to be. And she wasn't yet thirty — or thirty-three.

Chapter Fifteen

Jill handed Lulu a package with "To my Roomie" written on the wrapping paper. With Jill, gift giving wasn't limited to birthdays and Christmas. "Go ahead, open it." Inside was a monthly planner bound in red leatherette with a page for each week of the year.

"Thank you. It's beautiful." Even if she didn't reciprocate gift for gift, Lulu was at least learning to overcome her awkward feelings sufficiently to express gratitude. And she was grateful to Jill, not only for the planner but for her willingness, back when Lulu asked her in January, to help her become a better student.

Lulu pulled her chair next to Jill's desk and followed her roommate's lead as they filled in their planners, first with classes, then with social obligations. Lulu wrote in her library hours and the meetings of the dorm council and the Newman Club. "We'll put in assignments and quizzes and papers and exams as we go along," Jill said. She squinted at Lulu's calendar and frowned. "Whatever made you sign up for dorm council, Lulu?"

"To make the world a better place. When you consider all the Jim Crow laws and Indian reservations…"

"Lulu, dorm council is the biggest time waster in the world —Mrs. Hatch and a bunch of coeds talking about diddly things."

"Well, Dottie says…"

"Oh, Dottie! Lulu, Dottie's brilliant. So's Mimi. You and I aren't geniuses. We have to work hard to get good grades. We don't have time to save the world. Every single thing you do has to be for your own benefit. Forget about the starving children in China." Jill had the same prim expression she'd assumed the morning Lulu'd hesitated about joining a sorority.

Lulu felt the cold from the log in the woods as it moved from her buttocks and through her middle. She didn't want to be frozen out of Lovejoy. On the other hand, she'd promised Dottie. "Dorm council wouldn't be time-consuming, not like a play or Alpha O."

"Suit yourself, Lulu. Now, we need to pencil in study time."

"Two hours for every one hour in class, that's the rule of thumb." Lulu stared at her planner. "I don't have enough time for that."

"No, Lulu, no one does. That's what makes college hard. Not enough time. So you have to use shortcuts."

"For instance?"

"For instance, take good notes at the *Great Thinkers* lectures and read them over every Monday night and before every exam and underline the really important parts."

"I don't take such great notes."

"I know."

Lulu didn't care for the smug tone of voice, but she had an idea she needed to heed what Jill was telling her.

"You can look at mine Tuesday nights," Jill continued. "But not before exams. That's when I cram."

"When you cram, you don't retain the material for the long run."

"Who cares about the long run, Lulu? Either the subject will keep coming up or you'll never have to know it again. The important thing is to get a good grade on each exam and paper so that you get a good point average."

Wasn't the important thing to get a strong liberal arts education? Because Jill didn't attend the visiting lectures, she hadn't heard Dr. Livingston's opinion on this matter over and over the way Lulu had. But maybe Jill was right. Maybe Lulu would be better off to ease up on expanding her knowledge and concentrate on getting a strong point average.

The honeymoon was over, Veronica informed the pledge class, who were seated at her feet on the red and yellow braided rug in the Alpha O aerie. They'd had fun. Now they must prove themselves worthy of becoming Sisters. Her expression was not the one she wore at teas and mixers but the one she employed overseeing Gordon Linen.

The pledges must carry out a group project, learn the Greek alphabet and submit to an ongoing self-evaluation that would begin that very evening.

Lulu's heart sank. She didn't have time for a pledge project, nor — since she was pretty sure she wasn't going to major in Classics — for memorizing the Greek alphabet. Her planner exercise with Jill had shown her that she needed to budget her time as carefully as she did her money.

There wasn't much discussion on the pledge project. Veronica and Wendy, who was pledge president, had already "put their heads together" and come up with a proposal: volunteering at the children's hospital downtown. A quick show of hands solidified the decision.

The point of self-examination, Veronica explained, was to be the best sorority on campus and that meant excellence in every category. To begin, she asked the pledges to name an action each was going to take to make second semester more successful than first. She called on Wendy, as pledge president, to speak first. Wendy said she was going to lay out her clothes for the next day the night before so as not to waste time in the morning.

Veronica nodded approvingly.

Jill, when it was her turn, linked an arm through Lulu's and said she would speak for both of them and that they had filled in their schedules for the semester.

Veronica nodded approvingly.

Lulu felt proud and grateful.

Veronica said there was one important item of personal care she needed to address and that was the freshman fifteen.

The freshman fifteen?

The freshman fifteen, Veronica explained, was the poundage freshman coeds tended to put on over the winter. It made their spring clothes tight and, more to the point, their appearance at Greek Sing in June a little too pleasingly plump. "So, don't overdo the desserts, ladies!" She pursed her lips like a schoolmarm chiding a class of fourth graders.

Suddenly, she broke out into a big smile. "Now! Our final topic for tonight is Itty Bitty Buddy Week. It's an Alpha Omega tradtional and lots of fun!" We all, Sisters and pledges, put our names into a hat. The name you draw is your itty bitty buddy for the next week. Each day you do something to surprise your buddy, and each day *your* itty bitty buddy does something to surprise *you*. The little gifts you buy shouldn't cost more than a few dollars."

Lulu's heart sank. Itty Bitty Buddy Week sounded like the biggest time waster in the world, if ever there was one. And it would cost money, too.

Speech 101 was the first class Lulu took that was not made up entirely of freshmen. The first day the only other student she recognized was Marc. They exchanged smiles when she walked in, but not wanting to presume, she didn't take the empty seat next to him. She had chosen Speech to replace math because the teacher was Mr. Wilson. He'd worked to bring out the best in each of the actors in *Six Characters in Search of an Author*, so she figured he'd be a good teacher. "Mr. Wilson has the reputation of being kind of mean in class," Deb had advised her, "But he's an easy grader."

Mr. Wilson strode in looking more than ever like a European film star down on his luck. Lulu thought he must not have had a haircut since the day she first saw him at play tryouts. When he whipped off his filthy trench coat, she saw his familiar blue button-down shirt frayed at the collar and cuffs and the same tweed sports jacket hanging untidily on his skinny frame. He held up a copy of the *New York Times* and asked how many of the students had a subscription to it, his voice, raspy from cigarettes, containing an astonishing range of expression. Marc's hand went up. "There's my man," Mr. Wilson exclaimed. "The rest of you, for God's sake, hie yourselves to the library every single day and read the *New York Times* from front to back omitting nothing. It will be the best education you'll ever have. Forget about your classes — forget about this class — but see to it that every single day you read the *Times*."

It was all very well for Dottie to read the *New York Times* every day in January when she had nothing else to do except get together with Professor Goddard's group and talk about what they'd read, but with everything else she had to do, Lulu couldn't see herself reading the paper every day. Perhaps it would be enough if once or twice a week, she went into the library reading room where bamboo rods held the newspapers open on easels and glanced through the headlines.

Mr. Wilson's first assignment was to explain how something worked. Lulu thought of the sewing machines in Hesselton, the Women's Union. Her mother had tried to teach her to sew, saying it was an accomplishment she could draw on for the rest of her life. Although Lulu never did get good at sewing, she thought probably she could understand the workings of a sewing machine well enough to make it the topic of a short speech. Late that afternoon, she crossed the road to Hesselton and sat for an hour in front of one of the machines. She turned the wheel. She bent her head to watch the needle go up and down. She opened a drawer under the machine, took out a manual and studied the diagrams. She wrote down "needle," "bobbin," "slide plate" and other terms on a three-by-five card.

Committing the speech to memory was harder than memorizing lines for *Six Characters* because instead of a script Lulu had only her ever-changing, improvised conception of how a sewing machine actually worked. Standing in front of the class, she soon got as tangled as thread on a slide plate maneuvered by a monkey. "Good God," Mr. Wilson said in a stage whisper. He had taken a seat in the back of the classroom, and now he turned to Marc. "She makes it sound like a miracle."

Speech wasn't going to be the automatic A Deb had made it sound like, but Lulu was satisfied with C+ for her first speech. Surely, she'd be able to bring her final mark up to a B-.

Ike came by the reserve desk the first Sunday of the new semester. He leaned against the counter and talked about preparations for the spring musical. After awhile, he asked Lulu what her plans were for Winter Carnival. Soon after she replied that she'd be going to the OK house with Tony, Ike straightened up and said goodbye.

"Wow, you shot him down, all right," Rolf said.

"Oh, I don't think Ike was thinking of asking me to Winter Carnival."

"You're better off going with the OK's anyway. The Chopped

Livers might be hard to live down." Fraternities and sororities that hadn't filled their pledge classes had given out more bids, and Rolf had been invited to join one of the middling houses, which he declared to be the best on campus because it wasn't full of phonies like some of the more popular ones or losers like the least popular. Lulu was happy for him. She was happy also for April. Somehow, the fact that the Pea Greens had given her a bid assuaged the uneasiness Lulu had felt ever since Bidding Day when she had passed by April, alone and sobbing, in the phone booth.

Upon reflection, Lulu was afraid she had been callously indifferent to Ike's feelings, but the next Sunday afternoon, he once again paid her a visit at the reserve desk. As he talked about the upcoming lecture on the Peace Corps, she felt relieved to think that they were still friends.

In his introductory remarks, Dr. Livingston thanked the students for attending the first lecture of the new semester and reminded them that the visiting lectures, a crucial component of Lovejoy's community of scholars, played a key role in the acquisition of a strong liberal arts education. Next, the youthful-looking, hirsute visitor took the podium, and in a beguiling Boston accent urged the students to ask themselves what they could do for their country. To Lulu, it was almost like having President Kennedy appear in person.

Afterwards, walking back to Chubbuck, Dottie said what a wonderful opportunity it would be to join this new Peace Corps after graduation and travel to a foreign country to help the disadvantaged. Kateri said she'd rather do something to help the disadvantaged right here in the USA. Dottie beamed a sympathetic smile at her roommate. "Yes, of course. I could see doing that. On the other hand, it would be wonderful to go to Africa and help build schoolhouses and dig wells. Which would you rather do, Lulu?"

Lulu couldn't picture herself in Africa building a schoolhouse or digging a well. She couldn't see herself doing much of anything of that sort in the USA either. She'd be able to pick crops or do light housework or babysit or give an invalid a sponge bath, but presumably these were tasks the disadvantaged were equipped to do for themselves. She wasn't sure who in the USA Kateri had in mind — American Indians on Western reservations perhaps or Jim Crow Negroes in the South. She realized suddenly that she'd just as soon leave such good works to people who'd already had advantages. What she wanted to do after graduation were things for herself — buy herself a car, for instance, not a rattletrap like Old Nelly but something new and sporty. *An epiphany!* In the light of her friends' aspirations, however, that revelation would sound distinctly selfish. She searched her mind for a diplomatic reply. "I think everyone deserves the best possible."

Apparently, she struck the right note, because Dottie bestowed on her the same approving gaze with which she had endowed Kateri.

"Kind of fun, isn't it?" April had come into the lounge where Lulu was struggling with *Ovid's Metamorphoses* — simplified, Professor Snow had assured them. Lulu had left behind January's Elysian fields of pleasurable reading for the field-hand grind of translation. Having a set amount of lines to do before each class smacked of high school. French was bad enough, but she could skim whole chunks and still get the gist. In Latin, every word in a phrase had to be fitted in with every other word in the phrase and every phrase had to be fitted into its sentence. April rubbed a tissue against her nose, which either from the cold weather or from allergies, had been consistently pink since the return from Thanksgiving vacation. "Like a puzzle."

"I'd just like to finish so I can go to bed." Lulu hoped she didn't sound cranky.

"Me, too. If you like, we could work together." By far the better Latin student, April had apparently taken notice of her floor mate's struggle.

"Okay, sure." Working through the grammar with April, Lulu's interest sharpened so that she stopped thinking about how late it was getting. Slowly, the story line — Proserpine spending part of the year with her mother Ceres, the half-sorrowful goddess of the harvest, the other part as queen of the underworld — came into full view like mist rising off a distant mountain. *Was adult life as intermixed with sun and shadow, spring and winter, as the myth suggested?*

"That was fun," April said when they closed their books. "We could work together more often."

"Yes, let's." Lulu got to her feet and picked up her book and notebook. She felt as though she was forgetting something and then remembered to say, "Thank you, April."

April's nose turned a deeper shade of pink and she waved her wadded tissue in the air. "Don't mention it."

April's gesture was surprisingly graceful. Although she was timid and socially awkward and in spite of her too-pink nose, she was really quite pretty. Also, she was short. "April, if my friend Ike asked you to Winter Carnival, would you go?"

"Lovejoy seems so small," Wendy said. She and Lulu were taking the Saturday morning jitney into town to volunteer at the children's hospital. When Lulu had drawn Wendy's name for itty bitty buddy, Jill helped her pick out amusing, inexpensive presents and supplied wrapping paper, and Lulu found it was really kind of fun, after all, to be a bearer of gifts — and that small extravagances wouldn't break her budget. "Doesn't it seem that way to you?"

"Compared to where I grew up, Lovejoy is big." Central Maine was experiencing a cold snap. Under her coat, Lulu had on her wool cardigan, her warmest wool skirt and her highest knee socks

"Really? I'm thinking of transferring." Wendy was wearing one of her many cashmere sweater sets, one of her several wool plaid kilts, nylon stockings and a camel's hair coat.

"Where?" What could be better than Lovejoy?

"I wanted to go to one of the Seven Sisters." Wendy pulled off the black-watch plaid cloche that matched her skirt and gave her long curly blond hair a shake. "I could have gone to Northwestern, but when I didn't get into Radcliffe or Vassar, I decided to come East anyway. But Lovejoy is so remote."

"Where I come from, Lovejoy's the ultimate. I'm just hoping I can do well enough to keep my scholarship and stay here for four years."

"You're smart, Lulu. You're as smart as anyone in our English class. Why do you worry about doing well?"

"I don't do so hot on quizzes and exams and papers, even in

English class. If Lovejoy were always like the Jan Plan, it would be perfect for me."

"It's not perfect for me, Lulu. I'm not making any of the connections it's so important to make in college.

"What connections?"

"In my career. I'm thinking of going into finance."

"Finance!" At the reserve desk, the students who came for the Economics books were all men. "But you're so good in English."

"Oh, yeah, but that's stuff I can figure out on my own. I want to major in something that will prepare me for a career. What do you plan to do after you graduate, Lulu?"

Lulu had been giving so much attention to getting through freshman year she hadn't thought about what she'd do after she graduated. "Be a high school English teacher, I guess." Once she heard herself say it, she was sure of it. She'd make a terrific high school English teacher.

"Oh, teaching! Those that can't, teach."

Lulu felt stung. She'd just confided her life's goal and Wendy was scornful.

"Hey, don't get me wrong." Wendy sounded apologetic. "A good teacher's worth a million bucks. The thing is, Lulu, good teachers don't earn a million bucks. Good teachers, bad teachers and all in between — they're barely paid a living wage."

"You want to earn a million bucks, Wendy?"

"If someone's going to be paid a million bucks, why shouldn't it be me?"

Lulu had no answer to that question. "Is Tim going into finance?"

"Tim doesn't know what he wants. He's unmotivated. That's why we broke up. Besides, I want to be free to date guys from other fraternities."

It occurred to Lulu that, although OK might possibly be one of the other fraternities Wendy had in mind dating, Chopped Liver would most certainly not be. Lulu didn't know any Alpha Os who dated Chopped Livers, and that included herself. She and Ike were just friends.

The children's hospital was Our Lady of Sorrows pediatric ward on a large scale. Lulu and Wendy weren't expected to do any of the aide work Lulu was used to — taking temperatures, changing diapers, bathing and feeding. Instead, they sat on a rug in a large recreation room with several small wan-faced children. Wendy began singing "Hush Little Baby." She stood up and danced languorously, acting out the parts of the song. One by one the children and then, finally, Lulu joined in the singing and dancing.

"Will you sisters come again?" one little girl asked after Wendy had gone through a repertoire of cumulative songs and she and Lulu were putting on their coats.

"You can tell we're sisters?" Wendy said.

The child nodded solemnly.

Lulu felt flattered by Wendy's acceptance of the child's question. They were slated to be sorority sisters, of course, but Wendy with her expensive clothes and sophisticated manner was so much smoother and prettier.

On the Saturday morning of Winter Carnival, each of the four sororities built a snow sculpture on the lawn beside the women's union. The Alpha Os gathered early and Lulu did as she was told, which involved running farther and farther afield to scoop up armfuls of snow. Yael climbed onto the growing mound and sculpted. Soon a dog's pointed head appeared, then sloped shoulders, haunches and long floppy ears. Pieces of coal were stuck into the face and onto the ends of the ears. Snoopy the Beagle!

"We'll win!" Deb exclaimed. Everyone applauded with sodden mittens. Lulu had played in snow all her life and had made many a cockeyed snowman, but she'd never seen anything so remarkable as this Snoopy. She looked around at the other sculpture sites. The True Blues and the Posh Maroons were rolling up big balls for their foundations. The Pea Greens were still straggling onto the lawn. No other sorority had as many Sisters and pledges present as the Alpha Os did.

"We've won!" Veronica amended Deb's prophecy. She and another Sister had dragged a hose from the Women's Union and were spraying Snoopy to an icy sheen.

To belong to a group that expected to win, that acted like winners from the outset, that were so cheerful and fun-loving about it as though winning were their due — this was a novel experience for Lulu.

That afternoon, Lulu and Janet, who had both been invited to the OK toga party, took the jitney downtown and bought several yards of purple sateen. They lay the material out on the floor of Janet's room, folded it in half and cut out neck holes. They wrapped gold yarn around ivy plucked from the exterior wall of Chubbuck to make wreaths for their hair. That evening, they put on shorts and sleeveless blouses and then the togas, secured at the waist with lengths of braided gold yarn.

Tony and Janet's date Pete, like most of the other OK pledges, had obviously raided Gordon Linen for their costumes and looked more like specters than Romans. Unlike Lulu and Tony's previous dates, where a movie had occupied the better part of the evening, the first half of this one was spent dancing, the second half talking. The foursome sat on pillows on the floor drinking a mixture called purple passion and telling stories about their summer jobs. Tony and Pete had caddied; Janet had worked behind the counter at a dairy bar. Sipping her drink to make it last, Lulu described patients at Our Lady of Sorrows Hospital. When she imitated an old lady by pulling her lips over her teeth to look toothless and whined, "Ain't you got no tea?" the others laughed. She told about the befuddled old man who kept trying to get out of bed to bring in the cows and about the teen-aged Indian mothers who brought their babies in because they cried too much. She hadn't realized what a fount of hospital stories she possessed, and egged on by her companions' laughter she unearthed more and more, astonishing herself, even, with how funny it all seemed.

All the coeds had the same curfew that night and all First Floor Chubbuck came in at the same time, laughing and in high spirits. Each had attended a fraternity party, even Evie, who had gone with Marc, and April, who had spent the evening with Ike.

In bed, finally, Lulu almost laughed out loud remembering the hilarious reception her hospital stories had received. Whether due to the presence of Janet and Pete or the ambiance of the OK rumpus-room-turned-Roman-atrium or the drink of sweet, fizzy purple passion, it was the most fun she'd ever had on a date with Tony. In a few weeks, he'd be a Brother and could take her to the OK house every Saturday night. She said a prayer for that toothless old lady at Sorrows, and suddenly her mind filled up with patients, the funny ones at first and then the sad ones. Fifteen-year-old Roy would be in an iron lung for the rest of his life — if he was still alive. He'd been transferred downstate to a home for polio patients. He'd probably never see his beloved farm again — if he was still alive. Lulu welled up. She'd been so happy during the evening and suddenly she was desperately sad. Once when she and Alice were in eighth grade they got the giggles so bad during Mass they couldn't contain themselves. Afterwards, Alice's mother said people who laugh easily when young, cry easily when they got older. Lulu reached for a Kleenex and wiped her eyes and blew her nose. She fell asleep saying a prayer first for Roy and then others at Sorrows, by name, as they came to mind.

The next afternoon, the results of the snow sculpture contest were announced. Alpha Omega got first place. For Lulu, it was plain to see that Alpha O really and truly was the best.

Chapter Sixteen

"*I talked to Janet about Tony,*" Jill twisted her chair back-to the window where a prodigious number of baby spider plants sprang from their mother. Two weeks had passed since the toga party. Tony hadn't made a date for the following Saturday after they'd kissed and nuzzled that night, nor had he called. Lulu had felt too awkward to confide in Jill or anyone else, and it wasn't the sort of thing she could very well write to Wesley about. "If you want, Roomie, I'll tell you what Pete told Janet he said."

Lulu turned her chair to face Jill, whose expression was hard to read in the light coming from behind her. Lulu had a feeling if a guy stopped asking Jill out, she'd go right up to him in the library or Judson or Hades and ask him point blank what was going on. "Well, okay, shoot."

"Now, Lulu, I know that you like everybody and that Tony just doesn't get your sense of humor."

"What did Janet say he said?" Now that it had started, Lulu wanted to get the conversation over with. She felt her neck reddening and her hands trembling.

Jill's expression, as Lulu's eyes adjusted to the light, was what a kind adult might use with a child insisting on knowing whether Santa Claus was real. "Well, that you don't really like anyone and that you make fun of people in unfortunate circumstances."

The blush swept up to the roots of Lulu's hair. She clasped her hands to keep them from shaking. It wasn't in her to say: *This conversation is making me feel awful.*

"Oh, Roomie, I'm not saying this to make you feel bad." Jill stood, lifted her arms and walked toward Lulu.

Lulu, too, stood up. "Excuse me, I have to go now." She grabbed her coat and hat and left the room before Jill could put her arms around her and cause her to burst into shameful, angry tears. She walked quickly out of Chubbuck between the white pillars and past the wrought iron lamp posts rimed with ice. She passed the long violet shadow on the snow-covered slope beneath the chapel. At the path to the library, she veered off as though she had urgent business in the direction of the pond. She tucked her chin into her coat and shoved her bare hands into her pockets. The winter sun in the bright blue sky looked small and hard and cold. On the pond's surface, slush roughed up by the wind had refrozen in glaring lumps.

She'd had a real job during the summer, not a pastime for which she got paid in tips but a serious responsibility, life or death really. She might report for work and discover a patient she'd washed up and fed and talked comfortingly to the day before had died. Well, that only happened once, but once was enough. All the hospital workers employed humor to make their work possible. The trouble with Tony — and Janet and Pete and just about everyone else at Lovejoy — was that nothing very serious had ever happened to them, nor had they ever been witnesses to real tragedy. Keith Sinclair was so much more mature than Tony. He was in his twenties, he'd been in a war zone, he was studying to be a doctor. He'd had a wonderful way with Roy and other very ill patients, but in the kitchenette, in the depths of the night shift when everything was quiet, he could be wickedly funny about them. Compared to Keith, Tony was a child. He could hardly keep up his end of a conversation. That's why she'd done most of the talking on their dates. He'd acted amused, especially at the toga party. And now he'd turned her words against her.

Lulu drew in a shivery breath. She didn't need to cry. She didn't need to talk Tony over with anyone. She wasn't like Jill and Bridey and so many of the other coeds who went on and on about their boyfriends. And Tony hadn't been a real boyfriend anyway. Real boyfriends didn't stop with a date every Saturday night and a kiss. Real boyfriends pressed for more time together, more serious talk and more than above the neck kissing. Lulu wasn't sure she had time for a real boyfriend — or the desire. There was something a little frightening about real boyfriends. Ever since Christmas vacation, Jill had been anguishing over hometown Ronnie and Lovejoy Brad, with Bridey as her faithful confidante. Lulu had a limited amount of interest in going over and over the same ground. Besides, Brad, as the on-the-spot competitor, was clearly in the lead, and Jill came into the room after evenings with him with the flushed exhilaration Elise had displayed with Sammy. Surely, Jill couldn't continue with two boyfriends in two different locations.

Lulu walked back toward the library, breathing in the cold air more easily. With a real boyfriend, a woman could lose track of her real self — before she had time to figure out who that real self was. One day Lulu would be ready. In the meantime, she was better off using her Saturday nights to catch up on her reading. Still, Tony had hurt her feelings worse than she'd have thought possible.

"Oh, wind, if winter comes, can spring be far behind?" Lulu was pleased to recognize Fr. Flannery's reference to Shelley. "In the midst of Lent," the priest continued, standing tall at the lectern in Judson, "let us remember we are a Resurrection people. I suggest that you think of Christ not as dying for our sins but as rising to new life in order to set us free. Lent reminds us that much in life calls for sacrifice, not for its own sake but out of unbidden suffering or love for others. Jesus ate and drank with others right up until the agony in the garden after the Last Supper. After the Resurrection and before his ascension into heaven, he walked with his disciples on the road to Emmaus and ate with them; he cooked fish on the beach and shared it with his disciples. Life is meant to be shared both now and for all eternity. After suffering and death, comes the Resurrection. Let Christ be our guide, our Alpha and Omega, the beginning and the end."

Lulu walked out of Judson with Bridey and Kateri. Earlier that morning, Jill had picked up the perfume bottle on Lulu's desk and spritzed her roommate with the tangy scent of soap and cinnamon. She felt as clean and fresh as the newly fallen snow that draped the trees and lined the frozen paths.

"I was taught Jesus did die for our sins." Bridey sounded indignant.

"*Love God and do as you please.*" Kateri ran and slid on the ice under the powder, her hands raised for balance. "That's my credo."

Lulu recognized Kateri's credo as a quote from St. Augustine taken from one of Fr. Flannery's sermons. Appealing as it sounded, it didn't seem complete. "Don't you think God demands sacrifice?" Lulu had the uneasy feeling something was slipping away from her.

"Absolutely," Bridey said. "And punishment, too. I didn't get back into Lovejoy scot free. I had to spend a whole year in suspension." It struck Lulu as kind of funny to hear the usually light-hearted Bridey defend sacrifice and punishment.

"You girls go to Catholic school?" Tim Duggan, the Lamb Chop Wendy had broken up with, fell into step with the three coeds.

Bridey and Kateri both nodded. "Twelve years," Bridey said.

"No," Lulu said. "I went to Sunday school and Confraternity of Christian Doctrine."

"Must have been a piece of cake." Tim stopped, unzipped his parka, thrust one hand into his breast pocket, pulled out a pack of cigarettes, and proffered it to Lulu.

She shook her head slightly. "No, thank you." Out of indifference or discretion, Bridey and Kateri had kept walking.

Tim lighted a cigarette for himself, replaced the pack, and continued walking with Lulu as though he had nowhere else to be on a Sunday after Mass. "I went to high school with the Brothers. They believed in discipline. If you didn't do your homework, the Brothers made you pay, especially Brother Mathematics."

Lulu thought of when she'd had Mrs. Grove for algebra. For the whole first marking period, students who got even one homework example wrong had to report to her room after school where she re-taught the previous day's lesson, and they couldn't leave until they corrected their homework. "We had discipline."

"In a public school?"

"Sure."

"Not Catholic discipline, though."

"What do you mean?"

"Take Brother Mathematics. First thing each class, he'd say, 'Okay, let's get this over with. Who didn't do the homework?' And you knew you couldn't get away with anything. You knew it was sooner or later. So you got up and walked to the front of the room and bent over and grabbed your ankles."

Lulu was both horrified and fascinated to see where this story was going.

"Brother Math had a belt — 'The Viper,' he called it." As Tim talked, Lulu pictured him bent at the waist clasping his ankles, rows and columns of other boys looking on while a middle-aged man in religious robes flicked a belt in the air and snapped it against Tim's backside. It sounded like a scene out of the Middle Ages. Her scalp prickled and sweat trickled down from under her arms. She felt unclean. "That's not discipline. That's punishment."

"That's Catholic discipline." At the door of Chubbuck, Tim took one last drag, dropped his cigarette on the path and ground it into the snow. "Nice talking to you, Lulu. You want to go to the Lambda Rho party Saturday?"

Lulu couldn't stop grinning all the way through the door of 104. "Tim Duggan asked me out!" The words were out of her mouth before she knew she wanted to broadcast her news.

"Roomie, that's wonderful!" Jill twirled from the mirror and embraced Lulu.

"What did I tell you, Jill!" Bridey jumped up from a chair and joined the embrace.

"Well, no wonder he wants to date you." Jill pulled away and widened her eyes at Lulu. "Bridey and I were just saying you and Wendy could be sisters."

"I don't look anything like Wendy." Lulu slung her coat over her chair.

"You could if you wanted to." Jill took Lulu by the shoulders and turned her towards the mirror. "Look at yourself, Roomy. *You're a beauty, oh, what a beauty!*" Lulu's hair had grown past her ears and hung in a pageboy. Her former bangs were long enough to be tucked behind one ear. Jill removed Lulu's glasses and handed them to Bridey. "A little mascara, red lipstick, and voila! Another Wendy." Jill pushed Lulu into a chair and began applying makeup foundation.

"My hair was blonde when I was little."

"So was Wendy's. The thing is she helps it stay that way." Bridey brushed Lulu's hair into an upsweep and stuck two wooden chopsticks through it.

"But hers doesn't look fake like Rolf's."

"Rolf has no common sense. He probably dunks his head once a week in a bowl of Clorox. You could be a natural-looking blonde if you wanted." Jill brandished a mascara wand. "Open your eyes wide."

The door opened. Elise took one step in, looked at Lulu, took a step backwards and threw open her hands in mock surprise. "*She walks in beauty, like the night!*"

"Lulu has a date with a sophomore Lamb Chop." In the thrill of the moment, Jill was apparently too proud of Lulu to bother ignoring Elise.

"A sophomore Lamb Chop! That's one to hold onto, my dear."

As was often the case, Lulu wasn't sure whether Elise's pronouncement was serious or ironic.

That night in bed, the stained glass windows of Our Lady of Perpetual Help popped into Lulu's mind. Sister Carmel, so mild and loving, had been the director of the Sunday School for the entire time Lulu was in elementary school. Other Sisters came and went. One, a Sister Aloysius, had a benevolent side that was offset by a vicious temper which arose without warning and raged until it burned itself out. One Sunday afternoon in one of the basement classrooms, when she was preparing the fourth graders for Confirmation, squirmy, not-too-bright Robert Gervais, who didn't sit up straight and who hadn't memorized the responses, gave an audible yawn. Sister's face boiled up red as a madwoman's. She marched to Robert's seat, yanked him to the front of the room, hoisted him against the blackboard and smacked his head. Lulu never spoke of the incident to anyone. Nor did anyone else as far as she knew. *So maybe I did have a taste of Catholic discipline, after all.*

It was an ordinary Saturday evening at the Lambda Rho house. No pledges were there, only Brothers and their dates. In the basement rumpus room — well-lighted on this, Lulu's second visit — everyone sat drinking beer and eating pretzels, the couples talking only to each other. Lulu was wearing Jill's red lipstick and the perfume Jill had given her, but makeup and mascara had seemed too foreign to attempt. Her biggest concession to vanity was leaving her glasses back in 104. Although in the habit of always wearing them, she was not what could be called blind as a bat, only moderately near sighted. Squinting, she glanced around expecting to see people she knew — Deb and her boyfriend Ed, for instance — but none of the other coeds or the Brothers were more than acquaintances.

"That's mine!" Tim was pointing to a shiny wooden paddle embossed with Greek letters that hung on a wall full of paddles. "I painted and varnished it myself… I earned it, too."

"Earned it? How?"

"You wouldn't want to know!" He said he would tell her just one incident involving his initiation. He and another pledge were each given a dime and driven to a remote part of Maine a hundred miles away and told they had to make their own way back.

"How awful!" *No wonder more guys flunk out than coeds.*

"No, it's stuff like that that made us Brothers."

Lulu finished one can of beer and held onto her second. Unlike with Tony, she didn't have to do all the talking. In fact, Tim did most of it, and it was relaxing not to have to think of things to say. The first time she met him, at the Alpha O-Lamb Chop mixer, he'd reminded her of Wesley, only more stylish looking and talkative. He'd danced most of that night with Wendy and, although he'd nodded to Lulu whenever their paths crossed on campus, she'd never expected to be on a date with him. It was almost like dating Keith Sinclair or Jimmy Taylor.

When Tim snuffed out his cigarette and stood and held out his hand, she took it as though that were the most natural action in the world. He led her up the stairs to the first floor and into a dimly lit room furnished with wide, deep vinyl armchairs. He sat and pulled her onto his lap. He put his arms around her and lifted his mouth to hers. He smelled of beer and cigarettes and pine needles. Lulu shut her eyes and felt his tongue against her lips. She opened her mouth. Warmth started deep inside her and spread through her entire body like the poof of flame on balled-up newspaper that ignites kindling that penetrates a hardwood log. Open mouth kissing in Tim's embrace felt as though it could go on and on and on.

Apparently it did go on and on because Lulu was surprised when a male voice announced, "Curfew approaching." She opened her eyes, Tim let go of her and she stood. In the dim light, she saw other couples unfolding themselves from the chairs. She blinked when the lights came on. Her second can of beer stood, still half full, on an end table. In the entryway, Tim held her coat while she shrugged into it. The Brother who had announced the curfew stood opening and shutting the door to the cold as couples pulled themselves together and left.

The cold that seared Lulu's lungs didn't dissipate her inner glow. Without her glasses, the campus had the gauzy look of a winterscape on a sentimental Christmas card. A full moon dazzled the sky and the snow-covered ground. Tim, bareheaded and without gloves, held her hand as they walked briskly across campus. The illuminated, many-tiered steeple of the library lacked only figures of a bride and groom to look like a wedding cake. At Chubbuck, there would have been a few minutes before the final bell for Tim to linger. Instead, he squeezed Lulu's hand, said he would call and turned back into the night, his head scrunched into his coat collar.

Jill and Elise were already in 104 when Lulu walked in. "How was your date, Roomie?" Jill's smile was as proprietary as though she owned a stake in Lulu's love life.

"Fine." Lulu felt too awkward to try describing an evening that had consisted mostly of cuddling and open-mouth kissing.

"Roomie, you're blushing!"

"Has some guy done a snow job on our darling Lulu? Can it be she's in love?" Elise was being ironic, but Lulu didn't mind. *Is this what being in love feels like?*

In his sermon the next morning, Fr. Flannery said that deep-down yearning was something this world could never satisfy. Lulu willed herself to keep her eyes on the priest and not let them stray to where Tim sat diagonally across from her by the back entrance. "As St. Augustine says, '*Our souls are restless, Lord, until they rest in Thee.*'"

Lulu had heard the story of St. Augustine in Sunday School and about his mother St. Monica, who had prayed many years for his conversion. Augustine's problem, Lulu learned later in high school

CCD classes, was that he yearned to be celibate. His common-law wife, whom he loved, he came to view as an occasion of sin. Lulu couldn't see why Augustine hadn't given up his struggle to be celibate and settled down to family life.

What Fr. Flannery said about yearning, however, rang true. By senior year in high school, she and her classmates had been brimful of yearnings, whether it was to marry or join the service or go off to college.

When students lined up for Communion, many fewer than at the first Mass in the fall, neither she nor Tim joined the procession. When she looked his way after the final blessing, he was gone. *I'm just as well off to wait for his call.*

He didn't call that night or the next. When Jill asked if she was going out with him on Saturday, Lulu was too embarrassed to do more than mumble, "He said he'd call." When her roommate's expression changed from curiosity to concern, Lulu abruptly left the room. Jill didn't bring up the topic again. Saturday evening Lulu spent in the dorm slogging through a Montaigne *essai* and Latin vocabulary.

At Sunday Mass she sat with Bridey and Kateri in their usual location in the lower front of the auditorium and tried to keep her eyes off Tim near the uphill entrance. At Communion, he joined the line, his eyes lowered, his hands steepled in front of his chest like a little boy trained by the nuns. *Tim's gone to Confession because of me! He considers me an occasion of sin!* Before the final blessing, she whispered to Bridey that she had to get some air. As unobtrusively as possible, she stood, sidled past Kateri, made her way down the aisle, walked out of Judson and kept walking in the direction of the pond. *Why couldn't he have talked to me? I was doing something sweet and brave and exciting and he was committing a sin. Why did he talk to the priest instead of to me? As though this were something between the two of them instead of the two of us?*

During a question and answer period at a high school CCD class, a bold senior boy had asked whether French kissing was a sin. The curate made his audience laugh by asking why anyone would want to exchange spit with someone else. He hadn't said French kissing was a sin, just implied that it was silly or disgusting.

Kissing Tim had not felt silly or disgusting. Sitting on his lap, their arms around each other, their hearts beating against each other, their tongues entwining — it had all come about as naturally as though a gate had closed in the chamber of her mind where conscious decision making resided. Maybe it was a case of invincible ignorance, but what they had done didn't feel wrong.

So why did she feel as dirty as though they had gone all the way?

Later, when she was alone in 104 Chubbuck, she picked up the perfume bottle off her desk and buried it in her underwear drawer. She couldn't bring herself to discard something perfectly good. Besides, she wouldn't want to risk hurting Jill's feelings. Maybe she'd use it as a future itty bitty buddy gift. But she knew one thing. She wouldn't wear it again. It wasn't who she was.

Chapter Seventeen

Lulu sat at her desk reading the latest letter from Wesley, their letters alternating as regularly now as the ones she exchanged with her mother. She read through it a second time, opened the drawer that was filling up and dropped it in with the others.

"Ahem," Jill said. Lulu turned. Her roommate had tossed Ronnie's letter onto her desk unopened. How long had she been watching Lulu?

"What?"

"I guess you're not about to burn Wesley's letters."

"Are you going to burn Ronnie's?"

"If I do, you're invited to the ceremony." Jill opened her wardrobe and reached for her coat. She gave her dark curls a shake and pulled a knit cap over them. "I'm meeting Brad after his three o'clock. See you at supper."

The planner open on Lulu's desk instructed her to study French. She opened the weighty textbook to a de Maupassant *conte*. Then she reached into her desk drawer and drew out all of Wesley's letters, arranged them in chronological order on top of the de Maupassant and read through them all. Funny, the guy she had gotten to know best since arriving at Lovejoy was Wesley. She knew who his friends were, what he thought about certain books and films, what he wanted for a career. She had confided in him, and he had responded with advice and reassurance. The only thing that stood in the way of romance was a difference in religion — in spite of the fact that they were, after all, both Christians. Although they had never kissed, she knew him better than she did either Tony or Tim.

Lulu put her coat over her arm and walked down the hall to see if Bridey and Kateri were ready to walk to Mass. Their door was open and Kateri, dressed in a leotard, was standing side-to in the middle of the room. She no longer put rollers in her black-as-ebony hair, which had grown past her shoulders and down her back. She stretched her arms high and wide over her head and held them there. After a few minutes, she dropped her arms to shoulder height and, holding them straight out, pivoted from side to side. A moment later, a moment that might have been an hour or an eternity, she held her arms forward, palms up. Slowly, she pulled her arms to her chest and cupped her hands. She crossed her hands over her heart and bowed her head.

Lulu clapped and Kateri looked up, startled as a woods animal. "I like your modern dance routine, Kateri" — Lulu couldn't get used to saying "Kat." She and Kateri had both signed up for modern dance for the third-quarter phys ed requirement. Lulu had loved dancing free-form, but the assignment for the final class to choreograph, memorize and perform an original piece felt formidable. "It's a very mysterious feeling."

"Actually, it's a prayer."

"A prayer?" Lulu had been in church processions that were prayers of a sort but never a dance.

"A prayer to the Great Spirit."

"The Holy Ghost, you mean."

"I mean the Great Spirit, Lulu, the God of my people."

"Oh…shouldn't you get dressed for Mass?"

"I've already said my prayers today."

"Private prayers aren't enough for Catholics," Lulu blurted out. "You're supposed to go to Mass, too." She wished she didn't sound so self-righteous.

"Actually, Lulu, I've discovered I'm not a Lenten Catholic, and I'm not a Good Friday Catholic either. I can't believe in a God who would sacrifice his own son." Kateri spoke as blithely about religion as Jill had the first day Lulu met her. "I don't want anyone to have to die for me to appease an angry god."

"You're a Christmas-and-Easter Catholic."

Kateri gave Lulu a pleased smile. "I hadn't thought of it that way, but, yes, I'm a Christmas-and-Easter Catholic." She crossed to her desk and ran her fingertips over her totem. "And something more besides."

"Isn't that book due at the library by now?" Unwilling to hear Kateri expound further, Lulu pointed to *A Short Account of the Destruction of the Indies* that still lay next to the totem.

"Oh, Lulu," Kateri picked up the book and cradled it like a baby. "This isn't a mere book. This is a gift that gives me such compassion for my people and all that they've suffered."

Bridey came noisily into the room, set down her toilet kit and grabbed her coat. "Put some hustle in your bustle, ladies. For Mass to count, we have to get there before the gospel."

Later, in bed, when Lulu ran the sequence of the day through her mind, there was an empty spot where Kateri belonged practically dancing to Judson and back with her and Bridey, sitting, standing and kneeling at Mass, radiating the whole time her other-worldly smile.

Also, for the first time, Lulu was struck by the incongruity of a loving God demanding vengeance. She tucked that concept onto a shelf in her mind alongside heaven, turned on her side and fell asleep.

Kateri stood in the middle of the wide circle of students seated on the gym floor, her back straight, her hair pulled away from her bronze face into a single braid, and holding a basket like the ones Indians in Aroostook wove to sell to potato farmers. In a hushed, awestricken voice she said, "My dance is called 'Creator and Coyote.'" Miss Stinson placed the needle on the record and a loud electronic shushing noise was followed by the hypnotic beat of tom-toms. Kateri knelt and placed the Indian basket on the floor. She stood and drew herself up. Slowly, she moved about, looking all around with her customary beatific smile. Her eyes kept returning to the ceiling, and eventually she stood still and gazed upward for quite a long time. She held her upraised arms still and a puzzled look came over her face. Lulu admired Kateri's ability to hold her audience in silent tension. Just before the pause seemed over-long, Kateri bent and picked up the basket. Out of it she drew a large shiny blue star. She danced diameters of the circle, lifting the star at regular intervals. Then she placed the star back into the basket and, beholding the ceiling with her other-worldly smile, began to dance so sensuously that Lulu decided Creator must be female.

Suddenly, Kateri dropped her head and folded her arms. Lulu put her hands together to clap, then stopped because Kateri had lifted her head and was smiling a sly smile evidently conjured for the dance, not one Lulu was used to seeing on her. Kateri got down on all fours. She prowled and rolled and never stopped smiling the sly smile. She seemed to notice the basket for the first time. She sniffed it and lifted out the star and sniffed that. She raised her head and studied the ceiling. She stood and danced diameters again, looking up at regular intervals to where the stars would be. She began reaching up, lifting down imaginary stars and tucking them under her arm. When she seemed to have them all, she dropped them into the basket and danced joyfully, using the basket as a dance partner.

She stopped abruptly and contemplated the basket. Slowly, she reached in and placed imaginary stars back into the imaginary sky. Briefly, her expression changed to that of the dignified Creator. As she went along, however, her movements and her expression loosened to the point where she was gleefully flinging stars helter-skelter.

Suddenly she was Creator again. And then Coyote. Lulu was amazed at how Kateri could represent both characters almost simultaneously. When Creator gestured at the sky, Lulu could almost see the mess Coyote had made of it. When Creator scolded, Coyote cringed the way Lulu had seen chastised dogs do. Coyote slunk to one corner of the stage and lay down. Creator disappeared. After a moment, Coyote raised her head to the ceiling and opened her mouth like a dog howling. She remained in that pose until the tom-toms died down and the needle scraped across the record.

For a moment, no one clapped. For Lulu, it would be like clapping after the consecration at Mass. When Kateri stood and curtseyed, the spell broke and the circle applauded. "I hope Miss Stinson's not grading on a curve," Janet whispered to Lulu. "Because, if so, Kat's just about ruined it for the rest of us."

After Kateri's performance, Lulu and Janet's duet of a march struck Lulu as wooden and contrived. Miss Stinson congratulated the two on choosing music and movements suitable to their talents.

* * *

One Saturday afternoon, the Alpha O pledges sat in chairs arrayed against the walls of the dim third floor corridor that ran between the four sorority rooms. It appeared to Lulu that it must be by arrangement that none of the other three sisterhoods were using their rooms that day. The closed doors made the space rather breathless. No one spoke. The door of the Alpha O room opened, Sue stepped out, took Wendy by the hand, led her into the room and closed the door. Lulu hoped when it was her turn she wouldn't be asked to recite the Greek alphabet. When she tried on her own, she tended to get mixed up around Rho. When the door opened again, Yael came to Lulu and took her hand. Lulu found it reassuring to be guided by a Sister who was also from First Floor Chubbuck.

The room was dimmer than the corridor. At the far end, white robed figures stood in a half circle holding candles that distorted their features. An august voice came from the apex of the arc. "Sister, whom do you present for sisterhood?"

"A radiant maiden of the Spring. One who has proven herself worthy to taste ambrosia and sip nectar."

"Then she must first descend into the underworld to become acquainted with death and sorrow, the beginning and the end."

Yael led Lulu to a long, narrow box and helped her step into it and sit. Then Yael tied a bandana over Lulu's eyes. Lulu's heart rate sped up as she went from seeing dimly to not seeing at all. Yael put one hand at Lulu's back and indicated for her to lie down. What popped into Lulu's mind was the baby girl — Lulu thought of the baby as a girl — born on First Floor Chubbuck not so many years ago who went from its mother's womb to a suitcase in the trunk room where it died and decomposed and greeted with putrid fumes the first coed to open the door in May. Lulu hoped the box didn't have a cover. If she felt herself to be completely enclosed, she'd scream — or yank off the bandana.

No cover came down. Lulu relaxed. She lost consciousness of her body and of her thoughts and entered into the blissful daydream state that follows a restful sleep. She had lost track of time when the august voice said, "Arise, neophyte, to a new life of compassion and grace, the end and the beginning." Lulu felt Yael's hand in hers prompting her to sit, then stand, then step out of the box. Two hands on her shoulders turned her to face a particular direction and the blindfold was loosened and whisked off. She blinked. A robed figure, whom she recognized as Veronica, stepped forward from the arc of wraiths and fixed a sorority pin onto her blouse.

"Welcome, Sister." the august voice said. Tears came to Lulu's eyes and a flush to her cheeks. Yael and Veronica had stepped away. It was Lulu who was addressed as Sister. "Kindly join our assembly, Sister."

Lulu walked towards the arc. Someone slipped a white robe over her. A lighted candle was placed in her hands and she was ushered to the back next to Wendy. As Jill and Bridey and the other pledges suffered mock death and rose to new life, Lulu remained in a sort of happy dream state. After the last pledge was initiated, the arc shifted to a wide circle, the neophytes intermingled with their Sisters. "Let us extinguish our candles, Sisters," the august voice intoned. "And eat and drink with the immortals." Lulu blew out her candle and placed it at her feet as she saw the others doing. A large round cake was passed around and each Sister broke off a piece and held it until it had completed the circle. "Oh Divine Wisdom, giver of earth's good gifts," came the august voice, "We thank thee for the footfalls of our newest Sisters, the advent of Spring and a new beginning." Everyone ate. To Lulu, the morsel tasted like very sweet corn bread. A cup went around the circle, and she sipped what tasted like sweet cold peppermint tea.

Suddenly, the shutters were thrown open and late afternoon sun lighted up the room. Shouts of "Congratulations" and "We love you" filled the air. Lulu hadn't been hugged so much by so many people since the day bids went out.

Although that night she was without a date and sat alone at her desk in 104, Lulu had never felt more blissful. She was a full-fledged Alpha Omega. Jill and Bridey and Wendy and Deb and Veronica and all the other AOs were her sisters. Her mind teemed with the initiation: sitting waiting in the hall, being led in by Yael, lying in the box, sharing the common loaf and the cup, hugging her new sisters. *Compassion and grace*! She had been lifted to a new plane.

She had felt ditched by Tony and Tim, but maybe *she* was the one who had wronged *them*; maybe she was the one lacking in compassion and grace. She'd been content to carry the conversation with Tony, never trying to bring him out, taking no real interest in him aside from the thrill of his kisses. Dating him was convenient, that was all. And with Tim, she had engaged in her first-ever episode of French kissing hardly knowing the guy beyond what she imagined about him. Tony and Tim had been her folly. She was better acquainted with Ike, who continued to come by the reserve desk on Sundays, than either Tony or Tim — not that she felt like kissing Ike.

She could imagine kissing Wesley. She reached into her desk drawer and drew out his letters. She pictured him sitting across from her at a cafeteria table during the TV math class — his perfect features and the smile that crinkled the skin around his eyes and lighted up his whole face. She had liked being the one to make him smile. She felt once again his warm, solid, moist embrace at the hospital. She picked the letter about the bowl of milk and strawberries out of the pile and paper-clipped it to the inside back cover of her planner. She would see Wesley in person during Easter vacation.

"Dad, why are the French around here mostly poorer than the Irish?" Lulu had been deposited at her doorstep that afternoon by Jimmy Taylor, and her whole family was sitting at the supper table eating, as they did every Saturday, baked beans, brown bread and cabbage salad. In her French survey course and in *Great Thinkers*, the French were important contributors to Western Civilization whereas the Irish, Lulu's forebears, were hardly mentioned.

"Well, see, the Irish came speaking the language. Right off the bat, the Frenchman is at a disadvantage because his first language isn't English, and even if he learns English the fact that he speaks it with an accent gives him a backwards sort of an appearance."

Mickey chanted, *"Pea soup and Johnny cake make a Frenchman's belly ache."*

"Mickey!" Lulu's mother looked shocked. So did her father — although beneath his show of horror Lulu detected an amused smile.

"Do you want to be excused from the table without dessert?"

There was no hint of humor beneath Johnny's frown. From her vacation, fly-on-the-wall stance, Lulu saw the oldest of her younger brothers acting as the family guardian of good behavior.

Mickey looked down at his plate. Not even Neil was laughing at his little rhyme.

Lulu cleared the plates while her mother cut squares of yellow cake with chocolate frosting out of a sheet pan. "Dad, how come more of the French don't run things at church?"

"Well, up in the St. John River Valley they do run things. That's because everyone up there is French. Also, the priests and nuns are French and everyone talks French. They don't even know English, a lot of them, any more than we know French. But down here, see, the priests and nuns are mostly Irish. Either Irish American or straight from Ireland. Here, a brogue doesn't hobble a man the way a French accent does. But you're onto something, Lulu. Somehow, the French ended up with the short end of the stick."

"Dad, was Grampa Delaney prejudiced against the French?"

"Well, not exactly. He worked with them in the woods. And once he had his own lumber business he employed a lot of them — Indians, too. He thought the French were good workers. Of course," Her father laughed, touched his napkin to his lips with one hand and pushed aside his dessert plate with the other. "I'm sure he thought God was an Irishman. And now I must tend to my hyacinths." Lulu's father stood up from the table, and her brothers got up to run outside and play.

The invention of better weatherproofing for shoes was a winter activity. Now that spring had arrived, Lulu's father occupied himself with the seedlings he'd begun on St. Patrick's Day. Each morning, noon time and evening, he moved trays of small pots about the house and glassed-in porch, following the sun until the weather would be predictable enough for transplanting into the garden. The whole downstairs had the cinnamon smell of hyacinths and pinks, and the porch — when the sun was on it — had the warm, moist feel of a greenhouse.

Lulu squirted detergent into one section of the sink and filled both sides with warm water. She started with the glasses. "Mum, I don't think the Church has always been fair to women." She hoped her views wouldn't shock her mother too much.

Her mother rubbed a glass with the dishcloth. "No, I don't think it has been."

Oh, you knew that! Sometimes, Lulu felt she was the last woman in the world to put aside childish things — and childish thinking.

That night, reviewing her day, it occurred to Lulu that like a high school girl who gets herself a name for playing around, the Church, once a bastion of civilization, had somewhere between the Dark Ages and the Reformation lost its good reputation. The *philosophes* in French 202 were even harder on the Church than the writers in *Great Thinkers*. And, yet, something else she'd come to realize was that even before the Protestants broke away, the Church had always been made up of contending parties — Franciscans and Dominicans, friars and monks, bishops and dukes, right down to your Bishops of Portland and your Fr. Flannerys. So, maybe she and Wesley, both baptized Christians born and raised in Meduxnekeag and graduates of Dux High, weren't in impossibly irreconcilable camps, after all.

The day after Easter, Lulu walked to the Paradise Diner in Market Square to have lunch with Alice, who had left Little Donny with Marlene for a few hours. It wasn't like Lulu to spend her hard-earned Sorrows money on eating out, but she had an idea what it was Alice was eager to tell her, and if there was one thing she'd learned living with Jill it was that sometimes friendship required an expenditure of funds.

Alice was already seated in a red vinyl booth towards the front when Lulu walked in, and the glow in her eyes and skin confirmed her news. Lulu slid in across from her friend and, before shrugging out of her coat, leaned forward and said, "Tell me."

"The rabbit died!"

"Congratulations!" Lulu clapped her hands together. "How do you feel?"

"Queasy at first. Hungry all the time now." Alice was hoping for a girl this time — although a boy would be okay, too, and maybe more fun for Little Donny, seeing how close in age they'd be.

She could always have a girl next time. Lulu and Alice discussed boy names and girl names. Now that the first child had been named for his father and grandfather, Alice had a lot of leeway for baby number two. Lulu advised traditional names like Alice or John rather than novelty names like Lulu or Wade. The diner was filling up, and Lulu and Alice kept looking up from their hamburgers and French fries to greet people.

"Speak of the devil," Alice called out. "How do you like your name, Wade?'

Wade Carmichael stopped short and sidled into the booth next to Lulu. The glee in his open, freckled face seemed to convey that Lulu and Alice were the two people he had most hoped to run into, and although Lulu doubted that was the case, she couldn't help feeling flattered. "My name? Are you looking to name another little bundle of joy, Alice?

Wade was quick, Lulu had to hand him that. She hoped Mickey, who with his red hair and freckles looked something like Wade, would grow up to be as likeable — but not as reckless. Wade reacted to Alice's news with his customary charm and said he'd name a girl Corina or Peggy Sue, a boy, Elvis. When two of his classmates came in, he stood up. "You here the rest of the week, Lu? Wes decided to go back to Boston early."

"He's left already?"

"On this morning's bus. So long, Lu. Congratulations, Alice. Tell Donny I said hi."

Chapter Eighteen

Dear Wesley,
This will be my last letter to you. I prefer that you not write back. Since you couldn't make the time to see me in person when we were both home over Easter, I don't care to continue exchanging letters. I am not interested in pursuing a phantom friendship, which is what I consider ours to be. (Whether or not a real date would be against your principles, you could have at least invited me to go for a walk.)
I wish you well in all your future endeavors.
Sincerely,
Lulu

Sealing the envelope, Lulu felt as hard as nails. *Cliché,* Mr. Lunt would write in red if she used such a hackneyed simile in a paper. Well then, as hard as a railroad spike that could be pounded and pounded without bending. *There!* She licked and stuck and pounded the stamp. She didn't need Wesley. He could find a girlfriend among his Pentecostal classmates — Hazel, perhaps — someone who saw him only in a crowd and married him the day after graduation, not having spent one minute alone. Lulu walked to the lobby, shoved the letter into the pigeonhole for outgoing mail and dusted off her hands.

On the way back to 104, she went into the bathroom. Bridey stood outside one of the stalls speaking like a coach. "Point the tip towards your backbone."

"Right, okay." Jill's voice came from inside the stall. "Who just came in?"

"It's me — Lulu." Lulu went into the next stall.

"Oh, hi, Roomie. Okay, Bridey, what do I do next?"

"Take your longest finger and push."

"Ow! It hurts!"

"Are you sure it's pointing toward your backbone?

"Oh, I've got it! I've got it! It's in." In a moment, Jill emerged, her eyes shiny. She washed her hands in the sink next to where Lulu was washing hers. "Thank you, Bridey." Wiping her hands, Jill twirled about and hugged her coach. "This is fabulous! Lulu, you're next. Bridey and I will give you all the instructions you need."

That night Lulu awoke to Jill shaking her shoulder and whispering, "Lulu, get up, we're going to see the Dean."

"Whatever it is, Jill, it can wait until tomorrow."

"It can't wait until tomorrow. The Tampax's stuck in there. I can't get it out." Lulu sat up and looked at Jill, who had mounted the ladder to Lulu's bunk, tears running down her cheeks. "You've got to help me. We'll go see the Dean."

"We don't go see the Dean about a thing like this." Lulu kept her voice low. "Besides, she's not in her office now, and we don't know where she lives."

"The infirmary, then."

"Whatever we do, we have to get permission from Mrs. Hatch." Lulu and Jill put on slippers and muumuus, shuffled out to the lobby and knocked on the housemother's door.

The slight palsy that caused her lower lip to quiver constantly and the gravity that tugged on the lines on either side of her mouth accounted for Mrs. Hatch's behind-her-back nickname, "Hatchet Face." The door opened a sliver to her fierce expression and a head covered with pincurls. When Jill explained herself, Mrs. Hatch held the door wide for them to come in. They followed her to her bathroom where she reached into the medicine chest and handed Jill a jar of Vaseline and a pair of tweezers. "Let's have you try this first." Mrs. Hatch led Lulu back into the sitting room. Maybe it was something about the housemother's forthright manner, for, within minutes Jill came out of the bathroom smiling. Mrs. Hatch's expression also softened into a smile. "I don't know why you girls aren't satisfied with Kotex napkins. They were good enough in my day."

Back in her bunk, Lulu found her mind too full for sleep. She wondered why Jill had awakened her and not Bridey. How awful it must be to be a housemother, subject to being roused at any hour of the night. Lulu herself wasn't going to try Tampax any time soon. She felt like laughing, and just as suddenly like crying. She had come to think of herself and Wesley as kindred spirits. He had become her most cherished confidant. Without his beautiful letters with their funny little drawings and their compassionate observations, how could she carry on? How could she ever be happy again? Mr. Lunt would scorn such a mundane image, she knew, but her heart was broken into a million pieces.

"Lulu, wait up!" Elise strolled along the path towards Lulu with an ironic smile — or maybe a plain friendly smile. Lulu couldn't remember any other time when Elise had gone out of her way to speak to her outside 104 Chubbuck. "So, have you decided on a major?" Elise sounded interested, as though she and Lulu were actual friends.

"English, probably." Professor Snow seemed to assume his freshman students would all sign up for Latin 201-202. Every chance he got, he made a pitch for Greek 101 as though he viewed them all, even Lulu, as fit Classics majors. M. Diderot, in the high-toned French Lulu could follow more often than not, kept recommending the 300 level courses in his major. Lulu preferred literature either written in English in the first place or translated into it by someone other than herself. "And you?"

"I'm thinking of theology."

"Really?" Lulu didn't plan to take any theology courses at Lovejoy lest she lose her faith. If her scholarship had been to a Catholic college, she would have been required to take theology, Catholic theology, but she didn't think she would ever want to major in it even at a Catholic college because she wouldn't want to spend four years constantly questioning the meaning of life. Mainly, she didn't want ever to lose her way altogether and have a nervous breakdown like Holden Caulfield. Or her father. "Why theology?"

Elise tossed her head back and smiled down at Lulu. "I'm thinking of becoming a minister."

"Really!" For the umpteenth time that year, Lulu was glad she was a Catholic and not a Protestant.

In 104, after they'd set down their books and hung up their jackets, Elise for once instead of heading out to find Muffy or another of her crowd, sat sideways at her desk and fished a cigarette from her purse. Lulu had never seen her sitting facing the desk or reading any of the books lined up across the back of it. "How are things in little Mixed-up-de-burg?"

"Meduxnekeag, you mean." Lulu picked knee socks out of the clean laundry piled on her desk and opened a bureau drawer. She didn't like hearing the name of her town made fun of — not by Elise. "Everything's fine."

Elise lighted her cigarette, took a deep drag and exhaled. "It must be nice to come from a place where everything is 'fine' — like *Our Town*." Squinting past the smoke, she fixed Lulu with a gaze.

Lulu lifted three wash-and-wear blouses off the back of her chair and put them on hangers. "What?"

"You and I are a great deal alike, you know."

"Really, in what way?" Lulu paused, the hangers dangling from her hand.

"Well for one thing, we don't go in for that old school spirit."

"I've been to practically every single visiting lecture." The only one Lulu recalled seeing Elise at was when Paul Goodman talked about his book *Growing up Absurd*. She hung the shirts in the closet and sat on the edge of Jill's bunk facing Elise.

"I'm thinking of sports, Lulu. Rah rah team, Run Maine Down, Clobber Colby, Master Bates — that sort of thing."

Lulu wasn't crazy about spectator sports. She had gotten cold and bored at the one football game and the one hockey match she'd attended. The season in Aroostook, with the potato picking recess in the middle of it, was too short and the equipment too expensive for football. Every child in Meduxnekeag had skates, and the outdoor rink was popular whenever it wasn't colder than twenty below zero or stormy or in the midst of a thaw, but as far as Lulu knew, the town fathers had never entertained the idea of building a climate-controlled arena like the one at Lovejoy. Even if they had, the equipment looked as expensive as that for football. To Lulu, the two sports were as obvious and violent as a mean pick-up game of crack the whip. Even seeing Marc glide out onto the ice and whack the puck hadn't been enough to hold her interest. She could picture herself glancing at a game on TV while lying on a couch covered with an afghan and looking through a magazine, but just thinking about sitting on a hard bench getting colder and colder gave her the shivers. "It's true neither of us wants to freeze our fannies at football or hockey games."

"Another thing, we don't like the kind of guys who are attracted to us. Like all those little OK pledges your Mixed-up-de-burg friend sics on you."

"What?" Lulu felt the blood rush to her face as the realization hit that what Elise said was so true she couldn't believe it hadn't already occurred to her. It wasn't for herself that the OK freshmen had asked her out — and were still asking her out — it was because of Jimmy Taylor.

"The only guys we like are the ones we can't have."

How long and how closely had Elise, who appeared so aloof and indifferent, been observing Lulu's social life?

"Another thing, we're not mastered by our passions. We like to analyze other people and laugh at them. We find them amusing."

"I don't…" Lulu started to say and stopped. Elise was saying what Tony had said about her. She did enjoy laughing at other people. She had joined Elise in laughing at Jill.

"The thing is, Lulu, we don't need close friends, either of us, the way everyone else seems to."

"You have Muffy." Even as she spoke, Lulu realized that it had been a while since Muffy had come by 104 to pick up Elise.

"Oh, Muffy, fickle, fickle Muffy!" Elise tapped her cigarette onto the ashtray on her desk. "You and I don't need to have a 'best friend' the way Jill has Bridey. And we haven't come to Lovejoy to find a husband either — the way our dear little Jill has found her Jack."

Elise must have forgotten about writing "Mr. and Mrs. Franklin Samuel Thatcher III" all down a page in her Great Thinkers *notebook.*

"About roommates next year, obviously Jill and Bridey will be together. So, if you're interested…" Elise took a drag, inhaling deeply, and blew out a plume.

Lulu felt sick to her stomach.

"…I'm open." Elise kept her eyes on the smoke. "If I'm still here, that is."

"If you're still here?"

"I seem to have accumulated a pile of those pesky mid-semester warnings. Like what you got in math."

Lulu blushed anew at the reminder of her warning in the fall. At least she hadn't gotten a pile of them. And, with math out of the way, she hadn't gotten any warnings second semester. In English and *Great Thinkers* she was getting Bs; French was a C plus, and — with April's help — Latin might not slip from B minus into the Cs; Speech was harder than she'd anticipated and Mr. Wilson had revealed a dreadful mean streak, but only a mute could fail to get less than a B minus. Golf, her spring phys ed class, was too fussy and frustrating to enjoy, but no coed, according to Deb, ever got less than a B in gym as long as she showed up for class. "I'm sorry to hear that."

"Yes, well, it's sufficient cause for me to be summoned by Dr. Freud."

Lulu assumed Elise was referring to Dr. French, the school psychologist. She was glad she herself hadn't been summoned by him first semester. Apparently, just one warning wasn't sufficient cause.

That evening when Lulu tried to compose herself for her examination of conscience, the words that came to mind were: *I'm a failure.* She had come to Lovejoy eager to excel in her studies, make good friends and find a boyfriend. All around her, other coeds were succeeding in one, two or three of those categories. She was, at best, a mediocre student. She had made a mess of the boyfriend situation. She was easily bored by the guys who were interested in her — and chagrined to think that the OKs who asked her out did so only to please their senior Brother — and hung up on ones who were unattainable. As for friends, she had spread herself so thin that, although she gave the *appearance* of having many, the *reality* was that she had none. None of her Sisters in Alpha Omega had turned out to be like real sisters, not even Jill in spite of the closeness they had felt at the beginning of first semester. And it was Lulu's own fault. She hadn't given gifts and encouragement the way Jill had, and so Jill had drifted into a true friendship with Bridey. Lulu had always felt sorry for only children and glad for her brothers, but maybe being an only child was better preparation for developing friendships.

All the other AO freshmen, although friendly enough with Lulu, had paired off already. None had approached her about becoming roommates. Maybe they assumed she would room with Jill.

Elise was right. She, Lulu, lacked passion. In trying to be everyone's friend she was no one's. Perhaps being nice to everyone wasn't sufficient for true friendship. Jill loved Brad and hated Elise. Maybe there wasn't anyone in the world Lulu truly loved or hated. Maybe she didn't have and would never have kindred spirits — or arch-enemies. She would never know true love, never marry and have children, never have a woman friend who was like a sister. She would go through life on the margins of other people's lives.

After Pollyanna of storybook fame lost the use of her legs, she could no longer play the "glad game" she had so blithely recommended to others. Pollyanna was a know-it-all, Lulu suddenly realized, full of certitude about everyone except herself.

Lulu blessed herself and recited silently an "Our Father," a "Hail Mary" and a "Glory Be." Perhaps Wesley's — Elijah's — still, small voice had been within her all along, but either it had fled or it had burrowed so deeply she could no longer hear it.

"Everything okay, Roomie?" Jacket over her arm, Jill paused with her hand on the doorknob and looked searchingly at Lulu, who was seated at her desk writing.

"Yuh, sure." Lulu didn't feel like asking why Jill had chosen Bridey to room with sophomore year. Besides, the reasons were obvious.

"Heard from Tim?"

"No, that was a one-time thing, I'm afraid." Lulu hoped she sounded nonchalant. She certainly didn't want Jill ferreting out Tim's reasons for not calling — whatever exactly they were. "We're not each other's type, after all."

"Is that a letter to Wesley?"

"To my folks....Wesley is passé, I'm afraid. Like Ronnie with you."

"I got fed up with Ronnie's boring letters, Lulu, but you always seemed to love Wesley's." Jill slipped her jacket on and opened the door. "I have to meet Brad. But anytime you want to talk about Tim or Wesley — or anything, for that matter, Lulu — remember, I'm ready to listen."

Lulu finished her letter and opened her planner. She ripped Wesley's letter out of the inside cover and held it over the wastebasket, then dropped it into the drawer with the others. Her planner dictated English reading for Saturday afternoon, but she felt the need to get outside. She'd walk over to Judson to make her Easter duty.

Heavy spring rains and runoff from the surrounding woods had washed the campus clean of snow, and the lawns were greening up under the intermittent drizzle of the last few days. The ice that edged puddles like shattered glass would soon be gone. Mother Nature had returned the ducks to the pond from wherever it was they wintered. Any day now, Lulu's hay fever would put in its annual appearance. Her cotton wraparound skirt didn't wrap around quite as far as it had in the fall — no doubt the result of the freshman fifteen, although she thought it couldn't have been more than five pounds that she'd gained.

She hadn't been to Confession since she was home at Christmas. Although she couldn't see that kissing Tim was a mortal sin, she no longer felt in the state of grace, and it seemed somehow that making out with him — and being dumped by him and by Tony and Wesley — had as much to do with her heavy-heartedness as the fact that she had no real friends, merely acquaintances, at Lovejoy. "*Rien, rien n'avait d'importance,*" Meursault concluded in *L'etranger*. Lulu couldn't bear to think that nothing was of importance, nor could she allow herself to conclude that the life she was leading was absurd. To think like Meursault — or Camus speaking through Meursault — would be like succumbing to a nightmare instead of wrenching herself awake.

She walked up the side aisle of Judson to a seat behind the line of a half-dozen penitents. Naturally, there were no real confessionals like the carved wooden recesses at Our Lady of Perpetual Help. Instead, Fr. Flannery sat sideways in a straight chair towards the back of the stage. A penitent knelt on a prie-dieu, her back to the auditorium. After awhile, Fr. Flannery, still looking straight ahead, lifted his head and Lulu saw his lips moving. She bent her own head and tried to think how to word whatever transgression she had fallen into with Tim and what couple of run-of-the mill venial sins she could insert it between.

When her turn came, she walked down the aisle, her hands folded in front of her, mounted the steps to the stage, walked to the prie-dieu, knelt, blessed herself and spoke to the hunched profile. "Bless me, Father, for I have sinned. It has been three months since my last Confession. I accuse myself of neglecting to say my morning prayers about a dozen times, using poor judgment in my dealings with another person once and entertaining uncharitable thoughts about ten times."

Fr. Flannery sat up straight and without turning his head said. "Was that other person male, Lulu?"

Lulu felt her face color. Never before in her life had a priest called her by name in the confessional. She was surprised Fr. Flannery even knew her name. Whenever their paths crossed on campus, he merely nodded. But, of course, she'd always spoken up at the monthly Newman Club meetings where he sat apparently engrossed in his breviary. "Yes, Father."

"And did your poor judgment lead to a sin of commission or omission, Lulu?"

"Commission, Father." Lulu's entire moral status felt as muzzy as the weather outside.

"It's natural at your age, Lulu, to be seeking intimacy."

"Yes, Father."

"The important thing is to come to know others in their personhood, and not to use them for your own convenience — nor to allow yourself to be so used. Most especially, Lulu, every action you take should be based on this one criterion: will this help me become the person God is calling me to be?"

"Yes, Father."

"God loves you, Lulu. Say an 'Act of Contrition' now."

Lulu blushed again. "God loves you" wasn't something Catholics went around saying to each other. It was more like something Wesley would say — although he'd say "Jesus" instead of "God." "*Oh, my God, I am heartily sorry...*" She rattled through the prayer.

"And now, for your penance say three 'Our Fathers' and three 'Hail Marys.'" Fr. Flannery raised his right hand. "I absolve you of your sins in the name of the Father and of the Son and of the Holy Ghost…"

"…Amen. Thank you, Father."

At a seat in the back of the auditorium, Lulu leaned her forehead on her folded hands to say her penance. When she raised her head, she felt as though an entire freshman fifteen had evaporated into the atmosphere. She stood up feeling almost giddy at the thought that all the doctrines of the Church and all the wisdom of the Western World boiled down to the Golden Rule — being considerate of others and taking care of yourself.

Walking back to the dorm through the drizzle, she didn't think she could initiate the conversation, but she wouldn't make it any harder than it had to be for Jill to tell her they wouldn't be roommates. She wasn't going to room with Elise either. No matter what, she wasn't going to spend another year with someone she couldn't count on to acknowledge her outside the room. Briefly, she saw herself writing the matter all out in a letter to Wesley, and just as quickly she remembered that their correspondence was finished. A dark undertow pulled at the lightness of her mood. Until this moment, she had harbored the hope that Wesley would write back explaining himself, asking for her forgiveness, promising to spend time with her during the summer. She'd even pictured him surprising her by taking a bus up from Boston to talk to her in person. They'd walk around the campus and she'd point out all the things she'd written to him about. He'd tell her more of his plans for the future. Maybe they'd never become boyfriend and girlfriend, but they would at least be friends. She had thought they knew each other so well when it turned out she didn't know him at all and probably never would, and apparently that was okay with him.

Well, she could live with her disappointments. There would be no *deus ex machina*, but eventually she could be happy again.

Chapter Nineteen

One evening after she and April had finished the day's Latin translation and April had retreated to bed, Lulu remained in the parlor sneezing and wiping her nose. In English class, Mr. Lunt had gotten hung up on the subject of spring. For Spring Weekend, he explained, each fraternity rented a get-away, often a big old rambling cottage on one of the beaches in southern Maine. To spend weekends off campus, a coed needed written permission from a parent, known as "blanket permission," a term Mr. Lunt exploited for sexual innuendo. He made Spring Weekend sound like a bacchanal straight out of the Eleusinian Mysteries. "A lot of little honeymoons take place, especially among the seniors," he'd said with a wink and a smirk. The poems he read aloud in class were also about spring — cuckoo birds singing loudly and leaping deer breaking wind — and he had given an assignment to write a poem using earthy, sensuous language. Lulu had been composing in her head off and on for two days. She wrote quickly.

Spring
  by Lulu Delaney
Feathery bits of vegetable sex
Get all through my clothes
And up my nose
Scratching and swelling mucous membranes
I itch and twitch and sneeze
My throat tickles
My eyes smart
My face aches
At bedtime
I lean over a wet washcloth

Drape a cold pack
Over my nose and cheeks
Spray saline solution
Take aspirin and a steaming cup of chamomile
I sit up in bed
Pillows bunched under my head
And read until my head shrinks
And sleep comes.

She had taken poetic license with regard to her bouts of hay fever, which were actually much milder than the poem suggested. It was her little brother Mickey who suffered the full-blown variety. She read over what she'd written — aloud, as she was the only one left in the parlor at that hour — and judged it sufficiently sensuous and earthy to satisfy Mr. Lunt

Mr. Lunt mimeographed her poem and distributed it to the class. No one else had had two pieces of writing so honored. She felt like a bona fide English major. Briefly, she pictured mailing a copy to Wesley and just as quickly remembered, with a wave of seasickness, that their correspondence had come to an end.

Assembled in Mrs. Hatch's sitting room during a regularly scheduled meeting, the dorm council was taking up the case of Evie. The defendant sat a little apart from the council members dressed in a red and white striped shirt, a green and white striped blazer and a filmy black skirt with tiny white dots. Among the bangles on her wrist was Marc's silver chain-link expansion bracelet. Although the spring musical was over, Lulu kept seeing Evie around campus with Marc. Just that morning, walking past Hades, she had glimpsed them seated facing each other with inscrutable, soulful expressions that could have signified either a breakup or a plan to elope.

One night, Evie had remained with Marc outside the entrance to Chubbuck an entire half hour after curfew sounded. When she rang the doorbell, it was Nathalie, the dorm council president and guardian of the rules, who let her in.

"Marc and I needed to talk," Evie said quietly now looking down at her hands in her lap. "When the bell rang, we were in the middle of an important conversation. We needed to finish."

Lulu had expected Evie to come up with a better excuse and so, apparently, had Nathalie, who said, almost eagerly, "But you're sorry Evie, right? It wouldn't happen again."

Evie raised her eyes but not her voice. "No, I'm not sorry. And I would do it again." Her eyes flashed before she composed herself again. "I broke the rule. I'll accept whatever punishment you think fair." She lowered her eyes.

Nathalie told Evie to step into the lobby while the council decided her case. Lulu felt bad for Evie — and for herself that she had become part of a group whose job it was to mete out punishment. She looked around at the others. No one looked happy about disciplining the ethereal Evie. "The categorical imperative," Nathalie said firmly, although she looked as discomforted as everyone else.

Immanuel Kant — what applies to all must apply to the individual.

Mrs. Hatch put up one hand, her quivering lip and down-turned mouth giving her the fierce look of an Old Testament prophet. "In future, you should all know that if there is something serious you need to tend to when the bell rings, something like what Evie has described, you need only ring my bell and let me know you need an extension. As for Evie, I don't think we need to do anything about her minor infraction."

Lulu was astonished. Mrs. Hatch had set the categorical imperative on its head. Then again, maybe dorm rules were meant more for people like Elise who would self-destruct without them than for advanced souls like Evie. The mood in the room lightened up. "Let's play a joke," Nathalie said. Evie was called back in and sat with her hands in her lap, her head slightly bowed. "Evie," Nathalie said. "We've considered your case and we've decided you can't go to Spring Weekend."

Evie's head jerked up. Her eyes blazed. "I hate you all!"

"Only kidding, Evie," Nathalie said quickly. "Only kidding."

Walking back to 104, Lulu felt shaken to think that, in the moments before Mrs. Hatch intervened to explain, Evie was capable of hating everyone on the dorm council — herself included. Lulu had thought Evie cared more about the theater and writing poetry than about anything or anyone else. On the other hand, maybe it took a real live person, a guy like Marc, to stir her deepest passions.

Jill was alone in the room. She looked up from her notebook, a worry line between her eyes, and pursed her lips. "I need to ask you a personal question, Lulu."

Lulu hoped she wouldn't blush when Jill told her she wouldn't be rooming with her sophomore year. "Shoot."

"Would you mind being in a triple again next year, Lulu?" Jill spoke all in rush. "With Bridey. We've become really good friends and you like her too, don't you, Lulu?"

"You would room with me again next year?" Lulu felt her neck and cheeks redden.

"Of course, Silly. You're my roomie!" Jill jumped up from her chair and threw her arms around Lulu enveloping her with the scent of cinnamon and soap. Tears came to Lulu's eyes. To hide her relief, she stooped to hug her roommate back. They were friends after all.

"Ah, the Existentialists!" Ike had come up to the reserve desk where Lulu sat in front of her splayed-open French textbook and twisted his head to read. "More liberal ideas for you, Lulu!"

"Maybe the style, but their ideas are as old as Aristotle."

"For example?"

"For example, *we are what we habitually do*. Even Montaigne said what the Existentialists are saying — *a person is always in the process of becoming*. Even Ovid says it — *no man should be called happy before burial.*"

"You sound disappointed with these guys." Ike tapped a forefinger against the book. "Could it be that their anti-clericalism offends you?"

"Anti-clericalism?"

"Anti-Catholicism."

"Oh that." Lulu had a hard time equating the Church she'd grown up in — the Church of weekly Mass and frequent Confession, of treating one's body as a temple of the Holy Ghost and one's neighbor as oneself, the Church of May processions and Forty Hours devotion and rummage sales and potluck suppers and giving up candy for Lent — with its reputation with the French Existentialists and other great post-Reformation thinkers of the Western World. On the other hand, no one was asking her to reconcile the two views. The Church wasn't considered important enough to occupy central stage in either course. "Jill keeps telling me I don't have to figure out stuff that won't come up on a test."

Ike laughed and straightened up as though ready to continue on to the reading room. Then he leaned against the counter again and lowered his voice. "Lulu, would you go to Spring Weekend with me — just as a friend? I know my fraternity isn't as high up there as some of the other houses, but we're going to a really nice beach and you'd have a good time. What do you say?"

Glancing over at Rolf sorting books onto a cart at the other end of the counter, Lulu replied in a voice just above a whisper. "Ike, I thought you were dating April."

"We broke up. April's too darn sensitive, Lulu. I'm always hurting her feelings without meaning to. That's why I'd like to spend Spring Weekend with you. You don't get your feelings hurt over every little thing."

Lulu looked down at her textbook and smoothed her hands over the open pages. Blanket permission was no problem. Her mother had signed the form thinking Lulu might get invited to the home of another coed. Besides, her mother trusted her. The trouble was that Spring Weekend was for romance, and she had no romantic interest in Ike.

He must have read her thoughts. *Would she ever learn to control her facial expressions?* "As friends, Lulu, that's all. It'll be fun to get away from campus before we have to buckle down for finals."

"Thank you, Ike." She looked up into his earnest face, with its over-large nose and its incipient five-o'clock shadow. His eyes, she realized, were his best feature, large and brown and fringed with thick lashes. "Yes, I'll go with you."

His smile made him look almost handsome. "Thank you." As Lulu watched him walk towards the reading room, his feet shuffling slightly, the back of his shirt inexpertly tucked into his waistband, she was struck by how hard it must be to be a guy, to be the one to risk rejection, to have the courage to pursue a coed you were interested in, knowing she wasn't crazy about you.

"Spring Weekend with Chopped Liver, huh Lulu?" Rolf trundled a full cart to her end of the counter. He must have overheard in spite of their lowered tones.

"Yuh." She wished she weren't blushing as though a weekend with Ike's fraternity was something to be ashamed of.

"Don't worry, you'll have fun. Anyway, those are the guys that'll be heading up the professions in ten or twenty years. Meanwhile, the Lamb Chops will turn to fat watching sports on television and the OK's will find fulfillment mowing their suburban lawns."

Rolf was so caught up with talk of music and the doings of his fraternity that Lulu was always caught off guard when, like now, he seemed to catch her mood and offer reassurance.

That night in bed, the image of Ike shuffling towards the reading room came to Lulu's mind. Like Oedipus or Atticus Finch, Ike was a person of character — perhaps more than she was. She'd do everything she could to be a good guest, and she'd try not to think too much about the lowly status of her hosts, the Chopped Livers.

Lulu felt uneasy about clearing up the roommate situation with Elise, but one evening when it was just the two of them in 104, Elise broached the topic. "Dr. Freud and I have agreed that I need time off from school to find myself." She raised her eyebrows. "So, in June I'm leaving for Europe."

"Oh, I'm sorry." What Elise was describing sounded more like a failure than an adventure. "Why don't you go home? Couldn't you find yourself in New York City?"

"And live with my parents? I haven't done that since I was fourteen. No, Europe is the place for me."

"Your parents can afford that?"

"The family fund will pay as long as I sign up for courses somewhere. I'll use London or Paris or Amsterdam as a base and travel around. European universities don't hold students to phony schedules like American ones. Besides, I'm sick of reading all this stuff written by men." Elise waved her hand at the volumes arrayed across the back of her desk. "At dear old BS Hall, at least we read Sappho and Virginia Woolf."

Lulu had never heard of Sappho or Virginia Woolf, and it had never before occurred to her that everything she'd read freshmen year was written by men. "We read the classics, Elise. The classics were written by men."

"Men like Paul Goodman. He says women don't need creative lives the way men do because we're fulfilled by having children." Elise turned her head and looked sideways at Lulu. "Didn't work for my mother, I'm afraid," she said dryly. "Every copy of *Growing up Absurd* should have a big "Girls Beware" label stuck onto its front cover. No, dear roommate, I was locked up with a bunch of females for four years, and now I'm finishing up a year in the wilds of Maine being lectured to by men. Enough of curfews and mystery meat for me. It's high time I got out into the real world."

Lulu hadn't thought before about the fact that all her professors so far were men. "Don't men run the universities in Europe, too?"

"Maybe I'll find a place that's not set up like a penal colony. Of course, you're used to that sort of thing, Lulu. You've grown up with the Catholic hierarchy idea."

"Hierarchy? The word was new to Lulu.

"Hierarchy, the way everything is set up top to bottom from the Pope to the bishops to the priests, like a pyramid — a pyramid of men, no girls allowed."

"Isn't that what it's like in the Episcopal Church — except for the Pope, of course?"

"I'm a liberal, Lulu."

Lulu answered Elise's non sequitur with another — "I'll miss you, Elise"— and realized what she said was true. She blushed.

"Thank you, Lulu. I'll send you a postcard." She smirked. "And let you know if I find myself."

"What's Machiavelli's main advice to a tyrant?" Jill sat crosslegged on the lower bunk, her notebook open on her lap.

Lulu sat at her desk chair, her notebook also open, although her sparse notes didn't compare to Jill's meticulous ones. Lulu tipped her head towards the ceiling and recalled, "First, make the people afraid of you. Later, get them to love you."

"That's what most of the nuns were like in elementary school — high school, too." Bridey lay on her stomach on Jill's scatter rug. She took a thoughtful drag on her cigarette and exhaled a long blue plume. "It worked, too. Is that what your teachers were like?"

"What do we know about Hobbes?" Jill was willing to lead study sessions as long as it was well ahead of testing and everyone stayed on track. On the day or two leading up to a big exam she studied alone. The morning of, she would awaken early, skip breakfast to go through her notes one more time and engage in no conversation whatsoever. If Lulu were to benefit by studying with her, now was the time.

Lulu tried to recall the main idea about Hobbes — apart from the fact that she didn't like him, which didn't actually qualify as a fact. Bridey frowned as though deep in thought and tapped her cigarette against the rim of the small glass ashtray she carried with her everywhere. "The tyranny of the weak," she said. "Because Negroes can't get into fraternities and sororities in the South, Student Government wants to eliminate fraternities and sororities at Lovejoy."

Lulu was glad Dottie wasn't in the room. Maybe Bridey made a valid point about the weak ruining things for everyone else, but Dottie wouldn't like to hear Negroes portrayed as tyrannical. Kateri wouldn't like it either. In fact, they'd be so indignant they'd probably derail the whole study session.

"Also..." Jill looked down at her notes. "...life is SPABS."

"Spabs?" Lulu didn't think she'd ever heard the word before.

"SPABS — it's an acronym for "solitary, poor, nasty, brutish and short.""

"Oh, yuh!" Lulu wrote the initials in her notebook. "Nasty starts with an n not an a."

"But then you wouldn't have an acronym, Lulu."

"Anyway, I don't like Hobbes. I don't believe what he says about life." It occurred to Lulu that somewhere along the way, the great thinkers of the Western World had taken leave of the virtuous

Plato and Aristotle and Augustine, who, according to Fr. Flannery, was the author of the maxim "Virtue is its own reward," and entered into a dreadful situation where getting ahead at any cost took precedence over doing the right thing.

"What you believe doesn't matter, Lulu. What matters is that you have a way of keeping his main idea in your head so you can use it in an essay question….What's important about Hegel?"

Lulu would like to discuss the ideas they were studying the way she imagined the American Expatriates had in Paris cafes, more along the lines of a leisurely feast than a pie-eating contest. She had a feeling, however, that that kind of discussion was never going to be a regular occurrence in Chubbuck. At least not in 104. Jill and Bridey, on the other hand, had figured out shortcuts to getting good grades, and if Lulu quieted the ideas racing around her head and listened more than she talked she might get good grades, too. And she needed good grades to keep her scholarship and return to Lovejoy sophomore year.

"Thesis, antithesis, synthesis," Bridey said.

"An example, please." Jill threw open her hands.

"Scott asks me to Spring Weekend. My mother won't give me blanket permission…" Bridey frowned and squashed her cigarette into her ashtray.

"You shoot your mother." Lulu couldn't help herself.

Jill rattled her notebook and scowled. "I don't have time to fool around, ladies."

"Heaven exists; heaven doesn't exist; heaven exists but not in the way we previously imagined — or in any way we're capable of imagining." Lulu was trying to redeem herself.

Apparently she succeeded because Jill broke out in a genuine smile, then looked down at her notes again. "So, what's the main idea about John Stuart Mill?" She looked up and widened her eyes.

Lulu looked at her own notes. "He was tutored by his father and his uncle. They ruined his childhood by making him study all the time, and he had a nervous breakdown at 21."

Jill winced. "Lulu!"

Bridey laughed out loud. "*Great Thinkers* isn't an English

class, Lulu. Or psychology."

"Yeah," Jill said. "The main idea about John Stuart Mill is you have to know other people's opinions as well as you know your own. And from their point of view. Otherwise, you don't really know what you yourself believe."

The study session continued for another hour cumulating in the thoughts of Marx and Engels. "Their main idea," Lulu said, "was like the early Christians' — give according to one's ability, take according to one's needs." Growing up, she had surmised that Communism destroyed the family and enslaved the individual. So she had been surprised by how congenial the works of Marx and Engels sounded. Dottie loved them. Some evenings she'd drop into 104 to read passages aloud, her wiry blonde curls electrified, her eyes shining behind her thick glasses. "Only difference is, Communists don't believe in God."

"Bravo, Lulu!" Jill slammed her notebook shut. She unfolded her legs, stood up, crossed the room to her wardrobe and pulled her towel off its rack. "Excuse me, please, I have to go to the bathroom."

Tongues of icy water surged and retreated, sucking sand from under Lulu and Ike's feet, shifting the ground they stood on. On a distant bluff, evergreens crowded either side of a white house and a red barn. "It looks like a Winslow Homer," Ike said.

In his introductions to visiting lecturers along with a mention of "our own Sarah Orne Jewett," the 19th century Maine author, President Livingstone usually worked in a reference to the college's art collection, which contained several works by "our own Winslow Homer." At each introduction, Lulu made a mental note to visit the art gallery, but so far she hadn't managed to make the time. She had a feeling that the Maine of Homer and Jewett, the Maine of the pointed firs and the ocean, was to most people's minds the real Maine and that Aroostook County might as well be a Canadian province. She lay her head to one side and squinted. "I don't see how Homer — or any artist — could get so much sea and sky into one picture."

"Those buildings would be tiny boxes in the middle of the canvas. The trees would be tiny triangles. Everything else would be blue sky or blue sea."

"Wouldn't that be an awful lot of plain blue?"

"Not plain blue, Lulu. Look, the sky is not the same as the sea. And the sea keeps changing and the sky is full of other colors too."

"You have the eyes of an artist, Ike."

"Take Art 101 and 102 next year, Lulu, and you'll see like an artist, too. In fact, you'd love Art — all those Madonna and Childs, all those angels and cathedrals. Art is very Catholic. Up until the Reformation, that is. Liberals had better ideas than conservatives, if you don't mind my saying so, Lulu, but in the beginning their art stunk. All those full-length portraits of old burghers dressed in black. Everything opened up again with the Impressionists. They saw all the colors of the rainbow in sky and in water. Shut your eyes, Lulu, then open them and blink three times. Do you see it?"

"Oh!" The sky and sea swam, and she and Ike were specks in the suddenly scintillating seascape, tinier even than the tiny house and barn and trees in the distance. "But I wouldn't dare take art, Ike. I'm not a very good artist."

"That doesn't matter. You'd learn to see like one."

"I'll keep an open mind. But there're just so many other things I'd like to know more about — economics, for instance."

"Ecky would be a waste of your time. Read *An Intelligent Woman's Guide to Socialism and Capitalism*. George Bernard Shaw tells you everything an English major needs to know about economics." Ike took Lulu's hand and she ran with him, shrieking, into a towering, lace-capped wave.

The night before Greek Sing, which was the last big event of the year and for which Saturday morning classes were canceled, Lulu lay in bed reviewing her year at Lovejoy. There was another week of classes and then finals would begin and everyone would go about preoccupied and unwashed. Before her last exam, she would bring her suitcases up from the trunk room, pack, and — since Jimmy Taylor would be staying for graduation — get ready to take the bus home.

She didn't have the naïve confidence about grades she'd started the year with, but she wasn't afraid of flunking any of her exams either and she was going into them with decent grades. Next year she'd take math again with Miss Grundy, the spoon feeder. She'd sign up for biology and get to dissect a fetal pig, which would be like seeing the insides of a human baby — Little Donny, for instance. She'd be free of Latin and French, having completed the foreign language requirement. She'd definitely try out for the fall play. Maybe she'd finally make it downtown to the High Dive.

Pollyanna's sense of gratitude returned only when she was once again able to walk. It was a *deus ex machina* ending for sure. But, then, Pollyanna was written for children. Like the alternating happy and unhappy endings in *Ovid's Metamorphoses*, in real life some things worked out well and others didn't. And Lulu did have a lot to be grateful for — Jill and Bridey and her other Alpha O Sisters, Chubbuck First Floor, the Newman Club, the Tin Can, Ike, Jimmy Taylor and the freshmen OKs. So what if her OK classmates asked her out because of Jimmy? She'd had a good time — mostly — and it went to show what a good "big brother" she had at Lovejoy, all because she and Jimmy were from the same home town. God had been looking out for her all along, her God who entered into human life as spontaneously as any ancient god lowered into a scene by crane. If *l'enfer, ces les autres*, as Sartre had it, maybe heaven also consisted of other people.

To settle her mind for sleep, Lulu said God blesses for other people in random fashion the way she had when she was a child. Deb had gotten pinned by her boyfriend Ed, and the entire Lamb Chop house had serenaded her one night outside Chubbuck. *God bless Deb and Ed*. Ike and April were dating again. It turned out that, although April had enjoyed Winter Carnival and subsequent dates with Ike, the prospect of going off campus with him for the entire Spring Weekend had unnerved her to the point of making her querulous. *God bless Ike and April*. Lenore had written that she and Craig were "expecting" in the fall. Lulu was proud of Lenore for doing everything in the proper order: engagement, marriage, pregnancy. It just went to show the gossips back home. *God bless Lenore and Craig*.

Tears rolled down Lulu's cheeks and onto the pillow. Without Wesley, life was neither hell nor heaven, more of a purgatory. Could it be that he gave no thought to her? She could go for hours at a time without thinking of him and then without warning, like now, she'd be in tears. She couldn't bear to throw out his letters — or to reread them as she used to.

Too bad life couldn't be arranged so that attraction was always mutual. She had recovered that place inside her where she could retreat for sustenance; yet she knew now that she would never be done with yearning. It was an inescapable part of life.

And maybe having an inner retreat wasn't enough. Maybe it would help to confide in someone. The person Lulu most wanted to talk to about Wesley was Wesley himself, the one person she had come to put the most trust in. But that was impossible. She had been wrong to disdain all the talk Jill and Bridey made about their dating lives. Tomorrow afternoon after Greek Sing when Jill was getting ready to go out with Brad — Lulu herself had no plans — she would talk to her about Wesley.

The next morning was bright and sunny and Lulu felt the pathetic fallacy working in reverse — her mood buoyed up by the weather like a half-drowned log bobbing to the surface. "We have the best colors, the biggest smiles and the loudest voices," Veronica had told the freshmen AOs, who by now each possessed a red blazer with the gold Alpha Omega insignia. "So we'll win." Lulu noticed Veronica hadn't said they were the best singers. Nevertheless, Alpha O had thrown itself into rehearsals. Lulu had a terrible voice, she knew, and kept her voice very, very soft. Instead of making her feel bad, the Sister who played director said in front of everyone, "Your smile is wonderful, Lulu! Keep it up. It's smiles like yours that make us winners."

Each fraternity and sorority took a turn singing in four-part harmony on the steps of Hesseltine. When the Alpha Os stood ranged on the stairs ready to begin, their jackets and teeth blazing in the sun, the director mouthed, "Winners!" Lulu sneezed once, then not again. Alpha Omega won first place in the Women's Division. Walking back across the road with her Sisters, Lulu practically floated on the resounding conclusion of "The Naval Hymn," AO's final song: *Thus evermore shall rise to Thee/ Glad hymns of praise from land and sea.*

Next to one of the two white pillars outside Chubbuck, a guy stood squinting into the sun, his arms folded across his chest. A wave began in the pit of Lulu's stomach and swept up her body bringing tears to her eyes. As though she were all by herself, her Sisters mere shadows, she walked toward him. His curly hair was slicked back, his shirt buttoned to the top button, his square, perfectly symmetrical face ravaged with acne. When he smiled — a kind smile, revealing perfectly shaped teeth — the skin crinkled on either side of his gray eyes. He dropped his arms and held out a hand. "Hello, Lulu," Wesley said. "Would you like to go for a walk?"

Acknowledgements

So many eyes, ears and hands aided in the growth and development of "Lulu" that I'm fearful of leaving someone out but here goes. First off, a shout-out to the folks at NaNoWriMo.

Workshop teachers before "Lulu" was even conceived of include Karen Malpede of CUNY Graduate Center Continuing Education, who prompted us students to "drop into the scene," Jennie Fields of Park Slope Barnes & Noble, who read aloud excerpts from "the masters" for us to emulate, and Lore Segal of the 92nd Street Y, who taught us to ask, "What's this story *about?*" Once "Lulu" was birthed, Susan Breen of Gotham Writers' Workshop posed the question of who the audience would be. Madeline Eller, my teacher in the creative writing class of the Brooklyn United Federation of Teachers Retiree Programs, lavishly marked up an entire draft and counseled me to make an outline.

My thanks to Colby College friends who read, commented and, in some cases, performed extensive editing — Lynne Urner Baxter, Pam Plumb Carey, Helen Grand, Coral Harris, Susan Mahoney Michael, Earl Smith and Pam Taylor.

Thanks, too, to other reader friends — Nathalie Dupree, Ginger Ewing, Margaret Hagen, Brett Harvey, Madeline Lee, Judy Lysaker and Donna Reilly.

I thank fellow students in two Gotham classes for encouragement and occasional come-uppances. For their unstinting praise, I thank fellow retired teachers in the Brooklyn UFT Creative Writing Class, of which I've been a member since 2003.

My children, Matt, Liz and Jane, read various drafts in part or in whole and rendered suggestions and technical assistance. Thank you, my darlings.

My husband Frank, who has spent over forty years guiding yearbook staffs through the publishing process, listened in when I started talking with folks at CreateSpace and said, "I can do that." Thank you, sweetheart, for spouse-publishing "Lulu."